They Call Her
Mrs. Sheriff
A Wild Horse Pass Novel

Cynthia Hickey

ISBN-13: 978-1-0881-4738-2

Psalm 82:4

Rescue the weak and needy;

Deliver them out of the hand of the wicked.

ACKNOWLEDGMENTS

Thank you to my husband, who continues to support me and to my readers who anxiously await the next story..

1

Kansas, 1886

"You, Wilhemina Jackson, have potential."

Willie glanced around Rose McMurray, proprietor of the Kansas Gentleman's club. Two of Rose's lace-and-satin-cinched girls aided the madam in blocking Willie's path on the sidewalk, leaving her to either step into the muddy street, enter the saloon doors on her right, or barrel through the fragrant trio like a twister across the prairie. At least once a week since Sam's death, Rose complimented Willie's "potential." Never had a compliment felt so insulting.

"My answer is still no," Willie answered.

Rose patted her sky-high red hair. "With your face and those curves that motherhood only enhanced, you could be my best girl."

One of Rose's sentries frowned and tugged at her low bodice to show her irritation at Rose's words.

Willie rested her palms on the hilt of the gun

she wore at her right hip. "No today, no tomorrow, no forever." She took a step toward the street, but Rose blocked her.

Rose blinked her heavy lashes and maintained a genial smile. "Now, Willie dear, don't be a fool. We both know you need the money. Your pride is going to starve those babies of yours."

Willie winced. She didn't need a madam to tell her something she already feared. "I have something else in mind to put food on my family's table."

Rose laughed. "Like become a deputy? Just because you used to help your husband with policing Apple Grove doesn't mean the new sheriff here is going to give you a badge. My offer could be the easiest way you have of making a living, and a fine one at that."

Willie opened her mouth to argue, but Rose cut her off with the touch of her painted nails to Willie's cheek.

"You know where you can find me when you change your mind. And *you will*." Rose turned her nose up, smoothed the skirt of her canary yellow gown and slipped through the doors of the saloon, her sentries following.

Willie clenched her jaw and fought against the tears. No matter what Rose thought, she wasn't changing her mind. No matter what people said about the evils of pride, pride was what kept her from selling her body, shaming her children, and disgracing her dead husband's name.

With a shake of her head, she continued down the rough-hewn sidewalk toward the telegraph office, smiling at those pitying looks as she passed, keeping her shoulders level and head held high. She'd answered the advertisement over a month ago. Thirty-two days had never felt so long. *Please, Jesus, today, let there be an answer.*

A ruckus at the end of the street drew her attention. Willie hiked her brown calico skirt and rushed to see what was happening.

Two men scuffled in the dirt street. Their fists flew faster than whiskey the time the newest saloon opened and the owner had provided a free round to every man in attendance in celebration. A crowd of no less than ten surrounded the fighting men, several of the onlookers shouting encouragement, and a few of Rose's girls giggled and shrieked.

Willie pulled her gun from its holster. Marching through the crowd, she fired a shot over their heads. "Stop this nonsense before I fetch the sheriff." She reached for the whip that hung at her waist since she'd begun helping her late husband, Sam, when he wore the sheriff's star.

A hand clenched hers, stilling her from uncurling her whip. "I've got it, Willie." The new sheriff, Dan Thomas, stepped beside her and lowered her gun hand. "There's no longer any need for you to put yourself in harm's way."

Willie holstered her weapon as he shoved the fighters apart.

The crowd dispersed.

One of the fighters gave Willie a leering glance before leaving as well, one of Rose's girls possessively clenching his arm.

"I would make a good deputy, Dan," Willie

said. "You know I would."

"What I know is that a woman"—his hazel-eyed gaze moved south from her eyes, lingering—"like you needs to be at home tending to her husband…and children." He grinned. "I wouldn't mind you partnering with me in another capacity."

She stiffened. Him too? Being a widow did not put an open for business sign above her head. Still, she gave him her best smile. "Why, Sheriff Thomas, is that a marriage proposal?"

He whitened like a bed sheet. "I, uhh…didn't, uhh…"

Willie whirled, her skirt swinging around her ankles and left him to his muttered denials. What had the world come to? She marched to the telegraph office.

Pushing through the door, she prayed for a favorable response. Willie stopped at the counter. A burly man hunched over, writing words on a slip of paper as the machine tapped out the code.

When he finished, he smiled up at Willie. "Just the person this message is for." He handed her the note.

"Thank you, Mr. Mason." Willie gripped the yellow paper tight and dashed outside. Her heart pounded. After two years of scraping out a living on what she managed to hunt in the woods, after two years of eating what little their garden produced, after two years of raising a newborn and a toddler with no ones' help save her mother's, her hopes lay on penciled words hastily scripted. *Please, Jesus, please.*

She opened the crumpled paper and scanned

the message.

She blinked.

She read the message again to be sure she hadn't read it wrong, but the response from the mayor of the town was the same. The job was hers.

Willie clutched the telegram to her chest and leaned against the sun-baked front of the building. She closed her eyes and lifted her face heavenward. "Thank you, God."

She'd done it. After two years of widowhood, and what seemed like a lifetime of tribulation, she'd found a means of supporting her family. All she had to do when she arrived at her destination was prove she could do the job. After that, her gender wouldn't matter. Not a small feat, but one she was capable of accomplishing once she set her mind to it. She had to believe that.

She pushed off the wall and headed home.

Home was a ramshackle, one-room house on the outskirts of Apple Grove, Kansas. The sun cooked the walls and the winter cold entered uninvited through cracks between the board walls. Not much of a home, in her opinion, but since Samuel's death, they only had what funds they could get from Mama's sewing and Willie's hunting. Thankfully, the hunting provided meat for the table and rabbit furs to trade for supplies.

Being careful not to knock the door off the tattered rawhide hinge, Willie slipped into the house and enjoyed a brief moment of rare silence. With two-year old Bonnie, six-year-old Samuel, and a mother who talked every waking moment, peace was in short supply for the tiny shack's occupants.

She glanced one more time at the telegram in her hand before folding it and stowing it in her bodice, then stepped out the back door which took exactly twelve long strides from front door to back. "Mama?"

Her mother glanced up from where she weeded a small vegetable garden, her face bronzed from the summer sun. "What's put a smile on your face, Willie?"

"A job." Willie grinned. "A paying job that provides us with a house. Pack our things. We're moving to Montana."

"What? Why?" Mama straightened and wiped dusty hands on the faded green calico apron she wore.

"Life here is like sucking on a lemon." Willie glanced toward the thin line of trees separating the house from the creek. Her children's laughter rang through the air.

"It's not that bad."

"Really, Mama? What part of drippy ceilings and soup so thin it's not more than flavored water isn't 'that bad'?"

"Well … it can't be as bad as Montana. Bears walk boldly down the streets is what I've heard. It snows come September and doesn't stop 'til Easter."

"From whom did you hear that ridiculousness?"

"It doesn't matter. When did you decide to move to Montana?"

"Last month when One-Eyed Henry offered a

trade, and he wasn't talking about furs. Being a widow doesn't mean I'll sell myself to feed my children."

"I reckon you're right. When are you leaving?" Tears filled her eyes.

"Us. We are leaving, Mama. You're going with us. I want to leave as soon as possible." Winter was over, and they could be in Montana by the beginning of summer.

"I reckon I'd best say goodbye to my friends. I've lived here so long, it's a darn shame, is all I got to say." She bustled toward the house.

Willie marched to the fallen barn and studied the wagon. Maybe she could use boards from the barn to repair the wagon. No one would buy it in the poor shape it was in. The two oxen, skinny from sparse feed, might not make the long journey. No, it would be best to scrounge up train fare as far as they could go, and buy a wagon then to carry them the rest of the way. She hoped the old man at the livery would be willing to buy such sad looking beasts. She'd find out in the morning.

"I've some sewing to finish." Mama hollered out the door. "Wouldn't do to leave a job undone. Junior has Bonnie down by the creek. He said something about mud pies." She shook her head. "This is one of those times when we can thank the good Lord we don't have much. Two oxen, a rundown wagon, and children to make a trip across country with no men folk? Lord a mercy may the angels go with us!"

Willie let her mother rattle on and headed toward the creek. Mama knew how much she hated letting the children play there unsupervised. Sure, the water ran low this time of year, but accidents happened all the time on the prairie.

The sound of shrieks and laughter reached her ears before she saw her babies playing. She sat on a large rock and watched. Junior stood in the creek, water to his knees, and splashed his sister who jumped up and down on the creek bank and shrieked with glee.

How precious they were, and how sad that Sam had died before seeing his baby girl. She would have melted her daddy with one glance of her bluebonnet eyes. But, life went on in the form of these two children, thus giving Willie a reason to live. She was responsible for much more than herself.

Every time she moved, the telegram crackled, reminding her that her family had a future. Maybe she wouldn't wait until morning to try selling the oxen. "Children? Would you enjoy a trip to the mercantile?"

Junior stopped splashing. "Can we get a peppermint?"

She calculated the coins in the metal cigar box in the house. "Yes, I believe you can." After all, the journey would be long even by train, and the little ones would need a treat or two along the way. She held out her hands for them to grasp. "We're moving to a place called Wild Horse Pass, Montana."

"Why?" Junior yanked free. Tears welled in his eyes. "This is our home."

She grabbed a hold of his hand again,

swinging their arms. "Mommy needs a job. Our new home is a beautiful place with white picket fences nestled against a mountain that kisses the sky." According to the advertisement at least.

"How far away is it?"

"A long way."

"Then I don't want to go." Junior raced for the paddock. Bear, their Newfoundland, tore from the bushes and bounded after him.

An hour later, after clearing their money tin of most of their funds, Willie led the way to the mercantile, Bonnie's small hand firmly clasped in hers and Junior trailing behind kicking up dust. They stepped inside and were greeted with the homey smells of pickles, wood smoke, and shaving cream.

A wiry little man, Amos Elmore, wearing a striped vest, stepped from behind the counter. "Wilhemina Jackson, how may I be of service?"

Willie glanced around the store, mentally calculating how many supplies they would need. "I'm moving to Montana at the end of the week. I need to sell as much as I can.

Amos withdrew two peppermint sticks and offered them to Bonnie and Junior. " You've some credit left from that bundle of rabbit furs."

"No, sir, I'm sure—"

"Are you telling me I've kept a bad accounting of our business together?" He raised sparse eyebrows, and Willie realized what he was doing.

She looked away, fearing her eyes would blur at his kindness.

"Look, Willie, I know you've had a rough time of it since the sheriff's death, God rest his soul, but I want to do this. I'll box up a few things I think you'll need for your trip. You go purchase your train tickets. Also, I might have a buyer for that … house of yours. The land is worth something, at least. You got anything else to sell?"

"My husband's pistol." She pulled it out of her holster and set it on the counter. She could make do with her rifle and whip. She caressed the pearl handle. As much as she hated to part with it, it would bring a pretty penny. She should have sold it sooner.

"This will do fine. Ought to be enough to get you to where you're going and purchase a few extras once you get there."

Willie smiled. "God bless you, Mr. Elmore."

"No idea what you're referring to." He turned and started piling things on the counter. "These will be ready in an hour. Got that wagon fixed?"

She shook her head.

"I'll have these delivered at no charge. Consider it a going away gift. My boy will be over later to fix your wagon so you can fetch a good price."

"Thank you." It would be enough to pay for steerage for Bear. Tears welled in her eyes. "At least let me purchase a peppermint for each of my children."

He grinned. "It's a deal."

Please, Lord, let the citizens of their new home be as kind as this man.

When they returned home, Willie and Bonnie

entered the dark little cabin while Junior raced out to pet the oxen. She expected supper to be waiting. Instead, the stove was almost out. It'd be cold sandwiches tonight. She sighed and set Bonnie at the table then started slicing the bread. Mama must be delivering her sewing. Once she got a notion in her head, there was no dissuading her.

"Junior, it's time to eat," she called out the slit of a window over the washboard. She cut thick slabs of ham, placed them between slices of bread, then laid them on blue speckled tin plates and placed four on the table. Mama would eat when she arrived back home. No sense in making the children wait.

"Well," Mama said, rushing through the door and hanging her shawl on a peg. "I've said my goodbyes. There's a pile of crates outside, too. Didn't Amos holler howdy when he dropped them off?" She sat at the table and folded her hands. "Sorry the food wasn't ready, but I wanted to get the unpleasantness of leaving out of the way." She peered at Junior. "What's the matter with my boy?"

"Mommy is going to get rid of Ox and Blue." Tears fell anew.

"We have to, honey. I'll buy two more when we reach our destination." Willie sighed, a rather common occurrence lately, as it seemed life weighed heavier than ever. She'd pray doubly hard that night while lying down to sleep that their new town would come through on its promises. The luxuries they'd had to do without, and the painful choices she'd been forced to make since her husband's death, were unfair to the children. For Mama, and herself, too, if she were honest.

Later that evening, as crickets chirped from cracks in the walls and Willie lay on a simple pallet on the floor, she gazed at the roof over her head and prayed she was doing the right thing..

2

Thomas Miller stuck a horseshoe into the fire, pulled it out, hammered it into shape, then dunked it into a barrel of cold water. He'd never tire of the hiss when hot iron met cool water. Perspiration ran down his back in a steady stream. The heat of the fire on a warm day he could do without. He drew his arm across his forehead before the sweat ran into his eyes.

The new sheriff ought to arrive any day. Couldn't be too soon. Tom and the pastor were getting really tired of stopping vigilantes from taking the law into their own hands. Especially since most of those vigilantes were women. He shook his head and started on another shoe.

Women shouldn't tote guns and chase crooks. Why, they'd even planted flowers around the old hanging tree. That's not how the good Lord intended for things to work. The men kept the law and made the living, while the women tended the house and young'uns. That's the way things had worked since the beginning of time.

"Hey, Tom." Harvey Coffee, owner of the

town's mercantile, marched into the dim recesses of the livery. "Wife said to tell you she only has one more of those fancy yard thingamajigs left to sell and you need to make more. She also wants to know if you could go by the sheriff's house and make sure all the doors and windows are set right."

"Sure thing." He'd checked them last week, but Wilma was one of those women who wanted a man to double and triple check things. He pitied Harvey. "My supplies ready?"

"Yep. And the sheriff's. You can pick them up at your convenience. Good day, Tom." Harvey tipped his hat and left.

Tom banked the coals, then straightened and popped the kinks from his back, before stepping outside into sunshine. Spring was mighty pretty in the shadow of the Judith Mountains. Wildflowers dotted the landscape and peeked between boards in the sidewalk. He remembered his first glimpse of Wild Horse Pass. The town with its one road and white picket fences didn't portray the wildness of Montana, but winter had a way of bringing the harshness back with bitter cold, snow, and fierce winds. Yet, he knew now that hidden behind the beauty lurked the sins of man, but he had no desire to live anywhere else. In his eyes, Montana was a bit of Eden.

He scrubbed the dirt from his face, neck, and arms before untying his leather apron and hanging it on a nail by the door. He might as well check out the sheriff's cottage before Wilma Coffee took a switch to him. Being a former schoolteacher, the woman had never lost the stare she once gave unruly students.

Two daughters of the Simpson family twittered and waved from across the street. Tom shook his head. Poor Frank had four daughters to marry off. He didn't envy the man. Most of the town's citizens lived on outlying farms and ranches, but a few lived in town, and those were the ones a body had to worry about. Those were the ones who had their nose in everyone else's business.

Throwing a wave over his shoulder, Tom increased his pace, not wanting to get stuck in a conversation with two young ladies who only talked about hair ribbons and fabric. Especially since their mother had an eye on Tom to be a husband to one of her four. He shuddered.

"Afternoon, Tom." Pastor Mark Netser stepped off the porch and matched his pace to Tom's. "Where you off to?"

"Got to check the cabin again."

Mark scratched his chin. "Seems a bit redundant, doesn't it? Gloria was just there. She thought it would be nice to hang curtains on the windows, and she's been changing out flowers in a jar on the table every day."

"Sounds mighty pretty for an unmarried man's cabin."

"There's no dissuading the women of this town when they set their minds to something."

"Agreed." Tom stopped in front of the white clapboard cabin and stared at the white lace curtains. He raised his eyebrows and pursed his lips. It'd be a fine home for a woman or a married couple, but not a rough lawman. Oh, well. Curtains were easy enough to remove if the man didn't care for them.

Folks were excited and wanted things to look nice. They hadn't had a lawman for months. The poor fella would get a welcome he'd never forget. Hopefully, it wouldn't send him running for the hills.

Shoving his hands in his pockets, Tom walked the perimeter of the small plot of land, noting the freshly tilled garden spot and corral. He doubted the man was married. If he wasn't, there'd be no time for a garden. Not with traveling the ranches and keeping an eye on the town. But, the house used to belong to the mayor and was given over to the last sheriff when Mayor Bloomfield built that monstrosity on the hill. Not many people would turn away a free roof over their head, frilly curtains or not.

Back at the front of the building, he studied the white-washed siding and porch that stretched the length of the front. He tilted his head and considered what it might be like to live in such a place with a pretty woman by his side and a passel of kids running around. He could consider such a thing if it were the right woman.

Maybe.

"I still think you would have made a fine sheriff. You're the best shot this town has." Mayor Bloomfield stopped next to Tom and rocked on his heels, thumbs looped through his suspenders.

"I've got a job I enjoy, Mayor. I don't really

cotton to being a lawman." Not when it made people Tom's responsibility. That wasn't a task he felt qualified for. Not after Ma's death while he watched and did nothing to prevent her brutal murder.

"Still, it would have prevented us hiring someone from all the way in Kansas. I'm not sure a prairie rabbit has what it takes to keep the law in Montana territory. Guess the poor fool doesn't know what he's getting himself into, right?" The mayor laughed and clapped Tom on the shoulder. "The women of this town have a way of running off just about anyone."

Another reason Tom didn't want to be sheriff. The silly town bylaws stated the sheriff's life was open to scrutiny from the town's residents. While he had nothing to hide, he did value his privacy.

"Let's hope this sheriff works out. Soon enough, we'll be as lawless as the rest of the small towns scattered across this territory." Since everything looked ready at the house, Tom turned back toward his livery.

Two Indians in white man's garb tried to enter the mercantile. Wilma Coffee, the mercantile owner's wife, ran them off with a broom. Tom shook his head and ducked into his blacksmith shop. They rarely had tame Indians venture into town, and when they did come, he tried to avoid them at all costs. Seemingly civilized or not, he didn't trust them. People like that could turn on a man in a second, taking away everything one held dear. Good for Wilma.

The two men then shuffled toward the town's

one and only saloon, only to be barred from entering. Tom exhaled sharply. If the town's new sheriff were already in residence, the two could be run out of town. As it was, they'd get the idea soon enough when no one let them step foot inside their establishment.

Maybe it wasn't the Christian way to believe, but Tom had battled with his prejudice for over fifteen years. It wouldn't go away overnight. He set to work putting his blacksmith tools to right, then headed to the livery to make sure the boarded horses were settled for the night. He rubbed the nose of Stormy, a beautiful mare set aside for the sheriff's use, then fed a sugar cube to Nightmare.

The inky-black stallion nickered a welcome and nudged Tom's pocket for more. "That's plenty, big guy. Wouldn't want your teeth to rot out. What would all the fillies think?" Tom patted the horse's head and lumbered up the stairs to his room.

The first thing he spotted upon opening the door was his bed. Loneliness assailed him each evening as he stretched across the single bed. Other than where he slept, the room held a chair, a small table, a tiny stove shoved in the corner, and a few hooks for his clothing. Since he ate all his meals at Bloomfield's Best Vittles, he didn't need much. Maybe he should get a dog to lessen the solitude. Another body in the small space that Tom could talk to of an evening and discuss the day's happenings.

At one time, he'd thought of getting married and settling down someday, but that had been a long time ago. Before Ma's death and he realized he didn't have what it took to keep anyone safe. He sat on the edge of the bed and toed off his boots. Pa had died of guilt and a broken heart after that fateful day, leaving Tom alone at a young age.

He flopped back on the bed, banging his head against the wall. That's what he got for digging deep into a past filled with pain. He rubbed the back of his head. Maybe the knock was God trying to knock some kind of sense into him.

A banging on the door caused him to bolt upright and reach for his boots. No one knocked after dark unless they needed his help. "Hold on, I'm coming." He hopped to the door, one boot on and the other in his hand. He swung it open and came face-to-face with the mayor.

"Looks like there's a wagon stopped up on the bluff. Can you take a look?" Mayor Bloomfield's face was creased with worry. "Could be the new sheriff, could be someone up to no good."

"You want me to go now?"

"No time like the present."

"Give me a minute." He shoved his foot into the other boot and grabbed his rifle from a hook over the door. "If they've stopped, they must not be planning on coming into town tonight. I don't know why this can't wait until morning."

"We've got no one else to send, Tom, and the missus is concerned."

He sighed and closed the door behind him. "The sheriff can't get here fast enough." He stomped down the stairs and to the livery where

Nightmare greeted him with a whoosh of air from his nostrils. "Yeah, I feel the same way, boy." Tom needed to learn to say no to some things. Riding out after dark wasn't his job. Besides, the bluff was several miles away. The moon would be mighty high in the sky before he laid his head to rest for the night.

His bad mood increased the farther from town he rode. A cold breeze blew down his collar and the clouds decided to release a chilly drizzle. Not enough to dampen the dirt under his horse's hooves, but just enough to make Tom miserable. He pulled his hat tighter on his head and folded up his collar.

The mayor's request better not be a wild goose chase. One thing was for certain: Tom intended to give the new sheriff a hearty handshake when the man arrived.

3

Willie stopped the wagon on a high rise and set the brake. She wanted a glimpse of the town from up high before descending into the valley. But instead of a quaint town, she saw more land. Mountains towered in the distance, reaching into a sky so blue and so vast, a body felt insignificant.

"How many more valleys before we reach this new home of ours?" Mama huffed up the hill to stand next to her. "Seems like it's always just over the rise."

Although exhaustion weighed on her shoulders, and fatigue showed in her family's faces, Willie yearned to move forward. If she squinted, she thought she could see rooftops in the distance. They couldn't be too far. After all, they'd passed miles of fencing. That didn't appear without the help of a person. "I'd like to keep going, Mama. The town can't be far. This is the way the man at Fort Maginnis said to go."

"You said we were close yesterday." Her mother turned back to the wagon, her skirts rustling along the tall brush. "But, I agree. Best to go on, at least until dark. That hill over there probably hides the town. We can be there by supper time, God willing."

Willie glanced behind them at the wide eyes and eager looks of her children and the hanging heads of the tired oxen. While in no worse shape than when they'd left the farm where she purchased them, and Willie had done her best not to overtax them, the poor beasts of burden needed a good long rest. As did they all. She shook her head. "We'll move on in the morning."

The grazing was plentiful, they had a small amount of food left, and the temperature wasn't too cold. A rest would prevent all of them, family included, from arriving in town looking filthy and worn down.

"We don't know what type of varmints are out here, Willie." Mama planted fists on her hips. "Are you going to keep your shotgun close at hand?"

"Of course, I am." She hefted the gun against her shoulder and let her free hand rest on Bear's head, his fur soft and comforting under her fingers. The dog would warn them of anything coming near, and the shotgun would make sure that person, or animal, didn't return.

While Willie and Bear still gazed over the valley, the smells of frying bacon and baking bread drifted on a breeze. Although it grew chilly as the sun lowered and a slight mist fell from the sky, Willie didn't return to the wagon for her shawl. Not when the sun kissed the mountains and painted them with shades of marigold and daffodil. She could fall asleep every night to that wonderful sunset.

"Mama?" Junior handed her the frayed shawl. "Bonnie stepped on a thorn."

"Thank you, son. I'll tend to her. Heel, Bear." She turned and hurried to her little girl's side, propping her gun against the wagon. Bear plopped in the dirt, sending up a cloud of dust. "Sweetie, where are the moccasins I bought you at the fort? If you were wearing them, you wouldn't have stepped on a thorn."

"No, church."

"Honey, you have other shoes for church." If they weren't too small, and hopefully, there would be a church. A place described as wonderful as Wild Horse Pass had been portrayed would have one for sure. Willie pinched out a thorn and tossed it in the fire pit. "Let's put your moccasins back on until we reach our new home." She planted a kiss on her baby's head and straightened, catching the last glimpse of the sunset before the only light was from the moon, stars, and cooking fire.

"Sure is a pretty place." Mama handed Willie a tin plate of beans, bacon, and a biscuit left from the day before. "Don't frown. You'll have bread by morning. You can't eat something that ain't ready."

"True." Willie dug into the beans, forcing them past her teeth and trying to be grateful for something that had been the same day after day. Maybe her feelings of discontent were punishment for her lying about her name to get the job. Mama hadn't asked the type of job, and Willie hadn't volunteered the information. She didn't care. The pay was good, and the position provided a house. Those were the important things.

The bitter tang of guilt covered the taste of the beans. God understood her motives, right? She glanced in the direction of the town, hoping the citizens would.

Mama prattled on about the scenery they'd passed through, the miraculous arrival of the poor oxen they'd purchased for little money, and the small amount of food left hanging in the wagon. When she'd finished listing those things, she started on the condition of their clothing.

Willie shook her head. "I'm wearing the buckskin fringed skirt and vest tomorrow."

"No, you're not." Mama's eyes glittered in the fire light. "We are not arriving at our new home with you looking like an Indian."

"I *am* an Indian, Mama."

"One quarter, Wilhemina. That's all. Why advertise the fact. Some folks don't take kindly to mixed breeds. With your sky blue eyes, you could pass for anything. I've had a tough time of it and don't want my girl to suffer the same."

"I'm proud to be a mix of Cherokee and Scot." She set her plate on the rocks rimming the fire. "That's who God made me. My children will grow up to be proud of who they are. You shouldn't be so unhappy about grandma's people." She snapped her fingers at Bear, grabbed her shotgun, and returned to stand on the bluff, tired of the old argument she and Mama had too often.

The only thing Indian about Mama was her dark eyes. The chestnut hair threaded with silver and gold looked more Scottish, and somehow the high cheekbones of her ancestors had also skipped her leaving Mama with rounded cheeks.

Samuel had loved Willie despite her Indian blood. Others would, too. She wouldn't hide her ancestry from her new neighbors. Despite her eye color, her high cheek bones and raven-colored hair often gave her away.

"Don't be upset." Mama stepped beside her. "I'm tired of seeing you hurt by folks' blindness. I experienced enough for both of us." She crossed her arms and seemed to focus on something across the valley. "When was the last time you smiled? Or laughed? It pains me to see you drowning in sadness. Find your joy in the Lord, daughter. He won't let you down."

"I know He won't. I'll laugh and carry on once we're settled somewhere."

"You carry too much on your shoulders. I'll help find a way to make some money once we settle."

Willie shook her head, the wind catching the long strands of her hair. She pulled a piece from where it had stuck to her lips. "Watching out for my babies is enough for you to do and a huge blessing to me." It wouldn't do to have her new job cross into her personal life. Not if she could help it.

As twilight began to surround them, the scattered clouds dispersed, filling the sky with millions of stars. Willie stayed to gaze at them long after her mother returned to the wagon. She started at the sound of hooves glancing off rocks, then squinted over the ledge, making out the shape of a man on a horse. A cloud of dust rose as he galloped away. Since he headed in the opposite direction, she let her shotgun stay resting on her shoulder. No sense in alerting anyone to their presence. Not at night.

When all sounds from the wagon had ceased, and their supper fire burned low, Willie turned and headed to bed. Inside their weeks long home, she slipped off the faded and stained calico dress and hung it on a peg. A smile teased at her lips as the moon's light fell on her leather skirt. She'd live in it if she could.

Mama said, quite often in fact, that wearing leather wasn't womanly. Willie shrugged. Since it didn't hide the physical attributes of her body, she figured even a feed sack could look 'womanly'. Regardless, Willie intended to wear the clothes for their entrance into Wild Horse Pass. With her leather skirt and vest, large-brimmed hat, and shotgun, she figured folks might take her a bit more seriously than if she arrived wearing petticoats and lace.

After donning a flannel nightgown against the night's chill, Willie slid under the quilts next to Bonnie and pulled her baby close. The little one's curls tickled her chin.

Mama was half correct. Willie smiled all the time, in private with her children, but it had been ages since she'd laughed out loud. She yearned for a belly-aching laugh that made her cheeks hurt.

She could pinpoint the exact moment when laughter left her world.

When she'd watched her husband die in her arms. Watched the blood pour from his body and the light fade from his eyes.

She rolled on to her back and stared at the lightly billowing canvas overhead. Bandits had set upon them as they strolled along the creek bank after church one day. Samuel had shoved Willie into the bushes to protect her and their unborn child. He'd been shot, but not before fatally shooting the two outlaws. Willie hadn't even had time to draw her gun.

Could it be that Willie's new choice of profession was spurred by her husband's death? Why else would she have responded so quickly to the newspaper advertisement, so willing to uproot her family and travel across the continent?

The straw-filled mattress rustled under her as she flopped to her other side. Sleep would be slow coming, if it arrived at all. Nerves, anticipation, and a measure of guilt, filled her. Her stomach churned.

What would Mama say when she discovered in the morning what Willie's new job actually would be?

*

Tom thought of the figure he'd seen on the bluff the night before as he strolled down the sidewalk toward the livery. He looked longer than was proper at the woman with waist-length hair blowing in the breeze. He couldn't make out more than her silhouette, but the urge to see more of her had tugged at him.

Having spotted the smoke of a campfire, he'd volunteered to ride out and see whether the newcomers were friendly. One glance at a family with a wagon had put his concerns to rest. Either they'd drive on into town or pass on by. They didn't seem like a threat, despite the outline of a rifle on the woman's shoulder. Maybe he should've stopped and said howdy, offered to escort them to town if that was their destination.

He pushed open the double doors at the front of the livery, then headed to the back of the large barn to do the same with the rear doors in order to let a breeze blow through. Owning the only livery and blacksmith shop in town, he stayed busier than a one-legged dancer in a dance hall where dances were handed out free. He let the three boarded horses into the paddock and grabbed a shovel.

His guests did leave quite the mess each evening. Tom ought to consider hiring some part time help. Maybe one of the local boys would be interested in earning a few coins now and then. Or he could take on an apprentice. The thought had merit.

When would the new sheriff arrive? Tom mucked out the first stall, sending the manure and dirty straw into a pile outside the door to be carted away later. While he worked, his mind drifted to the types of cattle brands and pot holders he'd form for the mercantile. Wilma Coffee seemed partial to flowers and curly-cues, but she wasn't the only one purchasing Tom's creations. Many of the ranchers also used him to make their branding irons or something else depicting their brand to put on a fence post to point out to folks when they'd arrived. He shrugged. The extra work wasn't his priority. Just something he played with in a rare slow moment.

A shout of welcome rose outside the door. Tom leaned his shovel against the wall and joined the crowd converging at the end of the street. Coming from the other direction was a lone wagon pulled by two skinny oxen. Walking beside the wagon was a woman in leather fringe, her blue-black hair falling to her waist like satin ribbons. A wide-brimmed hat hid her face. A monstrous dog trotted by her side.

The mayor, Bernard Bloomfield, bustled past, hands tugging on his brocade vest. Tom smiled. The portly man always insisted on being the first to greet any newcomers. Tom increased his pace and stood beside the mayor when he stopped.

"Welcome. Welcome! I am Mayor Bloomfield. " He stood on tip-toe and glanced around the wagon. "You ladies alone?"

The older woman driving the wagon set the brake and stood. She said something low to the leather clad woman before turning to the crowd. "I'm Winifred Baxter and this is my daughter Wilhemina. Inside are my grandchildren, Samuel Junior and little Bonnie. Yes, sir, we're alone if you're mentioning our lack of menfolk. Never alone though as long as God is with us." Her dark eyes swept the crowd.

"Well said." Mayor Bloomfield offered her

help down. "May we treat you to a dinner at our fine restaurant? Best food in town if I say so myself."

Tom bit back a laugh. The mayor *would* say so since his wife ran and cooked for Bloomfield's Best Vittles.

Wilhemina stepped forward. She tipped her hat back revealing the prettiest face Tom had ever seen and sky blue eyes that made a man forget his words. She squared her shoulders and held out a hand to the mayor. "I'm your new sheriff. I go by Willie Jack."

A hush fell over the town.

Mayor Bloomfield's face turned the shade of a ripe tomato. "But…why…you're a woman."

The corner of her rosy lips curled. "We've eaten, but thank you for your kind offer. We'd like nothing more than to be shown to our new home."

Tom crossed his arms, certain the mayor would send her on her way. A woman couldn't be sheriff. The position was too dangerous. She was no more a Willie Jack than he was a Thomasina Millerson. Wild Horse Pass would be the laughing stock of Montana if she stayed.

"Sheriff?" Winifred's eyebrows almost disappeared into her dark hair, sprinkled with silver. "That's your new job?"

So, the lovely woman had deceived her family in addition to the town. Why wasn't Bloomfield sending her on her way? Surely he wasn't swayed by a pretty face and lovely figure. Was that a split skirt? The women in town would have fits for sure.

And still the mayor stared, not speaking. What was the man thinking?

"Miss…Jack—"

"Missus. I am a widow."

Bloomfield cleared his throat. "Mrs., uh, Jack. I'm afraid you've put us at a bit of a disadvantage. We'll need time to decide how to proceed. May I ask you a few questions?"

The group of townsfolk drew closer.

"While this is a wonderful place to raise a family, we do have our share of crime. How would you handle an armed man threatening one of our citizens, or, let's say, yourself?"

"If he didn't relinquish his weapon, I'd shoot him."

Bloomfield took a step back. "What if a group of…loose women tried to set up a house of ill repute?"

Willie Jack frowned. "Are these serious questions, Mr. Bloomfield, or are you toying with me?"

Tom suspected it might not be a wise thing to get on her bad side. The beautiful woman stood at least five-feet-seven, and her eyes grew colder with each question. From the way she held her gun, he suspected she knew how to use it and use it well.

"Oh, I am very serious, Mrs. Jack. I'm not sure where the misunderstanding came from about you being a woman, and I do apologize for any inconvenience this may have caused you and yours, but—"

"Are you saying my girl isn't good enough to be your sheriff?" Winifred marched up and poked him in the chest with her forefinger. "Because, I'll tell you right now, this girl can out-shoot any man here or I'll eat my dusty bonnet. Besides, her late husband was a sheriff, and I reckon my Willie learned a thing or two from him."

"Let's have a shooting contest," someone shouted. "Pit her against Tom."

"No." Tom held up his hands. "There's no need for that."

"Why?" Willie tilted her head, revealing a graceful neck. "Is it because I'm a woman?"

Tom swallowed past the mountain in his throat. "Well, yes."

"Mama," she said. "Watch the little ones. I've a contest to win."

"Make sure you do. That bonnet won't go down well without lemonade."

Willie Jack turned to the mayor. "I'll make you a deal. If I can shoot better than your man, here, then you give me three months to prove to you that I am capable of being your sheriff. If I lose, we'll find another livelihood somewhere else. Deal?" Once again she held out her hand.

This time, the mayor grasped it. "Deal." He released her hand, and then clapped Tom on the shoulder. "Get your gun."

This was craziness. He whirled and stomped back to his room above the livery. Within minutes, he was back by the woman's wagon. He couldn't bring himself to call her sheriff. With a jerk of his head, he invited her to follow him to where a row of stumps stood in a field, the same place the town held shooting contests on the Fourth of July each year.

The stumps were positioned at different distances. Mayor Bloomfield rushed to set empty bottles on each of the stumps.

"You first, ma'am." Tom waved a hand.

"Thank you." She raised her gun, took aim, and shot the farthest bottle, then worked her way to the closest, shattering each one. When she'd finished, she turned and raised an eyebrow. "Sufficient?"

Wow, the woman could shoot. "Can you shoot a moving target?"

"Of course. Do you care to run?" Her mouth twitched. "I can count to ten, if you'd like."

Tom opened and closed his mouth a couple of times, then laughed, a deep belly laugh that startled birds from the stand of trees behind the stumps. Without blinking an eye, Willie Jack took aim and felled three of them.

She turned to the mayor. "A deal is a deal, Mayor Bloomfield."

"Yes, ma'am it is. I see no reason for Tom to shoot." He turned to the crowd. "Residents of Wild Horse Pass, I introduce you to the new sheriff. At least for the next three months."

The crowd cheered. Well, the women cheered, the men glared. Tom shrugged. They'd all get used to the idea, and the time would pass quickly, God willing.

Even Tom would get used to the idea...eventually. Maybe.

4

The town's citizens followed them to their new home, filling the air with their murmurs and dust from their feet. All except for the big man, Tom Miller, anyway. His face had lost color, then darkened, and then he'd turned and stalked away. Maybe Willie shouldn't have shown off her skills quite so readily, but few things made her as angry as people doubting she could do something primarily because she was a woman.

"We hope this house will be satisfactory." Mayor Bloomfield rocked on his toes, fingers slipped into the pockets of his vest.

Willie studied the quaint cottage. Two rocking chairs graced a front porch. Flowers lined the foundation. "It's perfect." Even if all four of them had to share a bedroom, the little house was a palace compared to their former residence. The small house called a welcome, letting Willie know she'd come home.

"Well, then." The mayor pulled a ring of keys from his pocket. "For the house and the sheriff's office, which we're proud to say, houses two jail cells. There is another set of keys hanging in your office. We're a very progressive community." He grinned, gave a nod, and led the crowd away. They weren't out of sight before the murmuring increased in volume.

"Let's check out our new home." Willie swung Bonnie to the ground then took her hand. After unlocking the front door, she led the way into a small parlor. At her left were two rooms with beds, to her right was a small kitchen. The house was perfect for the four of them. She smiled at a jar of wildflowers on a square pine table. She ran her fingers across the scarred surface, envisioning many family meals there.

"Might as well unload the wagon and make this place ours. For three months." Mama bustled back outside, motioning for Junior to follow.

Willie's heart sank. Even Mama doubted her abilities to make a go of her new job. She sat Bonnie in one of the rockers and instructed her to stay. Bear plopped at her feet. The little one wouldn't go far without Bear barking a warning.

"Good morning!" A young, bird of a woman, skipped inside the house. "I'm Gloria Netser. My husband is the pastor of this fine town. I hope you enjoy the flowers and curtains. Although we weren't expecting a woman, these types of things make a place a home, don't you agree?"

Willie couldn't help but return the woman's smile. With the way she chattered, Mama would be in heaven, trying to get a word in edgewise. "I'm Wilhemina Jackson, and this is my mother Winifred Baxter. You may call me Willie."

"And me, Winnie." Mama thrust out her hand. "I just know we'll be great friends."

"Oh, I'm sure of it!" Gloria held out a covered dish she'd pulled from the basket hanging on her arm. "Apple pie?"

"Thank you." Mama accepted the gift and glanced toward the house. "I'm afraid we're not set up for company."

"Sure you are. The house is fully furnished, right down to the dishes." With a swish of her skirts, Gloria flitted around the kitchen.

Willie shoved her hat off her head. It hung down her back by the rawhide strands around her neck. She rubbed between her eyes. Goodness gracious, the town seemed filled with people of one extreme or another. Either they looked as if they resented her arrival or they treated her and Mama as life-long friends.

"See?" Gloria swept a hand at the table.

Mismatched china graced the space in front of each seat. Never one for formalities, Willie found the view welcoming rather than the stiffness matching china would've had. "Find the pump outside and wash up, Junior." Willie hung her hat on a peg and her shot gun over the fireplace where someone had conveniently placed a nice set of elk antlers. Through the kitchen window, mountains, topped with remnants of the winter snow, rose to kiss the sky. The advertisement had been correct in its assessment that Wild Horse Pass was a touch of heaven.

She'd do everything in her power to fulfill her obligations as sheriff. Uprooting her family again held little appeal, and she had a feeling the town of Wild Horse Pass grew on a person.

"Now, sheriff, don't forget to head over to the livery and pick up your horse." Gloria sliced the pie. "We always supply our sheriff with a horse. Should you choose to leave us, the horse is still yours."

"Even if the sheriff is on a trial basis?" Willie tried, but failed to keep the sarcasm from her words.

"Why should that be any different?" She tilted her head like the bird she resembled. "It isn't your fault we hired you not knowing your gender. Maybe those responsible for hiring our law enforcement should be clearer in their requirements. I read the advertisement. Nowhere did it say women need not apply."

They may not have much in common, and Willie might tower over the other woman by six inches, but she felt as if she'd found a cherished friend. Someone with like-minded ideas of the equality of men and women. She pulled out a chair and sat. Yes, she might find this place to be a genuine home after all.

"Who is the man I outshot today?" Willie cut off a piece of the flaky pie.

"That would be the livery owner and blacksmith, Thomas Miller. Isn't he handsome? And such a Godly man, too. He'll make a fine husband to some lucky woman."

Willie closed her lips around the fork tines. She recognized the match-making gleam in Gloria's eyes and refused to go there. After they unloaded the wagon, she'd fetch her horse and have nothing else to do with the man.

Two hours later, Gloria having returned home and Mama busy unloading their few belongings, Willie headed down Main Street with Bear at her side and her trusty rifle on her shoulder. The mayor hadn't given her a badge yet. Maybe she'd find it at the office. She'd check in the morning.

She stepped into the dim recesses of the livery and breathed in the comforting odors of horse, hay, and manure. "Hello? Mr. Miller?"

He stepped out from one of the stalls. "Hello, sheriff."

Gloria was right about one thing. The man was handsome. Large, too. Hair the color of the fresh hay he'd spread on the floor brushed his collar. Eyes the color of coffee stared impassively, and a cleft in his chin looked like it would be the perfect size for her finger. Her face heated. He might be harder to ignore than Willie had thought.

*

"May I help you?" Tom pulled a rag from his back pocket and wiped his hands.

"Gloria Netser sent me to fetch my horse." She lifted her chin, her blue eyes piercing under the brim of her hat.

He thought he detected signs of an Indian ancestry, but the eyes kept him from making a complete assumption. No Indian he'd ever seen had eyes the color of a summer sky. No, the pretty woman in front of him couldn't be part Indian. He wouldn't be able to abide living in the same town with someone with Indian blood. Not after what had happened to his mother. "But, you aren't the sheriff yet."

"I am for three months. She said there was no difference in me being in a trial period than if another sheriff moved on." She crossed her arms. "I agree."

Tom sighed and shoved the rag back in his pocket. He did have a horse meant for the sheriff. A beautiful dapple grey mare sixteen hands high. "Horse's name is Stormy. She's outside." He led Willie to the paddock. "Grey mare at the far end." He put two fingers between his lips and let out a shrill whistle. The mare trotted over.

"She's beautiful." Willie leaned against the railing. "And she's all mine." She glanced up at him. "Why does the town provide the sheriff with a horse?"

Tom shrugged, choosing his words carefully. He couldn't tell her how folks kept running the sheriffs off. Nor could he say how the town considered every action the sheriff made part of their business. In the hopes of keeping a sheriff longer than a few weeks, they'd started adding certain incentives. One, being the horse. Two, being a house. He opted for as much of the truth as he deemed safe. "Trying to get a sheriff to stick around, I reckon. Winters are brutal around here and some people can't handle the cold."

"Hmmm." Her frown told him she didn't believe he spoke the entire truth. "But, it doesn't bother you, does it?"

"I'm a blacksmith. I spend my life in a continuous state of perspiration, and even in the middle of winter, this place has a beauty that calls to a man."

"Why do you resent my presence, Mr. Miller?" She turned fully toward him. "Be honest. I have a tough skin."

"I don't resent you, sheriff, just the fact that you're a woman in a man's role."

She shrugged one shoulder and turned back to the horses. "Fair enough, but, you'll owe me an apology at the end of three months, I guarantee. Now, if you would be kind enough to fetch my horse, I'll be out of your way."

"Gladly. I'm sure you have a lot of work to do." Tom hopped the fence then grabbed a bridle from the post. The sooner he got the sheriff out of his livery, the better. The woman's stare made him nervous. Almost as if she could read his thoughts.

He saddled Stormy and offered the sheriff a hand up, which of course she declined. With a slap on Stormy's rump, Tom sent her trotting down the street.

"My wife told me she'd mentioned the horse." Pastor Netser leaned against the building. "I love her dearly, but the woman sometimes jumps ahead of things."

"She's correct in the fact we shouldn't discriminate." Tom headed back to the paddock to fetch the other two horses for feeding. "But, I don't see why we have to continue to give away the best horses in town."

"Take that up with the mayor, Tom. He's convinced a sheriff needs a spectacular horse with which to outrun the lawless." The pastor stepped back as the horses headed inside, then pulled the door shut behind them. "Do you think this Willie Jack can handle the job?"

Tom spun around. "She's a woman."

The pastor grinned. "True, and very beautiful."

"I hadn't noticed." Liar. "You don't agree that she's stepped out of what's proper?" Tom grabbed a bucket and dipped it into a barrel of feed.

"She outshot you, didn't she? I think that makes her capable."

"She didn't shoot fair." He dumped the grain into a feeder. "Shot before the signal was given."

"You would've been hard pressed to hit all three targets in such quick succession, and you know it. Besides, she out shot you fair and square. No cheating involved."

Tom laughed. "I think I might be feeling a touch of jealousy. Out shot by a woman. That still doesn't mean I approve of her being sheriff."

"Fair enough." The pastor clapped him on the shoulder. "Keep an open mind, Tom. That woman is part of God's plan for this town. Mark my words. She's going to make a difference."

Tom stared in the direction of the sheriff's house. The pastor was right, and Tom couldn't help but wonder what part Willie Jack would play in the town's future.

*

Willie hung the last washed shirt on the line, then stretched to pop the kinks from her back. Why Mama insisted on doing a load of laundry on the very day they moved in was a mystery. Still, it would be nice to start the morning fresh and concentrate on her new job as sheriff without domestic duties looming over her head. Most likely, there would be few times where she could lend a helping hand at home.

The scent of beef stew drifted through the open kitchen window. Mama wasted no time in raiding the pantry, filled by the lovely folks of Wild Horse Pass, and fixing something other than beans for supper. What a blessing she'd given Willie by moving in with her after Samuel's death. An arrangement that benefited them both. Mama had company as she grew older, and Willie had help with the young'uns. And, Mama's conversation helped keep the loneliness of being a widow at bay.

"Sheriff!" One of the men she'd spotted in the morning's crowd sprinted toward her, hat in hand, long greying hair flying around his face. "There's a fight on Main Street. You need to come break it up."

Willie started for the house, the man following. "What's the fight about? Any guns drawn?"

"Not yet, but one of the parties involved mentioned something about cutting the other one."

"Junior. Fetch my whip." Willie untied her apron and tossed it on the table. "Junior!"

"I sent him to fetch Bonnie for supper." Mama exited the kitchen, drying her hands on a towel. "The two are playing Hide 'n Go Seek."

Willie sighed, held up a finger for the man to wait, and then rushed to her bedroom, skirting around Bear who refused to move from the side of her bed. She'd start hanging the whip beside her gun to keep it within easy reach. Less than twelve hours in town and her services were already in demand.

The man stuck his head in her room. "Sheriff, we'd best hurry."

"Out." Willie pointed. "This room is off limits." Gracious. Did the town's citizens think they could wander through her house at will?

With her whip hooked at her waist, she headed to the parlor to fetch her gun. "Mama, don't hold supper for me."

Junior burst through the open door. "I can't find Bonnie. Mama, you gotta help me find her."

Willie's glance darted from her son to the man, her heart in her throat.

5

"Mama?" Willie bit the inside of her cheek. Her first work as sheriff called, yet she couldn't leave while her baby was missing.

"I've got her." Mama carried Bonnie into the front room. "She was hiding under the bed. I'll take care of the young'uns. You git."

Willie slung her rifle over her shoulder, called for Bear to follow, then dashed after the man who had summoned her. Thankful for the split leather skirt she had insisted on wearing which enabled her to run faster, the man stayed only a few feet in front of her. He led Willie down the one street, proudly named Main Street, and onto the fringes of town where a false-fronted, three story building painted a cheery red and boasting a sign stating it was the only saloon in Wild Horse Pass provided a backdrop for a crowd of the town's residents.

Out front, two men grappled in the dirt, one of them clutching a long bladed knife. Willie took a deep breath, prepared to prove she could handle the job bestowed upon her, and stepped forward. "Stop that this instant."

The men continued fighting as if she hadn't spoken. Several heads turned her way, smirking, silent challenges on their faces. A few of the women raked their gazes over Willie's split leather skirt and curled their lips. Let them judge. She'd like to see how well they acted as sheriff in petticoats.

Willie unhooked her whip and cracked it over the fighters' heads. "Break it up!"

A woman screamed as the whip cracked like lightning over the heads of the men on the ground. The men glanced up and struggled to their feet. The older man, clearly drunk and unsteady on his feet, kept a firm grasp of his knife, while the younger man who didn't look old enough to be out of school, swiped his arm across his bloody lip.

Willie bit the inside of her cheek. Since she had yet to sit down and read the town's bylaws, she was unclear as to how to handle the unruly fighters. Sam would have barged in, taken them by the arm, thrown some punches if needed, and hauled them to jail. Regardless, it wouldn't hurt for them to sleep the drink off in the town jail. Willie just needed to get them there. "Let's go, gentlemen." She motioned her head down the street.

"I ain't going anywhere with no injun woman sheriff." The man with knife stepped toward her.

"Is that so?" Willie snaked her whip around the wrist holding the knife. "Guess I'll lead you then." She yanked, causing him to stumble and drop his knife. She kicked it toward the blacksmith, and then motioned for the younger man to walk ahead of them. "Watch him, Bear." The dog bared his teeth. The man jumped back, then skirted around Bear to follow Willie.

With the crowd following, they headed to the small unpainted wooden building which housed her office. She turned to face the crowd from the top step. "Go on home. I'll take care of things from here." She shoved the door open and escorted her first prisoners inside. Bear padded along beside her, never taking his dark eyes off the men.

The man with the whip around his wrist cursed and struggled. "You're cuttin' off the blood flow."

She bit back a remark of how the blood flow to his brain had been cut off long ago. Her dear departed Sam had believed in treating prisoners with care, and Willie wanted to do the same, even if it meant keeping her mouth shut a lot of the time. "You're in here." She gave him a push into one of the cells and loosened the tautness of the whip in order to remove it from his wrist. The younger, quieter man stepped willingly inside his cell and closed the barred door.

"I need your names." Willie wound her whip and rehung it on her belt, thankful she hadn't had to draw her gun.

"Mine is Henry Larson." The young man plopped on a cot, sending a cloud of dust into the air. "That loud mouth is my older brother, Oscar. He's a mean drunk, if you haven't noticed, but I reckon he's all right when he's sober."

"I've noticed what kind of a drunk he is." Willie studied the two, one belligerent, the other contrite. Good-looking young men if you looked past the blood-shot eyes, scrapes and dirt. "You two sleep it off and I'll be back to release you in the morning." If they didn't escape first. The doors to the cells hung crooked and were missing one or two bars. At least the townsfolk had seen she meant business when someone stepped out of line. She'd ask the blacksmith to repair the doors and pray the town had the funds to pay him.

Thankfully, Mama hadn't been there to hear the man's remark about an Indian sheriff. The townsfolk hadn't seemed to notice either. Mama, taking such care to hide that half of her ancestry, would have melted with shame.

"Stay, Bear. Keep them inside." Her trusty friend plopped down between the cells, his eyes shifting from one Larson boy to the other. "This here, gentlemen, is my deputy. Rest assured he will keep you company until I return. I wouldn't advise you stepping out of your cell."

Oscar scowled. "That's the devil's dog."

"Call him what you like, but he *will* follow my orders."

She took a look around the dusty room that was her office, noting the desk propped on pieces of wood to make it level. A gun rack was placed over a small wood-burning stove and hooks lined one wall, she supposed for coats and gun holsters. A glass-fronted cabinet with a rusty lock showcased two rifles and a pistol. Next to it hung a ring of keys. She shook her head at the fact no one had stolen the weapons. Maybe Wild Horse Pass was the tame town the advertisement had proclaimed it to be. She couldn't help but wish they had made the sheriff's office as welcoming as the house, though. No matter. Her and Mama would have it to rights in no time.

She tried the keys until she found the one that unlocked the cabinet, then removed the pistol and holster and a box of bullets. After a good cleaning, the handgun would be easier to tote around than the rifle slung over her shoulder. She stepped into the night, locking the door behind her.

"Good evening, Sheriff Jackson." A plump woman in a dark purple dress waited at the bottom of the steps. In her hands, she clutched a board on which was tacked several sheets of paper. "I hope you don't mind if we use your full name to address you by."

"No, ma'am." Willie pushed her hat farther back on her head.

"I am Gertie Bloomfield, the mayor's wife and proprietor of Bloomfield's Best Vittles. Here, I have a list of the town's laws. I trust you will study them and make sure the residents abide by them in addition to the territory laws, of course." She thrust the board at Willie. "We have a town meeting every second Wednesday evening of the month to discuss any concerns that need addressed. It is mandatory that you attend."

She flashed a grin. "The women's auxiliary is thrilled to have you here. We've been fighting for women's rights for years now, and have been fighting lawlessness by ourselves. We call ourselves the Wild Horse Pass Women's Vigilante Group." She leaned closer and lowered her voice. "Only, the menfolk don't know it's us that has been keeping the law. At least I don't think so."

"There is no longer a need for a vigilante brand

of justice, Mrs. Bloomfield." The last thing Willie needed was a group of eager women butting into her job and putting themselves in danger.

"Oh, but Mrs. Sheriff, I mean Sheriff Jackson, you are going to need our help." She eyed Willie's clothes. "It might help you be accepted if you wore proper women's clothing. The leather, uh, well, it doesn't do much to disguise a woman's curves. It wouldn't do to tempt the town's menfolk." She smiled again and bustled away leaving Willie standing with her mouth open. What had Willie gotten herself, and her family, into?

She clutched the board of laws to her chest and headed toward the light shining through the livery stables doors. Not only did she need to engage the blacksmith's services, but she needed to retrieve Oscar's knife. She stepped through the open doors. "Hello?"

"Back here."

She marched down the aisle between horse stalls to where Tom Miller sat hunched on a three-legged stool while digging a pebble from a horse's hoof. "Mr. Miller, I'm wondering whether I can trouble you for a job repairing the jail cells? Does the town provide funds for those type of services?"

"Yes, ma'am. You don't need to worry about paying for the job." He stood and wiped his hands along his tan pants. "What do you need done?"

"While the actual cells themselves seem to be in good repair, the doors are hanging crooked. I had to leave my dog in order to make sure the Larson brothers stay put."

"So, you want new jail cell doors?"

"If it wouldn't be too much trouble?" The lantern's light cast shadows across his face and reflected in the dark pools of his eyes. His coloring was so different from Sam's green eyes and dark hair. While Sam hadn't been a small man, actually a few inches over Willie's own five foot seven, Tom Miller towered over her. His sheer strength and size left her feeling safe in his presence.

A feeling she found she rather liked. A feeling she would also fight to ignore. There was no sense in getting attached to any of the town's residents. Not with her uncertain future.

"Not too much trouble at all. I'll mosey by in the morning and take a look at what needs to be done, and please, we don't stand too much on formalities around here. Call me Tom."

"And I'm Willie. Thank you." She thrust out her hand.

"Folks have taken to calling you Mrs. Sheriff." A corner of his mouth quirked.

"Yes, Mrs. Bloomfield slipped and did that very thing a few moments ago." She sighed. "I'd rather hoped they would take me a bit more seriously."

"They take you seriously enough."

*

She cocked her head and fixed those amazing eyes on his. "Do you?"

"I reckon I do. You handled the Larson boys well enough. No one was hurt." He pretended to be busy arranging his tools on the wall, fidgeting under her stare. What was it about her that made him so nervous? Was it the eyes that stood out in such contrast to her mane of dark hair or was it his suspicion that she possessed Indian blood? Maybe it was her calm self-assurance that set his nerves on edge. He'd never met a woman like her before; One that carried a whip and a gun or one that dressed in buckskins and walked around with a beast of a dog.

Wilhemina Jackson was a widow and a mother, yet shot a gun as if it were an extension of her. Still, many sheriffs had come and gone, some because they no longer wanted to live in Wild Horse Pass and all that entailed, and others because a bullet found them. If men couldn't handle the rigors of living in Montana's lawlessness, how could a woman believe to be any different?

"You have reservations about whether or not I can do this," she said. "That's fine. I will show you and the town that I am more than capable. Good night, Mr. Miller." She marched away, the fringes on the bottom of her skirt swaying with her hips. She stopped at the door, and spoke without turning. "I had hoped we could be friends. That you would possibly consider being my deputy, if the need arose. I see that I am mistaken. Please leave Mr. Larson's knife on my desk." She stepped outside and the dark engulfed her.

Tom was a cad. He'd hurt her feelings and had no idea how to make things right. A man couldn't help how he felt about things. He only needed to find a more prudent way to express those feelings.

He extinguished the lamp and headed across the street to the jail. As one of the town board members, he possessed a key to most of the buildings in town and might as well check out the cells before heading home.

He unlocked the door and stepped into a dark jail. The sheriff's beast growled from the shadows. "Easy, boy." Tom lit the wick on a lamp on the desk.

The cell doors weren't the only thing that needed fixing. The sham of a desk should be tossed out and a new one built. He laid the knife on the scarred desk top.

"Tom!" Oscar clutched the bars. "You've got to let us out of here. That … thing growls every time I try to move."

"You created a drunken spectacle in public, Oscar. You know that isn't allowed here." Tom held the lantern higher. Henry snored from his bunk. "Go to sleep. You'll be out in the morning."

"You know I wouldn't have stabbed my brother, Tom. He's the only blood family I have. Don't tell me you're siding with that woman."

"Yep, guess I am since she's the sheriff." At least for the next three months. With the condition of the cell doors, he'd have to replace them. They couldn't be fixed. Bloomfield would have an apoplexy at the cost. Still, while the Larson boys might not be too dangerous, they had seen their share of vagrants passing through and a good jail provided safety for the entire town. It would be a warranted expense. "See you in the morning, Oscar."

Tom skirted around the watchful dog and headed home, his head full of ways to improve the sheriff's office. Not to mention her mention of him being a deputy. He honestly couldn't say how he felt about that. While, he'd done his share of trying to keep peace in the town, he doubted he wanted to wear a star on his shirt, thus putting a target on his back. But, could he stand back and let a woman be a target alone? Tom wasn't a coward, and tried to do what was right in the eyes of God and by the town, but he felt as if someone had shoved him between two large boulders and left him.

He knew what Ma would have said. For him to step up and be a man and accept the woman's cry for help. Was it a cry for help? Willie Jack didn't strike him as a damsel in distress. He stomped the dirt from his boots and headed into his one room cabin. He toed off the boots and padded in stocking feet to the stove to heat up the beans left from lunch.

Would Ma have wanted him to be deputy to an Indian? After her brutal killing, he wasn't sure he could stomach it, but Ma also prided herself on judging folks individually. Of course, he'd only be called upon once in a while, hopefully. Willie did seem capable of taking care of minor skirmishes. His head ached from all the thinking. He banked the fire in the stove, put his boots back on, tossed the beans out the backdoor, and then grabbed his hat. Maybe the pastor could clear up the fog in his head, because Tom couldn't see through the murk.

Pastor Mark Netser and his wife, Gloria, sat in rocking chairs on their front porch when Tom arrived. "Howdy, Tom."

"Pastor, Gloria." Tom propped one foot on the step. "I've something on my mind maybe y'all can clear up."

"Be glad to help if we can, and outside of Sunday, I've asked you to call me Mark."

Tom sighed. It wasn't fitting to call such an important man by his first name. "It's about the new sheriff."

"Don't tell me you have a problem with her being a woman?" Gloria rocked faster. "Are you upset that she outshot you?"

"I didn't get off a single shot." Tom removed his hat and slapped it against his leg. "But, her gender does have a bearing on what's bothering me. That and the fact she might be Indian. You know what they did to my ma."

"Those Indians weren't this one, Tom. The sheriff can't be more than a smidgen Indian, anyway." Mark stood and placed a heavy hand on Tom's shoulder. "You can't judge one group by another. It'll eat you up inside. That horrible incident happened when you were a child. It's time to give that hatred to God."

Tom hung his head. Hatred? He didn't hate Willie Jack, the opposite in fact. He found himself intrigued by her. Yet …

"Riding into town in buckskins isn't exactly like she's hiding who she is," Gloria said. "In fact, I'd say she has embraced who God created her to be. How can we do any different? I suspect there may be more to your coming here tonight than her blood line. Am I right?"

Tom nodded. "She wanted to ask me to be her deputy, but changed her mind when I said I wasn't fully ready to accept a woman sheriff."

"Because of your mother?" Gloria asked.

"Yes." He didn't want to talk about his mother anymore. He should have done something, a young boy of fourteen or not, then things might have turned out differently. If they'd lived closer to town … he could spend hours on 'what-ifs'.

"Come sit, Tom." Mark waved toward an empty rocking chair. "Just sit in our company and listen to God's leading. Let God heal that terrible ache inside you."

"No, I reckon I owe our sheriff an apology. Might as well do it before laying my head on the pillow. Thanks for listening." Tom turned and marched toward the white cottage in the distance.

The moon lit up the street, making his way easy. The only sounds were the tinny music coming from the saloon and the nicker of the horses tied out front. He gave a small smile at thinking of how the women of the town had picketed in their vain effort to keep the saloon from being built. They'd finally relented and let it be built on the town outskirts and close to the church, but would not agree to saloon girls or any form of entertainment other than elderly Bob Mellon playing the piano.

Tom hadn't stepped foot inside the place other than to build the foot rail along the bottom of the bar, and he had no intentions of ever doing so again. Still, he'd reckon the sheriff would have plenty of occasions to venture inside. Another reason why a woman shouldn't be sheriff. They didn't belong in places of debauchery.

He stepped up on the porch of Willie's house and knocked. She answered the door in a pale yellow gown, her raven hair falling down her back, and her looking the least like a lawmaker than anyone he had ever met. He swallowed against the dryness in his throat.

"May I help you, Mr. Miller?"

"Tom, please. Could you step outside for a minute?"

"Do I need my gun?"

He closed his eyes and took a deep breath. "No, ma'am. Not unless you plan on shooting me."

"I reckon that depends on what you've come to talk about." She stepped outside, pulling the door closed behind her.

"While I am not yet used to the idea of a female keeping the law here, I do owe you an apology. I've jumped to conclusions without giving you the agreed upon time to show yourself capable of the job. I apologize." There. He'd said it. Now, he could sleep easy.

She took her full bottom lip between pearly white teeth, sending his heart racing. He focused his gaze at the stars rather than on how pretty she looked or the fact she stood in front of him without shoes, her milky toes shining in the moonlight.

"Does this mean that you'll be my deputy should the need arise?"

6

Willie plopped in a rocking chair on the front porch as the sun rose the next morning, casting a rosy glow over the town. She admired the view of the mountains kissed with coral and sipped her coffee, the town rules in her lap. She should have read them last night, but all she could think of after Tom's visit was his apology and the way his eyes had widened when she answered the door in her calico dress.

She smiled and ran her hands over her buckskin skirt. While she wasn't opposed to dressing like a woman, full skirts and petticoats wasn't logical attire for a sheriff, but, when a man's eyes widened at the sight of her leather, it was usually in shock, rather than admiration. She confessed to rather enjoying the attention femininity brought her. She sighed and set her coffee on a sawed off tree turned into a side table, then transferred her attention to the rules it was her job to enforce.

"While these laws may not be listed on the law books for Montana," she read, "they are the rules we expect Wild Horse Pass to abide by and are posted in addition to Montana territory law." What crazy nonsense would she read in the next lines?

"No person is allowed to spread gossip about another person unless it is information that will benefit the town of Wild Horse Pass." That left things wide open in Willie's opinion. "No married woman is allowed to fish alone on Sunday. No single woman is allowed to fish alone on any day of the week." Her lips twitched. What could possibly have happened for the town to enforce that particular law?

"There can be no more than one saloon in town, and that saloon is forbidden to hire any females. It is also unlawful for a female to enter through the doors of said saloon." That might make things a bit difficult for Willie, since she was a female sheriff. Surely, though, that law didn't apply to her. "Drunken misconduct is strictly prohibited within town limits."

"What are you reading?" Mama set in the chair next to Willie and set the chair to rocking.

"The town laws, or rules as they are most often called. Some of them are quite ridiculous. Listen to this one." She tapped a finger on the page. "The sheriff's life and doings are open to town inspection and could result in said sheriff's dismissal."

"What kind of foolery is that?" Mama leaned closer to get a look at the words. "No wonder they can't keep a sheriff."

"Looks like there will be some things I'll need to address at the next town meeting." Willie pushed to her feet, setting the laws on her seat. "I'm heading to the sheriff's office to release the Larson brothers."

"I've got a breakfast and coffee made up for them." She rushed into the house, returning moments later with a woven basket. She handed the basket to Willie. "That side pistol looks good on you." She nodded at the holster hanging around Willie's waist. "With that and your whip, you shouldn't have any trouble keeping this town in line, silly laws or not."

"I hope not." With the basket hanging on one arm, and her leather hat hanging down her back, Willie marched down the street to the place she would call her second home for at least the next few months.

She pushed open the unlocked door, surprised to see Tom there before her and measuring her desk. "Good morning."

"Mornin', Sheriff. I noticed you needed a new desk, and I've some scrap lumber behind the livery. I hope you don't mind." He straightened and tossed his wide-brimmed hat on the desk top. His mussed hair reminded her so much of Junior when he woke in the morning.

"Not at all." She fought the urge to keep from reaching over and smoothing the blacksmith's hair back into place.

"Mrs. Sheriff!" Oscar Larson yelled from his cell. He gripped the bars and pressed his face against them. "Can you call off your beast now so I can go home to my wife and younguns'?"

"Come, Bear." Her best friend padded toward her and nosed the basket on her arm. "There might be something in there for you, you big brute." She scratched behind his ears and set the basket on the desk. "You men come on out and have some breakfast before heading home. There's coffee, too."

"I ain't never had no lawman, er, woman, give me breakfast after a night in jail," Oscar said, skirting around Bear.

"Well, there's a first time for everything." The town had never had a woman sheriff before, either. Willie opened the basket and pulled out tins of biscuits and gravy and a carafe of hot coffee. "You hungry, Mr. Miller?"

"It's Tom, and while I've already eaten, I wouldn't mind a cup of that coffee."

"My stomach ain't up to food this morning," Henry stated.

"I don't imagine." Willie poured coffee for the three men then sat at her desk. "I want you two to lay off the drink. It's against the law to get so addled within town limits. Next time, I'll lock you up for two days, and I might lock my dog in the cell with you."

Oscar paled. "I'll do my best, Mrs. Sheriff, but can't make any guarantees. That whiskey calls to me like a lover's smile."

Willie winced. "Just Sheriff will suffice, Mr. Larson." The man should be ashamed of himself carrying on the way he had with a family waiting at home.

The Larson boys scarfed down their food faster than Bear ate the steak Mama had packed, Oscar grabbed his knife from the desk, and they skedaddled as if Willie would change her mind about releasing them. She grinned and shook her head. They sure had different attitudes when their mind wasn't clouded with whiskey or their heads pounding from too much imbibing. "I thought Oscar said Henry was his only kin?"

"Nah." Tom shook his head. "They're close is all. Oscar gets sentimental about his little brother when he's been drinking."

"Sentimental enough to fight him." Willie sipped at her coffee.

"What's on your agenda today?" Tom asked, setting his empty mug back in the basket.

"My husband was sheriff of a small town in Kansas. He believed in the sheriff being visible and easily accessible if the town residents needed him. I intend to do the same." She couldn't help but think his question arose from the silly town law of the resident's having the right to know everything the sheriff did. The thought bothered like a burr under a saddle blanket. "I'll walk the street, then collect my horse and ride the outskirts."

He nodded. "Should be safe enough."

"Excuse me?" She crossed her arms and shifted in her seat in order to face him.

"Uh, nothing." His face reddened.

"There will come a day, Mr. Miller, when you will feel very foolish for doubting my abilities." She stood and snapped her fingers for Bear to follow. She didn't want to spend another minute in the company of a man who thought her nothing but a silly woman who was in over her head.

Her boots beat out a steady rhythm on the

boarded sidewalks lining Main Street. Her march took her past a mercantile/post office, a diner, a barber, a dressmaker, a telegraph office, and a bank. The other side of the street contained the livery and a boarding house, not to mention the saloon off in the distance but still visible. No music drifted from its swinging doors. Good. She wouldn't have to worry about drunks stumbling from it until at least early afternoon. The church, parsonage, and schoolhouse sat at the end of the street completing the horseshoe effect. Not bad for a small town in the middle of Nowhere, Montana.

Willie made her way to the livery to collect Stormy. Since Tom was busy at the jail, she was perfectly capable of saddling her own horse. She'd been doing so since she was a child, after all. Horse saddled, and Bear trotting at her side, Willie rode out of town and headed west. Without a map, she used fences and smoking chimneys to alert her to where folks lived.

A few residents stopped plowing fields to look up and wave, others just stared. While it would take a while for her to be accepted, it still rankled that she wasn't readily accepted just on the basis of her professional standing. She kept her head high, smiled and nodded, and continued riding through the beautiful landscape. Mountains, trees, farms, they all made a pretty picture. Again, Willie counted herself blessed to be in Wild Horse Pass in a house that didn't allow light to enter through the holes in the walls. God had seen fit to give her a job that put food in her babies mouths and clothes on their backs.

She glanced heavenward and gave a simple prayer of thanks, the sun warm on her face. Bear barked, pulling her from her musings. The dog's neck bristled as he stared into a thick stand of trees. With her hand on her pistol butt, Willie slid from the horse's back, using Stormy as a shield. Her neck prickled, her hands grew clammy.

A ride down a road lined heavily with trees had resulted in Sam's death. They had been so involved in conversation they hadn't spotted danger until too late. Willie gulped, her throat seizing. What if history were to repeat itself now, with her?

She peered into the shadows. Would she suffer the same fate? Maybe she wasn't cut out to be a sheriff. But, what else was left for her? She could barely sew a straight hem and her cooking left a lot to be desired. Other than finding another husband right away, being the sheriff of Wild Horse Pass was the only option left to her. She could do this. She took a deep breath and stepped around the horse.

If someone lurked in the bushes, Bear would attack. At the very least his growls would increase. Most likely it had been nothing more than a rodent scurrying among the dead leaves on the forest floor. Still, she kept a tight grip on her gun, fought to control her trembling limbs, and swallowed her fear. A sheriff could not show weakness.

*

Something had happened on her ride. Tom watched as, with trembling hands, Willie unsaddled her horse and fed her oats from a nearby pail. Her dog sat and guarded her with dark, unblinking eyes until Willie turned and left the livery.

Tom came out of the stall where he had sat repairing a bridle. So deep in thought had she been that Willie hadn't seemed to notice him, yet he suspected very little escaped the woman's notice normally. He followed and stood in the livery doorway as she shuffled across the street and into the sheriff's office. Had someone accosted her on her ride? Made disparaging remarks toward her?

This was why a woman should not be the one to uphold the law in a place such as Montana Territory, especially a mother with two young children. He plopped on a barrel and rubbed both hands over his face, once again seeing his mother plowing a field alone because Pa was busy herding cattle. In his mind, he saw the Indians ride across the field and butcher her, heard her screams and her order for him to stay hidden. He should never have cowered behind the barn like a coward. Young or not, he should have fought and died alongside her. Now, Willie being part Indian or not, he was again facing the dilemma of protecting a woman in a man's role.

How could he not keep an eye on her? There were those, even in Wild Horse Pass, that would take advantage of her, even kill her if the need arose and she stepped between them and their nefarious goals. He groaned. The pastor and Gloria were right. Tom would have to set aside his prejudice in order to keep Willie safe. It was almost too much to contemplate.

Spirit heavy, he headed to the blacksmith side of the livery and stoked the fire. He might as well get started on some of the ornate iron work Wilma Coffee wanted to stock at the mercantile, not to mention the order for a new branding iron for a rancher in Billings. Thankfully, work was steady. In a few years, Tom would have a ranch of his own. Then, he might consider finding himself a bride.

He donned his heavy leather apron and slid the anvil closer to the fire. He picked up an iron rod and used the vise to clamp it to the anvil so he could hammer and punch it into the shape of an L with a curved line underneath. The cattle on his ranch would someday carry the brand of the Lazy M. He smiled as he dreamed and let habit guide his hands.

Once he finished the iron and set it aside to harden, he started on the cell doors for the jail. He could have them ready in a day or two if he focused, which, now that he was working on the sheriff's job, made it hard for his mind not to dwell on her.

What had brought her to Wild Horse Pass? He knew she was a widow, but weren't there other jobs available for women; ones that weren't so dangerous? He sawed a bar to the proper length, set it aside, and grabbed another one. How long had she been widowed? With her looks, there should have been plenty of fellas lined up to marry her. In fact, he was surprised she hadn't received one or two proposals since arriving in town. Obviously the men in that area were intimidated by a pretty face that could shoot and crack a whip.

His stomach growled, reminding him it was past lunchtime. He set aside his tools, removed his apron, and then washed his hands and face for his daily trek to the diner. With Bloomfield's Best

Vittles being the only place in town where a bachelor could purchase a meal, he was doubly glad the food, and prices, were reasonable.

He stepped through a door, sending a bell jingling over his head, and waited for Gertie to lead him to an empty table. One family, strangers, and a few lone men occupied one half of the room. No single women dined anywhere in sight, not that the town had many, but its silly laws about what was proper behavior for unmarried women kept most of them behind closed doors. If a man was on the lookout for a wife, he'd have to find her at church.

"Howdy, Tom." Gertie bustled toward him. "Heard you're helping the sheriff out with some repairs. That's mighty nice of you."

"I'm getting paid for it." He winced at his surly tone. He would have repaired the cell doors for free.

"Well, sure you are." She patted his arm. "I guess the town was so busy readying the house, we plumb forgot about the jail. Come sit over here." She led him to a small table with two chairs in the corner, and then handed him a slate with the day's menu written on it in chalk. "I'll be right back."

He glanced up as Willie strolled past the window, her son and dog at her side. Tom thought of his need for help at the livery, but the boy looked too young. With school not starting for a couple of months, what did the lad do all day? None of his business. They most likely wouldn't be around when school started. He perused the menu, deciding on elk stew and biscuits.

Gertie approached his table, her gaze on the window. "That sheriff is a good-looking woman.

We'll have to keep an eye on her and make sure she abides by the laws, sheriff or not."

"She still has to do her job," Tom said, handing her the slate. "She'll need some leniency."

"I guess we'll have to take that up at the next meeting."

"I'm one of the chairmen, Gertie."

"I know, but it will still need to be discussed." She took his order and flounced away.

Tom shook his head. The married women in town needed to keep their noses at home and out of everyone else's business. He'd said so once to the mayor, who replied that if Tom knew how to control a woman, he could make a fortune selling the knowledge.

As if Tom knew anything about women. The only thing he knew with any certainty is that as the years passed, more and more women were stepping out of their familiar roles of wife and mother and entering the work force. Case in point: the sheriff.

Gertie plopped his lunch in front of him, spilling some onto the table, and marched away, clearly vexed that he had not readily agreed with her. Well, she was Bernard's problem. Tom wasn't in any hurry to settle down.

All four of the Simpson girls, escorted by their mother who rarely left home, sashayed past the window. One of them, the oldest, he thought, glanced in the window, tossed her springy blond curls away from her face, and waved. He pretended not to see and shoveled in his food instead. If he were in the market for a wife, it wouldn't be a young girl just out of short dresses with nothing in her head but fluff.

When he'd finished eating, he tossed a few coins on the table, and headed back toward the livery. From the direction of the schoolhouse, Willie marched with not only her son in front of her, but two other young boys, and none of them were smiling.

"Know where I can get some whitewash, Mr. Miller?" She asked. "Seems these three thought it would be fun to draw on the sides of the schoolhouse with charcoal."

"I think I have a bucket and some brushes in the livery." He bit back a grin at the boys' contrite faces and went to fetch the supplies. Pail and brushes in hand, he stepped back outside. "You aren't going to arrest them, are you, Sheriff?"

"The thought crossed my mind. Lucky for them, you had the items they need to get to work. Let's go boys." She whirled, leaving them to follow, and marched back the way she'd come.

Tom chuckled and jogged after them. Bear snuffled up at him, then trotted at his side. Maybe the dog wasn't so fierce after all. Tom scratched behind the dog's ears. His reward was a goofy dog grin and a swipe from a large wet tongue across his hand.

Across the side of the schoolhouse, the boys had written "School is stupid" and drawn a face with a tongue sticking out. Willie set them to work with brushes to first remove as much of the charcoal as possible, then to painting over their artwork. She leaned against a tree, crossed her arms, and kept her gaze firmly planted on the boys.

She rested her head back against the trunk, emphasizing her slender neck. Her hat hung down her back, giving him a clear view of her profile. High cheekbones, sweeping dark lashes, and hair so dark it reflected the light. With her eyes closed, he could study her at his heart's content. Only problem was, his heart raced fast enough to outrun a twister. The woman was downright beautiful and looked as out of place in their town as much as she seemed to belong. When she turned and cast those remarkable eyes on him, he tended to forget where he was. He tried to swallow against the sudden dryness in his throat.

"That boy needs a job," she said.

"Uh?" He blinked.

"A job. My son needs something to do to fill his summer days." She cocked her head.

"He's a bit young, don't you think?" Tom leaned beside her, breathing in the scent of lilac. The wind lifted silky strands of her hair and blew them across his face. He shoved his hands in his pockets to keep from tucking them behind her ear.

"Yes, but he's mischievous and easily led astray. Mama sometimes has trouble keeping an eye on him. Do you need your stables mucked? It might take him a good long while, but he'll get the job done. He could also run errands for you."

"I've been thinking about hiring a boy, but I'd thought on someone older."

She slapped her hat on her head and peered up at him from under the brim. "My family is all about proving ourselves, Mr. Miller."

He laughed. "I reckon you are. Okay, I'll give

him two weeks to prove himself. Have him report to me in the morning." He pushed off from the tree and still grinning, headed back to work.

Yep, Mrs. Sheriff was going to ruffle some feathers, and possibly break some hearts, in Wild Horse Pass.

7

"What were you thinking?" Willie marched Junior down the street after sending his cohorts home. "Whose idea was it?"

"Not mine." Junior stopped and planted his short legs shoulder-width apart and glared up at her. "I told you who else was involved. Can't we stop with the questions?"

Tears burned her eyes. She'd failed as a mother. Since Sam's death she'd worked too hard for too long and neglected her family. "I've got you a job at the livery. You start tomorrow."

"I'm only six, Ma! Ain't that slavery?"

"If you're old enough to get into trouble, you're old enough to work. Besides, it's only temporary." She glanced across the street. Several women gathered in front of the post office. Their rigid spines and waving arms alerted Willie to the fact it may not be a peaceful gathering. Again, work pulled her away from dealing with one of her own. "I need to be able to trust you to go straight home."

"Yes, ma'am." Junior kicked a rock down the sidewalk, his skinny shoulders slumped, and trudged away from her.

"I'll check with Grandmama when I come home to make sure you did what I said." Willie strolled across the street, motioning for Bear to follow. "Ladies, what's going on here? The law clearly states no rioting or loitering. This is clearly bordering on both."

Gertie Bloomfield faced her. "It also states no single woman can walk the streets of this town unescorted. And this woman," she pointed at a pretty young girl in a pink-ruffled dress, "is loitering and alone and making eyes at Tom Miller."

Willie glanced around her. Tom was nowhere in sight. She studied the girl in the center of what could only be described as a mob of feathered hats. "Miss, what is your name?"

"I'm Sally Simpson. My Pa owns the bank. I'm not loitering." She stomped her silk encased foot. "I ran an errand to the mercantile and these vultures pounced as soon as I came out the door." Tears shimmered in her blue eyes. "And my ma taught me better than to make eyes at a man." Her gaze cut to Tom's figure passing in front of the livery doors.

Willie bit back a grin. It looked as if her ma's lesson didn't take very well. When Tom stepped onto the street and headed for the bank, little Miss Sally's head almost swiveled in a complete circle. Not that looking at a handsome man should be against the law or anything. Willie did plenty of her own gazing at Tom when he wasn't looking. She'd loved her Sam, but God didn't make many men as nice to look at as Tom Miller. "Head on back to your Pa. Go on now."

Since Tom was headed in the same direction as the girl, Sally hefted her skirts and set off at an unladylike run. Willie took a deep breath and turned to the crowd of red-faced women. "Congregating is also in your list of laws. Time to break things up, ladies."

Gertie puffed out her chest, looking every bit like a flustered chicken. Willie couldn't pull her gaze from the peacock feather bobbing on the woman's hat. "Look, sheriff, we made those laws. We know perfectly well what they say. Before we hired you, the women of this town kept things running smoothly. We don't aim to stop doing our civic duty."

"Did you or did you not hire me to keep the law, thus enabling you to fulfill your other responsibilities?" Willie tipped her hat higher on her head. "As important as all of you are, I'm sure there are other things that require your attention?"

"Well, of course," she sputtered, "there are committees, feeding the poor, church, but we can't—"

"Then it must be a great relief to know I have things firmly under control so you can attend to that list of good pursuits. Good day." Willie nodded and moved past them into the sheriff's office. She grinned at their open mouths and stunned faces. She had successfully put them in their place without ruffling their feathers. A job well done. This female vigilante group needed to stop before someone got hurt.

"We can handle it, can't we, buddy?" She

patted Bear's head. Sure, they could, despite the misgivings that tickled at the edge of her consciousness. Samuel would have approved of her accepting the job as sheriff, wouldn't he? After all, he had taught her everything she knew.

Now what? She sat at her desk and stared at the walls. The place could use a good cleaning, but there was probably something in the town laws that stated the sheriff shouldn't clean her own office. She laughed and grabbed a broom from the corner. Soon, she sent clouds of dust flying out the front door.

"No need to cover a guy in dirt." Tom dragged a new cell door inside. "I'll have the other finished in a day. I've keyed the lock to work with the key you already have."

"Thank you." She propped the broom against the wall. "You work fast."

"So do you." He gave her a crooked grin that set her heart into somersaults. "The town womenfolk are all a buzz about the bossy new sheriff."

Willie rolled her eyes. "They need to mind their own business." She averted her eyes from the way his muscles rippled under his blue shirt as he lifted the door into place. She didn't have time to contemplate anything resembling romance. "Accosting a young girl for looking at a man or running errands for her father, alone, is ridiculous."

"I agree. Most of the laws were in place before I became a member of the board."

"You're on the board?" Why did she not know that? Maybe Tom could be her way of making improvements to the laws.

He glanced over his shoulder. "Yes, ma'am. The reason for the single women ban against walking the streets alone is for their own protection. The only ones exempt from that law are women with grey hair. Seems the opinion is that they are less likely to be approached by a man intent on immoral advances."

"My mother might take offense to that." Mama prided herself on still being a comely woman. To know that she was considered undesirable because of a few grey hairs would not sit well. "Are the men in this town the sort to bother a woman walking down the street?"

He shrugged. "Hasn't ever happened before. The law is a preventive. They're posted at the post office, the mercantile, and the saloon."

No wonder the town couldn't keep a sheriff. "Does that law apply to me? I do have a regular escort." She motioned her head toward Bear. "I doubt anyone will bother me with him around."

"I'm sure of it." He tested the door on its new hinges. "Smooth as a rabbit's ear."

"Willie." Mama tromped into the office, Bonnie on her hip, and Junior at her side. "I need you to watch these two for a minute while I run to the mercantile for some things."

"Sure. Can you pick me up some fabric for a new blouse or two?" Willie held out her arms for her daughter, breathing deeply of a freshly washed little one. She rested her cheek against Bonnie's silky curls. "Junior, you can see whether Mr. Miller needs any help. He's the man you'll be working for."

Mama nodded. "You bet. We're all in need of new clothes. This boy," she ruffled Junior's hair, eliciting a scowl from him, "is growing like a baby bird." With a kiss on each of the children's foreheads, she bustled back outside and down the sidewalk.

She had no sooner left than Gloria Bloomfield, escorted by a woman Willie hadn't met, ducked inside. "Mrs. Sheriff." Gloria narrowed her eyes. "The jail is no place for children."

"It's only for a few minutes, Mrs. Bloomfield. Besides, my son will be working for Mr. Miller, and we are going over the details." Willie shifted Bonnie to her other hip. "They aren't here all the time." Were the women hiding around the corner, waiting for Willie to break one of their injunctions? Sometimes, it was all she could do to hold her tongue and be respectful. She needed the job too much to voice her opinion.

"I'm Wilma Coffee, my husband and I own the mercantile." The tall thin woman peered down her long nose. "I must admit your behavior is a disappointment. We had hoped that, upon hiring you, that with you being a woman, you would enforce the law better than the men we've had in the past."

"I intend to." Willie sat Bonnie in the chair behind her desk. "But nowhere in your laws does it say I cannot have my children with me at the jail. Since I have no one incarcerated at the moment, I see no harm in it."

"How about they come with me?" Tom

scooped Bonnie in his arms. "Come on, chief." He clapped Junior on the shoulder. "Let me show you the horses."

The two meddling women nodded their approval. "What a wonderful idea," Mrs. Bloomfield said. "Solves the problem."

"I don't see a problem." Willie tossed her hat on her desk.

Keeping her temper under control was like keeping a lid on a pot that threatened to boil over. If she expressed her opinion in any manner other than a subdued one, she most likely wouldn't be able to stay the agreed upon three months. As things were moving now, she probably wouldn't be allowed to stay on as sheriff past the allotted time. For now, she'd keep her mouth closed and make a list of things she wanted to address, and possibly change, at the next town meeting.

*

Tom headed to the livery before he could get dragged into the women's problems. Why had he volunteered to babysit? He knew virtually nothing about children. Didn't this only serve to prove his point about women doing a man's job? Women belonged at home tending to the babies, not plowing fields or carrying a gun as a lawman.

The sheriff's eyes had flashed blue lightning when the other women criticized her decision to watch the children for a few minutes, but he admired her self-control. Most women would have shot verbal bullets with both barrels. But then, Willie Jack wasn't like most women.

He sat the little girl on a hay bale. She stuck

her thumb in her mouth and stared at him with eyes the same alluring shade as her mother's. The boy, Junior, crossed his arms and gazed around the livery. Instead of blue eyes, the boy had the dark eyes of his grandmother. Gazing at their fair skin, it was easy to forget Indian blood flowed through their veins. It was also easy to believe all Indians weren't capable of the type of violence that had robbed him of his mother.

He rubbed his hands over his face and forced the unpleasant thoughts away. They were the innocents in life, made more so by the fact their mother needed to work outside the home for a living. What kind of job could she get at the end of her three months trial period? Other than remarrying, there was nothing for widows to do but move on or open a business and the laws of Wild Horse Pass strictly forbade any single woman to own her own business.

"So, who wants to feed the horses?" Tom returned the children's stares. Bonnie remained silent.

Junior cocked his head. "Big one or little one?"

"Excuse me?"

"Mama only lets me around the ponies. I want to feed a big horse." He marched down the aisle, peering into the stalls until he got to Tom's horse, Nightmare, a large blue-black stallion. "This one."

"Uh, well, son he tends to bite folks he doesn't know." Tom rushed forward and pushed the stallion's massive head back over the door.

"He won't bite me."

"How do you know?" Tom stayed firmly

between the boy and the horse. Nightmare neighed.

"Because animals like me." Junior climbed on the door and reached his hand out to the horse. "See?"

Nightmare sniffed his hand and drew back, then came closer and allowed the boy to pet him. Huh. Maybe it was only adults the horse didn't like. Tom fished a sugar cube from his pocket and handed it to Junior. "Keep your hand flat and your fingers out of the way."

"I know. I'm not stupid." Junior grinned, his dark eyes sparkling. "He loves me."

Tom was pretty sure it was the sugar the horse loved. Bonnie toddled toward them and tugged on Tom's shirt. "Potty."

The blood rushed to his feet. Why hadn't he thought of the child needing the privy before offering to watch her?

"I'll take her." The sheriff's mother hurried toward them. "Thank you for rescuing my daughter. I'm Winifred or Winnie as I'm most commonly called." She hefted the child to her hip. "Don't let my daughter see you letting her boy around that monstrous horse. She's quite the protective mother."

"The boy doesn't really take no for an answer." Much like his mother in that regard, come to think of it.

"Yeah, we're a stubborn bunch." She smiled. "Come on, child. You can carry my packages. Good day, Mr. Miller. I'll set an extra plate at the table tonight to repay you for your kindness. See you at five."

Before he could protest, she was gone. Had she invited him to supper and left without his response? He reached under his hat and scratched his head. Who were these people, and why did they want him to belly up to their table? He hadn't done anything to help more than most people would have. He felt as if he'd stepped into quicksand and sunk up to his armpits.

Rather than dwell on the mess one small act of kindness had gotten him into, he set to work on the other cell door. Maybe he could have it installed early in the morning and not have to see the beautiful sheriff for a day or two. It would be hard enough having those eyes settle on him across the supper table. A body couldn't tell what she was thinking until she said so. She looked at a man as if she weighed him and often found him lacking.

Maybe he should run across the street to the diner and purchase a pie. He shouldn't show up empty handed. But purchasing a whole pie would raise questions he wasn't sure he wanted to answer. If the town found out he'd shared a meal with the sheriff, tongues would wag faster than a dog's tail at the sight of a bone. Still, his mother had taught him well. A body never showed up for a dinner invitation empty handed. He wiped his hands on the legs of his pants and marched to the diner.

Gertie's daughter, Violet, every bit as plump as her mother but twice as sweet, greeted him with a smile. "Kind of early for supper, isn't it?"

"I'd like to buy a pie."

"Apple or cherry?" Her round face dimpled.

"Uh, both?" There went every cent in his

pocket.

"Well, aren't you hungry?" She took his money and then placed one apple and one cherry pie into boxes. "Having company?"

He shook his head. "Nope. Just in the mood for pie." He rushed out before she asked more questions.

He had over an hour until the appointed time. Getting from the livery to the sheriff's house, carrying two pies without being seen, would be a difficult task. He hurried home and set the pies on the table before heading for the wash basin. He had a shirt that wasn't too dirty. He'd only worn it once. After scrubbing everything from the waist up, he donned the dark brown shirt. He needed a shave, but that would have to wait. No sense in putting too much care into his appearance. He didn't want it to look as if he'd gone courting, more like he was headed to church. Carrying pies.

Why did simple things have to be so difficult? He glanced out his window. Gertie Bloomfield marched down the sidewalk, Wilma Coffee pulled the door to the mercantile closed, and the Simpson girls trailed behind their father. All signs it was five o'clock and the town was locking down for the evening. It was now or never.

Tom picked up his pies and stepped outside. What if he rode over on the back of Nightmare? Would folks think he went on official business? He should never have given into the impulse to take a gift. Wait. He hurried to the livery and set the boxes in his tool crate. There. If someone asked, he could say the sheriff needed to borrow a hammer. As the town's confirmed bachelor, he didn't want to cause any confusion.

Steps lighter now that he had a fool proof plan, he backed onto the street. A few men headed toward the saloon, but other than them, the street was empty. Tom slapped his hat on his head, and whistling, set off toward the sheriff's house.

"Howdy, Tom." Mayor Bloomfield stepped out of his office. "Where are you going looking so spiffy?"

"Just dropping off some tools at the sheriff's house."

"Do I smell cherry pie?"

Tom didn't want to lie. He forced himself to shake his head no. "Maybe it's drifting from the restaurant?"

The mayor's brow furrowed. "I don't think so. Maybe my wife is in a good mood and made something special for supper. You have a good evening."

Tom released the breath he'd held. That was a close call. He continued a bit further, only to have himself stopped by the Simpson family. "Care to join us for supper?" Frank Simpson asked. "The missus and I are taking the girls to the diner as a treat."

"No, thank you. There's something I need to do." Was everyone who lived within walking distance going to stop him? What happened to the virtually empty street he'd seen only moments before?

"You work too hard, son." Frank nodded rapidly. "Too hard. Need to take a break now and then. My girls are sorely disappointed, aren't you girls?"

They nodded as rapidly as their father, eight eyes fixed on Tom's face. They stopped giggling and ducked their heads.

"Yoo hoo, Mr. Miller. Supper's done!" Winnie waved from her front porch. She ducked back out of sight.

Tom groaned as heat rose from his toes and settled on his face. The whole town would know where he'd hung his hat for supper by morning.

8

Willie opened the door and greeted a red-faced Tom. "Come on in. Your timing is perfect. Supper is ready. Go ahead and hang your hat on the hook."

His face paled as he removed his hat and handed her a tool box. "There are pies inside. I didn't want to come empty handed."

Pies in a toolbox? She accepted his offering and glanced down the street before closing the door. Several of the townsfolk stared in their direction, whether because Tom was coming to supper or because she wore a regular dress. Either way, she understood his attempt at camouflage. Shaking her head, she closed the door. Nosey people.

"We aren't formal here." She led the way to the kitchen. "I hope you don't mind eating in here."

"Not at all. I eat most of my meals at the restaurant. This is a treat." He shifted from foot to foot and eyed the table where Junior and Bonnie already sat. "Is that belt to keep the little one in place?"

Willie nodded, eyeing the strap of leather

around her daughter's waist and then linked around the chair back. "Keeps her from running off and from falling. Why? Do it think it cruel?" Maybe her attempts at keeping her child in one place long enough to eat might not sit well with others.

"Ingenious, really."

"Sit at the head of the table, Tom." Winnie waved a spoon, dripping gravy on the front of her apron. "I hope you like steak and potatoes."

The man seemed to have lost his tongue. While Willie wasn't excited to hear her mother had invited him to supper, there was nothing to be done about it now. Tongues would wag. Hopefully, she could dispel the gossip by replying that it was a way to pay him back for his kindness in building the cell doors.

He stared, open admiration shining from his coffee-colored eyes. She narrowed her own. He didn't have to look so surprised every time he saw her in a dress. She smoothed her skirt of blue. She was a woman after all. The leather was strictly for work and hunting. While Willie would wear the more comfortable clothes all the time, she had made a compromise with Mama.

She set plates filled with steak, potatoes, and corn in front of each seat and reached for a pitcher of fresh lemonade. Next to it sat a cup of sugar.

Mama needed to slow down her spending at the mercantile. She'd purchased enough fabric for Willie to have two blouses and another dress, not to mention pants for Junior and fabric for clothes for Bonnie. Add in the food supplies since their garden wouldn't produce for a few months, and Willie hated to think what the tally was. They needed to save in case the residents of Wild Horse Pass sent them on their way in a little under three months.

Tom pulled out a chair for her at the opposite end of the table from where Mama had told him to sit. Her face flushed. It had been a long time since a man had made such a chivalrous gesture toward her.

"Doesn't that dress bring out the blue in Willie's eyes?" Mama asked, sitting to Willie's right. "I had quite the struggle getting her to purchase it."

For crying out loud. Willie rolled her eyes. The reason for Mama's good will toward Tom was out in the open. She was playing matchmaker. It wouldn't do her a bit of good. Willie had no intentions of getting hitched again. Few men other than Sam could understand her independent streak. What were the chances she could be blessed enough to find another like him?

Mama's comment had stolen what little of Tom's speech he seemed to possess. He stared at the food on his plate like a man confused.

"Would you care to say the blessing, Tom?" Mama grinned. "Then we can eat before the food gets cold."

He bowed his head and said a short prayer blessing the food and the hands that prepared it. Poor thing. He looked like a rabbit caught in a trap. Willie would set Mama straight at the first opportunity. Tom might very well be the only friend in town for Willie, and she wouldn't have him scared off by the scent of romance.

"Were the young'uns any trouble for you?"

She asked, grabbing a biscuit from the basket in the center of the table and breaking it in half for Bonnie. "They can be quite the mischief makers." She picked up her fork and scooped up some potatoes.

"No, they were fine."

"I fed Nightmare," Junior piped up. "He's a big black horse that likes to bite people."

Willie's hand froze halfway to her mouth, potatoes falling from her fork. "You put my boy in danger?"

Tom's head jerked up. "No, ma'am. I stood right beside him. If he's going to be at the livery most days, he needs to become familiar with the animals."

"I figured he would muck out stables or run errands." She couldn't survive if she lost one of her children. Maybe she should think of something else to fill her son's days.

"I'll take good care of him, Mrs. Sheriff. He'll do nothing too dangerous for his age."

She sighed. "Don't you start with that ridiculous name too. It's Willie or Mrs. Jackson or plain Sheriff." She wanted to smack the first person who had started that ridiculous title. "I'm a woman, a widowed mother, and I'm a sheriff. The three can go together without causing such a ruckus." She stabbed a piece of meat several times in an attempt to get rid of her frustration.

The tinging of the metal tines against the plate filled the room. When she finally got the meat on her fork, she glanced up to see the others staring at her. "What? While there isn't a lot of lawlessness in this town, I've handled what has come up admirably. No one should have any complaints about my performance so far and should give me the respect the position deserves."

"The town isn't exactly … as simple as it seems. We have our share of scoundrels. You'll see before the time is up." Tom buttered a biscuit.

"If you mean people breaking those ridiculous town laws—"

"More than that." He held up a hand to stave off her words. "We have unsavory characters pass through here all the time. You've been lucky so far. That's the main reason for the law about single women being out alone. It's for their protection. Nothing wrong with a town only having one saloon. It cuts down on the menfolk drinking or gambling away their earnings. Men should be at home with their families in the evenings. Women should be caring for the house and children."

Willie stared at him, waiting for a grin to show he was joshing. When one didn't come, she tossed her fork on the table. "Sometimes, life doesn't play along with carefully set rules, Mr. Miller. While I would enjoy cozying up around a fire with a husband, that choice was taken from me. If I don't provide a living for my family, then who will?"

"The church is responsible for widows and orphans. The Bible says so." He stopped buttering and met her gaze. "Deadly accidents happen when women step out of the role God planned for them."

"Hurry up and eat, children." Ma pointed at Junior's and Bonnie's plates. "Things are going to get loud around here. Your Mama is liable to fetch her whip."

Willie took a deep breath, willing her temper to cool. She would not embarrass her mother or frighten her children because of a difference of opinion. What had happened to this man for him to believe such things? "No worries, Mama, I've lost my appetite." She shoved away from the table and marched into the front room. She grabbed her hat and her rifle before heading for the front porch.

A woman's role! What kind of town had she landed in? Back in Kansas, women worked alongside their men in the fields, hunted the woods, and set traps in the prairies. When no good thieves came around, the women grabbed the guns and defended the homestead right along with their husbands. She plopped onto a rocking chair. She would change the mindset of these people or die trying.

Propping her feet on the porch railing, she stared past the town to where the sun started its descent behind the mountains. God had brought her to the beautiful town of Wild Horse Pass. Surely, He had a greater plan than to have her ridiculed and run out of town at the end of three months. Or maybe she had heard him wrong. It was quite possible that what she had thought was God's leading had been nothing more than her own wishful thinking.

She lifted her mane of hair off her neck to catch a breeze. She needed a lot more cooled off than just her neck.

"My apologies, again." Tom joined her. "Mind if I sit?"

"No one here but a woman to stop you, and everyone knows that is impossible."

"I never said you were incapable, Willie, only that you've stepped out of your God-designed role for a woman."

She snorted. "You leave my relationship with God out of this." She set the rocker into motion with a sharp jab of her foot. To think she had considered him a friend.

"Your Ma has cut the pie. Aren't you going to have a piece?"

"I'll pass, thank you." She turned to study his profile in the gathering dusk. Such a handsome man to have such a sad way of looking at the world. Something was going on in that blond head of his. Something that caused pain to radiate from his dark eyes. Well, it wasn't her place to find out what. She had a job to do, and a job she intended to do well.

*

Why couldn't Tom keep his opinions to himself? He continued to drive a wedge between him and Willie without having a clue what he'd done until it was too late. Would it be so bad to have her as the sheriff for three months? He could keep her safe that long, couldn't he? He was no longer a young boy forced to hide while his mother was killed. Part Indian or not, Willie was a beautiful woman who was in over her head whether she wanted to admit it or not.

"Sheriff, I have a complaint." A portly woman dressed in clean but patched clothes, her gray hair falling out of its bun, bustled toward the house. "Howdy, Tom."

"Mrs. Mahoney." Tom tipped his hat.

Willie stood. "What's wrong?" She grabbed her gun.

"Someone is stealing my chickens. I've lost the fifth one this week. I count on those chickens for food and funds." Mrs. Mahoney crossed her arms. "I want to know what you're going to do about it."

"As the town sheriff," Willie said. "I intend to find the thief. I'll be by your place in the morning."

"Bring that beast of a dog with you. He can track the culprit." With a swish of her skirts, she marched down the road out of town.

"Is it safe for her to walk alone at this time of night?" Willie stepped off the porch and watched her go. "Or are you only worried about the protection of the young women?"

"She's safe enough." No one in their right mind wanted to mess with Mrs. Mahoney. She could scare the ticks off a dog with her sharp tongue.

Willie resumed her seat on the porch. "Tell me about her."

"She's widowed and has three worthless sons who do nothing but drink and gamble. Her place is about a mile down the road, then you turn right at the junction. Can't miss the farm. It's falling into disrepair. The women vigilante group has tried to get the Mahoney's to clean their place up, but once Mrs. Mahoney ran them off at gunpoint, they've let her be." Tom scratched the scrabble on his chin. "She's mouthy and loud, and stays to herself most of the time. She won't hurt you none, unless you try to harm her or say something bad about her boys."

"I wasn't going to hurt her." Willie turned as fast as a rattlesnake. Her eyes flashed in the moonlight.

He held up his hands. "I didn't mean it that way." Couldn't he say anything right to her? He didn't normally have trouble talking to anyone. He stood. "Thank you for the meal. I'll fetch my tool box and go."

"You haven't had your pie." Winnie stepped outside, a plate in each hand. "I've brought you both a sliver of each."

"Thank you, Mama." Willie took her plate and sat back down. "I've something to check on in the morning. Can you watch Bonnie? I'll send Junior over to Mr. Miller's livery."

"I'll be working in the garden. I'll close the gate so she can't get out. We'll be fine." She patted Tom on the shoulder. "See, Tom. Us women got it all figured out. You men can relax now."

She went back inside, leaving a lump in his throat and his face as hot as the July sun. Embarrassed or not, he had nothing to say to Winnie's comment. Working a garden and tending a child were safe enough pursuits. He wanted to volunteer his company when Willie ventured out the next morning, but didn't relish getting his head shot off.

He wolfed down the pie like a starving man, then grabbed his tool box. "Thank you again, Willie." He couldn't leave fast enough. The longer he stayed, the more chances he'd say something else that would rile her.

"Wait." Willie grabbed her hat and rifle. "I still

need to make my evening rounds. I'll walk with you. Come, Bear." The ever present dog padded to her side.

He closed his eyes for a second, catching a whiff of something flowery when the breeze blew her hair. First supper, now an evening stroll around town. The gossip would fly for sure. If it weren't for the fact that ducking into the livery would leave her alone with dark descending, he'd make his excuses and head home.

"Well, good night." Willie stopped in front of the livery.

"I'll accompany you."

She shook her head. "I'll be just fine with Bear. Go home, Mr. Miller. As your sheriff, that is an order. This town has a curfew after all. Unless you plan on spending time at the saloon, you aren't to be on the street."

"I'll be with the sheriff."

"I'm refusing your offer." She slapped her hat on her head and, with one hand on Bear's head and the other clutching her rifle, she set off across the street.

Fine. Tom would watch from the shadows of his livery. If he heard one cry of alarm, he'd be at her side faster than a falling star.

He watched as she patrolled the sidewalk, the soft thud of her boots echoing in the still night. She stopped at the saloon, peered inside for several minutes, and then turned toward the school and church. Once she had walked the perimeter, she once again stopped at the saloon. Surely she wasn't contemplating going inside? After several seconds, she pushed open the swinging doors and went inside, leaving the dog lying on the sidewalk.

Once he got his mind to register what he had actually seen, Tom sprinted in her direction. What was she thinking to step inside such a place? His heart pounded in his throat as he barged through the doors.

Willie approached a round table surrounded by men playing cards. "I've heard rumors of gambling," she said. "Gambling is against the law in Montana territory. We need to break this game up, gentlemen."

One of the Mahoney boys pushed his chair back with a screech. "Well, if it ain't the purty little sheriff. Look here, boys, she's wearing a dress like a real woman and thinking to stop our game. She don't look so tough now, more like a prairie flower."

Willie straightened, her beautiful face hardened. "Knock it off or I'll lock you up. Your choice."

Tom put a hand on her arm. She shook him off and glared over her shoulder. "Do not interfere with the law, Mr. Miller."

He took one step back. The men had stopped laughing, their expressions glassy with drink, their expressions belligerent.

"One little woman ain't going to stop us." Mahoney gave her a two-hand shove.

Bear burst through the door, growled and leaped, latching on to the man's arm. Willie raised her gun, aiming it, in turn, at each man seated around the table. "Down, Bear. Now, this is the way it's going to play out, gentlemen. Either you disperse or my dog will eat you. I think jail or a bullet might be preferable to his teeth."

Chairs scraped back, as one-by-one, all except Mahoney sidled up to the bar. "You," Willie motioned toward him. "My Mama will tend your bite if need be, otherwise, I suggest you head on home."

He cradled his arm to his chest. "You'll regret this. Mark my words. Sheriff or not, I'll see that you pay."

"I look forward to seeing you again, sir." Willie gave a shaky grin, then, with a nod to the other patrons, marched from the saloon, leaving Tom to follow.

"Are you plumb loco?" He grabbed her arm. "We allow the gambling here in order for the men to have an outlet for blowing off steam. Now, they'll cause all kinds of ruckus."

She yanked free. "Gambling is against the law. I've been hired to uphold the law. I suggest you remember that."

"That was Iris Mahoney's oldest boy. Not only have you alienated half the men of this town, but she's going to have it out for you, too."

"I am not afraid of an old woman." She snapped her fingers for Bear to follow, then marched up the street.

He jogged to her side. "That family doesn't play fair, Willie." He shot out a hand to stop her again. "They won't meet you face-to-face. They'll hide in wait and shoot you in the back."

She paled. Her hand trembled as she brushed

wayward strands of hair out of her face. "Then I will be on my guard. Good evening, Mr. Miller. Head home now or be arrested for loitering."

Dismissed and left standing in the middle of the street, Tom closed his mouth. Feisty and strong-willed or not, Willie Jack had put a target on her back. One he wasn't sure he could keep someone from putting in the crosshairs of a rifle. "Fine, I'll be your deputy!"

The wave of her hand was his only answer.

9

Thankfully, Tom was nowhere to be seen the next morning when Willie saddled Stormy. Agreeing to be her deputy or not, the man had work of his own to do. She didn't need him following after her like an over-protective husband.

Sam had never stifled her. Instead, after Mama came to live with them, he had let her work side-by-side with him until her pregnancy advanced too far to be considered safe. After two years, she still missed her best friend. She had hoped Tom might fill the void in some small way, not as a husband, but as a kindred spirit. Instead, he wanted to smother her. She yanked the cinch on the saddle tight and glanced to where Junior sat on an overturned barrel.

"You wait right there, until Mr. Miller arrives. I mean it, son." She peered through the open livery doors. While she needed to get to the Mahoney farm, she hated leaving a rambunctious boy unsupervised. She bent and laced her knee-high moccasins tighter. If a person might need to sneak up on someone, the soft soles of her moccasins were better than boots.

"I'm here." Tom strolled in, wiping his hands on a cloth that needed a good washing. "Junior, why don't you head on home? I'm going to escort your mother this morning."

"No, a deal is a deal, Mr. Miller. I'm only going to investigate some stolen chickens. I don't need a deputy for that." Willie planted her fists on her hips. "Junior is here to work and so he shall."

A muscle ticked in Tom's jaw. "After you angered those boys, I don't think it's wise you call on the Mahoneys alone."

"I'm the sheriff." She slapped her chest. "Me. When I need your help, I'll ask for it." She planted one moccasin-covered foot in the stirrup and mounted her horse. "Be a good boy, Junior, and work hard. Mama loves you." Without glancing back, she rode into the morning light, keeping her back straight and her temper reined.

As the horse plodded out of town and into the surrounding countryside, Willie's nerves calmed with each muffled thud of the horse's hooves against the hard-packed dirt. Birds sang in the Ponderosa Pines, and the sun's gentle rays pushed the morning chill away. Willie pushed her hat off her head to hang down her back and lifted her face to the sun.

With her attention diverted, she almost missed the turnoff. She guided Stormy to turn right. The path to the Mahoney place was over grown, the trees thick enough Willie could stretch her arms out on both sides and touch the branches, giving the illusion the trees were closing in on her. It was the perfect place for an ambush.

She shuddered and urged the horse forward, emerging from the forest to stare at a ramshackle house. She thought their former home had been a shack. Even Tom's warning hadn't prepared her for what she saw.

The roof missed several shingles, and the porch sagged on one end. A log wedged under the eave was the only thing that kept it from falling. To the left of the house sat a chicken coop pieced together with bits of wire and assorted sizes of lumber. No wonder there were chickens missing. A three-legged mixed breed hound barked a welcome from the porch.

"Stay Bear." Keeping one hand on the pistol at her waist, Willie dismounted and approached the house. "Hello? It's the sheriff."

"About time you got here." Mrs. Mahoney came from around the corner of the house. "The sun's been up for hours. I sure hope you aren't one of those folks who sleep the day away."

"No, ma'am." Willie fought to keep from rolling her eyes. "Let's take a look at those chickens." She followed the other woman to the coop. She might as well keep the subject rooted where it should be and not on Willie's sleeping habits. "Have you noticed any tracks that don't belong to you or your family?"

"Not a one." Mrs. Mahoney leaned against a post. "Heard you got into a tussle with my oldest? The money he brings in from gambling helps keep a roof over our head. I'd like you to look the other way same as the previous sheriffs."

"I can't do that." Willie met the woman's cold gaze. "The law is the law. Your sons will have to find other means of making an income."

"Jobs aren't real plentiful in this town, Mrs. Sheriff. Ain't that why you accepted the one offered to you? A job meant for a man? Why, I reckon if you hadn't of come, maybe one of my boys could have been sheriff." She glanced at something over Willie's shoulder. "Don't you reckon?"

Willie took a step back, once again reaching for the gun in its holster. "If the town had gone looking within its own residents, then yes, possibly, but instead, they placed an advertisement. Am I really here about stolen chickens?"

"Of course, forgive me." Mrs. Mahoney opened the coop and stepped inside, her boots sinking into several inches of offal that should have been shoveled out long ago. "I'm missing four hens and a prize rooster. My best layers, too. Gone without a trace. Someone came and took them right out of my coop."

"Do you mind if I take a look around?" Willie turned to look behind her. Only the prickles on the back of her neck signified anyone was watching. While the disappearance of the chickens seemed suspiciously like an excuse to badger her as to the reason she accepted the job as sheriff, it wouldn't hurt to do a little investigating.

"Sure, go ahead. I'll leave you to it," Mrs. Mahoney said. "I've some vegetables to put up. Just holler if you need me."

"Are your boys around?"

"Sleeping, the lazy fools. The one complains

about your dog biting him. They're both babies." She stomped toward the house, yelling for the dog to stop barking before it raised the dead.

Willie rubbed at the beginning of a headache between her eyes, then called for Bear to follow. His bounding toward her set the hound to yapping again. Bear leaned against her, his tongue hanging out, and peered into the trees. It must not be a person intending harm since he didn't growl. The sun's rays highlighted a head of gold. Willie rolled her eyes. "Come out, Mr. Miller. You've been spotted."

Tom emerged from the trees, a sheepish grin on his face.

"Where is Junior?"

"Your Ma took him home. Said a couple of hours of work was enough for a young boy."

Willie sighed. Mama was most likely right, and if she knew her mother, she would give her grandson a few chores around the house to make up for coming home early. It also allowed Tom to babysit Willie. Whose side was Mama on?

"Follow me and be quiet." She glanced at Tom's boots, then down at her moccasins. Somehow, she didn't think he would take kindly to a suggestion of finding more suitable footwear for traipsing silently through a forest. "Step where I step. No sense in alerting someone to our presence."

He frowned at her feet, visibly struggling with something whirling behind those gorgeous eyes. Oh. The realization hit her upside her already pounding head with the strength of a hammer. He didn't have a problem with her being a woman, at least not totally, it was something else. Something that stabbed a knife into her gut. "You resent me because I'm part Cherokee."

"No." He wouldn't meet her eyes, instead focusing on something at his feet.

Willie's spirit crashed. "No wonder you're following me. No wonder you resent my role as sheriff. You hate Indians."

"Hate is a strong word." The muscles in his neck bulged. He finally raised his wounded gaze to hers. "I don't hate you."

"I won't deny who I am, but if it helps you, maybe you could think only on the three quarters of me that is a Scot." She slapped back a branch, letting it fling back toward his head. It might knock some sense into the fool.

She choked back tears. She would not cry in front of him. The realization that she had lost possibly the only friend she had in town, ripped at her gut. No wonder he kept such a close eye on her. The man didn't trust her two feet in front of him! What did he think she would do? Massacre the town members in their beds? Steal their medicinal whiskey?

For an hour, she ignored the man behind her and followed signs of broken branches and dirt scuffs on rocks. Someone had come that way, and recently. She sniffed and stopped. She recognized the sour odor. Parting the brush ahead of her, she froze. She held up a hand signaling Tom to halt.

In front of them was an operating whiskey still. The scent of fermenting mash, sour and sweet, filled the air. Bags of sugar and corn lay stacked against a lean-to. To the side of the still, an improvised chicken coop held five chickens. They had found the stolen birds, and more. She was pretty certain making moonshine was against the town's laws.

Tom let out a soft whistle. "So, that's where the saloon gets their drink."

"You suspected?" Willie glanced at him from the corner of her eye.

He shrugged. "It had to come from somewhere. Mention of it would have only set the women vigilantes sniffing around. I couldn't let that happen. Whiskey runners are dangerous folks."

"Have you always taken it upon yourself to be the town's mighty protector?" With Willie on the job, he no longer needed to decide what was best for people. At the first sight of the women vigilantes actually acting on something dangerous, she'd shut them down or lock them up.

*

Did he think it was up to him to keep the town safe? Yes. He'd thought the hiring of a sheriff would lessen his burden, instead, the pressure increased. He should have fought harder to send Willie on her way and post another advertisement. He hadn't missed her attempts at keeping tears at bay, either. Women were emotional creatures not meant for such stressful situations.

While he had never meant to let her know how he felt about Indians, she had surprised him with her accusation. Besides, it was only when he saw her dressed head-to-toe in fringed leather that his years old resentment against the Indians rose. When she wore a feminine gown, he could only focus on her beauty. Tom Miller was a mixed up man for sure.

"I reckon I have. Most of the other men turn their heads at their wife's shenanigans."

"Then it isn't your place to meddle." She let the branches fall back into place. "Let's head back to town while I figure out how to handle this."

"As your deputy I have the right."

"You weren't my deputy then, and you're only my deputy now when I need you." Sparks flashed from eyes the color of the morning sky. "Don't overstep your boundaries, Mr. Miller." She marched off, leaving him to follow like a scolded dog. Bear glanced over his shoulder as if he sympathized with him.

He followed the sway of her inky mane back to the road leading to the Mahoney place. Since she approached her horse without calling out to the house, he figured she didn't want the residents to know she had located the chickens. They didn't need some headstrong young men taking matters into their own hands, after all. Once on the hard surface of the road, he jogged to her side.

"Go back to work. I'm headed to the office and can handle things on my own." Willie increased her pace, her face set, mouth grim.

He laid a hand on her shoulder. "I'm sorry, Willie. I have a lifetime of hurts to get over. I didn't mean you any harm."

"Your apology for something not said outright, speaks louder than if the words were actually spoken." She shook him off. "No harm done. My family is used to that type of bigotry. You might want to have a conversation with God about why you feel that way. Good day." She swung up onto her horse, called to Bear, and left him standing next to Nightmare as she rode off. Her pain showed in every line of her posture as she sat straight in the saddle.

Why hadn't he denied her accusation? It would have taken very little effort to tell her she was wrong. Lying didn't come easy to Tom, still, in this case, maybe a small white lie would have served a greater purpose then wounding someone he was beginning to admire. While there could be nothing more than friendship between them, her strength and strong moral beliefs in right and wrong often made him forget the blood that ran through her veins.

He swung onto Nightmare's back and plodded back to town, staying several yards behind Willie. She wouldn't welcome his company. It was best to let her be for the time being. Somehow, he would find a way to heal the hurt he'd caused.

"Howdy, Tom." Frank Simpson, surrounded by his daughters, waved from the bank's doorway. The man's wife might be seen on a rare occasion, flitting around town in her fancy gowns, but the girls seemed to be constantly underfoot. Simpson paraded them like prize cattle to be sold at auction. They simpered and wiggled their fingers at Tom as he dismounted in front of the livery. If Frank wanted to marry them off, sending them to the city for schooling might be his best bet.

Tom tipped his hat in their direction and entered the coolness of the livery. Stormy was already in her stall with her saddle still in place.

Tom sighed. Usually Willie rubbed the horse down herself. She was obviously stating loud and clear where she thought his job lied. After their morning exchange, he deserved her anger.

Leading Nightmare to his stall, Tom got to work removing saddles and brushing down coats. When he'd finished, he headed to the mercantile. Maybe Harvey Coffee could tell him whether he had sold large quantities of sugar and corn lately.

He entered the store, breathing in the aroma of pickles and peppermint, not entirely surprised to see Willie standing at the counter. The woman had a quick mind, quicker than a lot of the men Tom knew. He should have known she would have questions of her own for Harvey.

"You haven't sold any large quantities?" Willie worried her bottom lip. "Has anyone been in trying to sell you moonshine?"

"Nope and nope. The wife would have my hide if I sold that liquor. Not to mention Bart Johnson wouldn't care for the competition." Harvey folded his hands over his large paunch. "Of course, that doesn't mean someone didn't make the half day's ride to Livingston to purchase supplies. Are you saying we got moonshiners in our fair town?"

"I'm not saying anything of the kind." Willie took a deep breath. "I appreciate your time, Mr. Coffee. Please let me know if you hear anything." She turned, her soft steps scuffling along the wood floor as she exited back to the street.

"What was that all about?" Harvey transferred his attention to Tom.

"I don't reckon I'm at liberty to say." Tom

rubbed his chin. "It's sheriff business. I'm nothing but a once in a while deputy."

"I thought her dog was her deputy."

Great. Tom ranked with her dog. He probably came in second place, too.

The bell over the door jingled. Winnie bustled in, holding Bonnie's hand, and Junior trailing behind. "Hello, gentlemen. Have either one of you seen my daughter? She said there were some things she wanted me to purchase, but I can't remember what."

"Sugar or corn?" Harvey asked, the corner of his mouth twitching.

Winnie shook her head. "No, I've got plenty of that."

"I think she was headed for the sheriff's office," Tom ruffled Junior's head. "Good work this morning, little man."

Junior grinned, then hopped on the railing running the perimeter of the counter. He eyed the licorice sticks in a jar.

"How about I buy you one for your work today?" Tom nodded at Harvey. "One for the little girl, too."

"I don't think Willie expects him to be paid, Tom." Winnie frowned. "Working for you is discipline for vandalizing the schoolhouse."

"One licorice stick won't hurt him." Tom dug in his pocket for a coin. "I'd best be getting back to work. Harvey, tell your missus I'll have some more of those thingamajigs for her by morning." He ruffled Junior's hair again, tweaked Bonnie's nose, and stepped outside.

Maybe he was remiss in not planning on a family in his near future. He might not know much about children, but he'd done all right while watching those two. The little one's serious gaze reminded him a lot of her mother's, and both left him feeling as if he had dirt on his face.

He glanced both ways. Willie exited the telegraph office, slapped her hat on her head, and headed for the saloon with purposed strides. Uh-oh. She planned on asking questions of the owner. Nothing good could come from that interview. He loped down the street, entering the saloon on her heels.

"Go home, Mr. Miller." Willie whirled. "Leave me be."

"But—"

She whipped out her pistol and aimed it at his head. "You are obstructing justice. Go home."

"You wouldn't shoot me." His mouth dried up. What if he were wrong and the woman was unstable? Then, she might very well pull the trigger.

"No, I wouldn't." She slid her gun back in its holster. "But you sure do try my patience." She marched to the counter. "I'd like to see the proprietor."

"You're looking at him." Bart Johnson, a tall, thin man with dark hair and a handlebar mustache, wiped a glass with a white cloth. "But we ain't open yet. Come back after the supper hour."

"I'm not here to purchase a drink." Willie stood ramrod straight. "I'd like to know where you get your whiskey."

"I don't reckon I can tell you that." Bart turned

to wipe the necks of bottles lined against a mirror.

"Why not?" High spots of color appeared on Willie's cheeks.

"It ain't none of your business." Bart faced her, his eyes hard. "I abide by the laws of this here town, so I shouldn't have to confess to every little detail. Why, next thing I know, you'll ask what time I go to the privy each day."

Willie cocked her head. "Seems to me the honest folks of this town have a right to know about the businesses here. After all, they allow you to be here with no competition. That should bring you in a nice tidy profit each month. Now, I'll ask you again … from whom do you purchase your whiskey?"

He leaned over the counter, whiskey-laden breath washing over Tom. "Get her out of here."

Tom grasped Willie's elbow. "Come on, sheriff. It's best we leave."

"Not until I get the information I came for." She tried pulling free.

He tightened his grip and leaned close to her ear. "You press the fact, and you might not make it home tonight."

10

Willie lay in bed the next morning and stared at the white-washed wood slats making up the ceiling. A bird twittered from the tree outside her window. A cool breeze ruffled the gingham curtains. A beautiful morning, yet there she was after a sleepless night, thinking on Tom's words at the saloon. What was hidden behind the smiles of the Wild Horse Pass residents? Surely an evil lurked that had yet to show its face. Otherwise, why would Tom be so worried about Willie's welfare? Was it really because she was a woman?

She crawled from bed and headed for the wash basin on her bureau. The splash of cold water against her face helped dispel the last of her drowsiness. She dressed in her leather, strapped her pistol to her thigh, hooked her whip on her belt, and then headed to the kitchen for coffee before going to work.

Mama had a cake on the counter and cookies in the oven. "Good morning, daughter. I'm having a group of women over for a meeting. Some kind of club, I think." She tossed a dishtowel over her shoulder. "It might help me make some friends in this town."

"We probably won't have the opportunity to stay, Mama. I wouldn't get too attached." Willie poured a cup of coffee.

"Why not? What did you do?"

"Nothing. Well, other than try to find out where the saloon gets its liquor, shut down the gambling, and keep the vigilante group from stirring up trouble." She plopped into a straight-backed chair and cradled the hot cup between her hands. "I don't reckon I'm very popular here. Tom Miller resents my Indian blood, did I tell you?"

Mama's eyes widened. "Why did you have to go and tell him? It'll be all over town before long. There goes my chance at friendship. What about the children? Did you think of them before blabbing?" She popped the towel against the counter.

Willie winced. "I confronted Tom about his distrust of me. He all but confirmed my suspicions were right." It still hurt like an open sore. She stared at her pale hands, then up at Mama's slightly darker skin and eyes. "I've said before, I won't deny who I am."

"Oh, phooie. Tom doesn't resent the fact you're part Indian. He doesn't like having a woman sheriff, is all. You've just made your job of being accepted twice as hard." Mama turned away from her. "I don't know how I can hold my head up in this town now. Once the ladies find out … well, there's no telling what they'll do."

"God gave us our Cherokee blood, Mama. I wish you were prouder of the fact." Willie carried her coffee onto the front porch. Leaning against the railing, she stared down the silent street. There never was any reasoning with Mama. After Papa married her and turned her more white than half-Indian, she had done everything in her power to live up to what she thought she wanted to be. It made Willie's heart ache.

She needed to visit the telegraph office again and send along the information to Billings that she had discovered the still. Yesterday, the operator had been "indisposed". No other information, just a hand scribbled note informing folks he'd be back in the morning. Not that she wanted help, but rather that she felt it her duty to let the Marshall's office know. She sipped her coffee, watching as Tom stepped from his livery, stretched his arms over his head, and waved upon seeing her.

The man probably thought things could go on as before. Tom Miller was a patronizing, bigoted worm. After stomping on her feelings and then adding further mortification by dragging her from the saloon as if she were a wayward child, she could care less if she said two words to him all day.

Wonderful. He headed her way. Now, she'd have to offer him a cup of coffee. She definitely didn't want to add rude to her list of faults.

"Good morning, sheriff." Tom grinned up at her from the bottom of the steps.

"Good morning." She peered at him over the rim of her cup.

"Tom!" Mama joined them, handing him a cup. "Have some coffee. You're just the person I wanted to speak to."

"Mama," Willie warned.

Tom glanced her way, then back to Mama, his handsome face creased with curiosity. "Ma'am."

"Well." Mama twisted her apron between her hands. "This might sound strange to you, but, I'd like for you to keep quiet about … our Indian heritage." She lifted her chin. "Some folks don't think too kindly on those of us with mixed blood."

Willie stomped her foot and stormed to sit in one of the rocking chairs. Of all the people for Mama to have this conversation with. She glared at Tom over her glass. He paled, his smile fading. Good. Let him be uncomfortable for once.

"Ma'am, I'm not a gossip. I have no intention of saying a thing."

Probably because he can't stand the subject. "What about the ridiculous rule stating the town is entitled to know everything about the sheriff and his or her family?" Willie cocked her head. "As a member of the town board, doesn't that mean you shouldn't withhold such vital information? After all, my small tribe might revolt and massacre the town."

"Look, sheriff." Tom squared his shoulders. "I apologized for my behavior. What else would you like me to do? I agree with you that some of the so-called laws are ridiculous, but even the town sheriff is entitled to some privacy."

"Well, thank you for that." Willie started rocking hard enough to almost take flight off the porch.

"Perhaps this is something we can address at the town meeting tomorrow night," Tom said.

"Not if it means bringing up our Indian blood."

Mama crossed her arms. "I'll deny every word of it. I've worked too hard to be accepted. My hair is lighter than Willie's, and my skin just as fair. No one needs to know."

"Don't be silly." Why couldn't Mama love who she was? Willie left her chair and tossed her undrunk coffee off the side of the porch. "It will all come out at some time, right, Mr. Miller?"

"Not by my lips." He met her stare.

"Enough of this. I've work to do." Willie spun and went back in the house to get the children ready for the day. "Junior, Mr. Miller is here to pick you up."

"May I speak with you in private, Willie?" Tom followed her into the house. "Maybe we could step out next to the corral?"

Without turning, Willie nodded and continued through the kitchen and out the back door.

Ox and Blue, Junior had insisted on naming the new oxen same as the old, snorted from the center of the corral before plodding toward her. She reached out and rubbed Blue's nose. It still amazed her as to how the two ancient beasts made the trip all the way to Montana Territory without keeling over dead. Sure, they'd only had to travel a few days, but they'd been knocking on death's door when she bought them. Now, they'd plumped up and looked years younger. If only the journey had worked the same for Willie. Instead of the hope she had once had about providing a better life for her family, despair threatened to choke her. All she had worked for was in danger of being trampled under the boots of the town residents.

Tom sighed and leaned against the fence, his arms resting along the splintered wood. "It seems as if you and your mother are on different sides of the road on this issue."

"Always have been." Willie plucked at a loose piece of wood sticking from the fence. Tom was the last person she wanted to have this conversation with. "I've chosen to embrace who God created me to be. Mama has chosen to hide certain aspects." A splinter embedded in her finger. She hissed.

Tom took her hand in his and with his fingernails, plucked at the offending sliver. "I don't think the majority of the folks will mind."

"No, but you do." She tilted her face, not at all sure why she should care what he thought. She was also very conscious of the way her hand fit in his work-roughened one.

He tilted her hand this way and that making sure he got all of it, then sighed and rubbed the splinter off on the side of his tan pants. "Something happened when I was fourteen that clouded my view of certain people." Tom folded his hands and sighed again as if the weight of the world had landed on his head. "My pa was always away, out hunting and such, trapping furs for extra money. That left the running of the farm to me and Ma. One day, while she was out plowing in one of our fields, three Sioux warriors came upon her." A muscle ticked in his jaw. Willie's stomach plummeted, knowing the outcome before he spoke the words.

"She screamed for me to stay hidden. They butchered her, right in front of my eyes, but not until they took turns, well, you can fill in the rest."

He turned glistening eyes toward her. "My ma should not have been in that field, Willie. My pa should have been, or me. Not a woman. Maybe we could have fought them off."

"You were just a boy, Tom. Her dying thought was of you staying safe." Willie laid a hand over his clenched fists. Tears clogged her throat. "Where I come from, women work and fight right alongside their men. I worked as a deputy beside my husband. You have to let this hatred go. Look at me."

"I am."

"No, really look at me."

His gaze traveled from her moccasin encased feet to her leather hat. It took all her will power not to squirm under his study. "I am not those men. Not all Indians are like them. You cannot judge all of us by those three. I'm sorry about your ma, but when you look at me, I want you to see Wilhemina Jackson, a mother and a sheriff, not a woman who carries Indian blood in her veins."

"I'm trying." His gaze focused on her lips before he grabbed her and pulled her roughly to him. His lips descended over hers like a man dying for a thirst of water.

She tried to push him away, then gave into the sheer wonder of his kiss. Her arms snaked around his neck, pulling him closer. She missed the physical affection between a man and a woman, and while she knew Tom's kiss was one of desperation, one from a man wanting to know that a part of him he'd thought dead still lived, she gave into the moment and just enjoyed.

*

A frozen part of Tom's heart melted as he claimed Willie's lips. She returned his passion with equal fervor, until the slam of a door shook him free of his trance, and he pulled back. "I'm sorry. I shouldn't have done that."

She smiled softly. "Do you feel better?"

"Oh, boy." He laughed. "If I thought a kiss could have done that, I would have tried it sooner."

Her cheeks darkened. "There's a time for everything, Tom." She placed her finger in the cleft of his chin, sending his heart soaring. "I've got to get to work. Please watch out for my boy." She strolled away, the fringe on the legs of her split skirt swaying with each step. She stopped to say something to Junior, then turned the corner of the house, Bear trotting along beside her.

The kiss might have dispelled any notions of Tom looking at Willie as anything but a beautiful, desirable woman, but it sure didn't lessen his need of watching out for her. If anything, the kiss had strengthened it. Not that he would tell her of his thoughts. It would be a hot day in January before he could tell her that little truth.

"Come on, boy, we've a load of work today. I have some things to deliver to the mercantile and could use the strength of a big boy like you." He put an arm around Junior's shoulders and led him in the direction Willie had gone. She was just entering the door of the sheriff's office when they stepped onto the street. Just in time too, because a pack of women were descending on the sheriff's house. It was time for Tom to make himself scarce.

It took longer than usual to load the wagon

with the iron yard doodads, Wilma Coffee wanted for her store, but the satisfaction on Junior's face when they finished made it all worthwhile. Tom let the boy handle the reins and drive the wagon down the street until they reached the mercantile. Without a pa, there were things only a man could teach him and for now, Tom was happy to be that man.

"Afternoon, Tom." Harvey stood behind the counter. "Those women have been over to the sheriff's place for a good long while."

Tom stacked his work against a wall. "I saw them descending like a pack of hungry wolves. What are they up to?"

"That's the vigilante committee. Don't tell me you didn't know." Harvey stepped over and inspected Tom's work. "I'm thinking they're recruiting Mrs. Baxter."

"Don't tell the sheriff. She's likely to take her whip to the whole lot."

Harvey laughed. "Now, that I would like to see. That committee causes more trouble than it fixes." His grin faded. "I heard tell Mrs. Sheriff had a run in with Bart Johnson. That woman has grit, that's for sure."

"Yeah, I was there. She didn't make a friend."

"Most sheriffs don't have a lot of those." Harvey moved back to the counter. "Can I get you anything else? The eighty twenty split still good for you on those items?"

"More than fair." Tom nodded at Junior. "I'll take a licorice stick for my hard working partner and one for myself. Put it on my tab." Maybe he should alert Willie to what was going on in her house. There was no telling what those ladies were up to.

He led the way to the sheriff's office where Willie studied wanted posters. She set them aside to wrap her son in a hug. "What brings you two by here?"

Tom scratched the back of his neck. "Thought you might want to know the women's vigilante group is meeting at your house. They've been there since this morning."

"Really? So that's what my mother is up to." Willie grabbed her hat. "Come on, Junior. I'll walk you home."

"Mind if I tag along?" Tom asked. He wouldn't want to miss Willie standing up to the women of Wild Horse Pass for a whole bag of candy, licorice in particular.

"Sure. Since you have some all-fired ideas about what's proper behavior for women, maybe you can talk some sense into them." She wiggled her eyebrows and hand-in-hand with Junior, marched out the door.

He doubted it. Their husbands hadn't managed very well so far.

Willie kept up a fast pace all the way to her house and met the women as they stepped off the porch. The group included the elusive Mrs. Simpson, Wilma Coffee, and Gertie Bloomfield. Thank goodness the pastor's wife had sense enough to stay away. Tom knew for a fact that she was often right in the thick of things.

"Ladies." Willie blocked their path. "I have it on good authority that this was a meeting of a group of vigilantes. I thought we had talked about this."

"Tom Miller." Wilma crossed her arms. "You're nothing but a loose-lipped snitch."

"No name calling, Mrs. Coffee." Willie lifted her chin. "I'm ordering you ladies to put a halt to this nonsense, and do not drag my mother into your shenanigans."

"Too late." Winnie joined her friends. "I've already joined. Besides, we're a women's auxiliary group doing good for the town. Whoever said we were vigilantes was telling a falsehood." She speared Tom with a look harsh enough to wither the strongest stalk of corn. The other women nodded hard enough to set their feathered hats to fluttering.

"That's right," Gertie said. "We're planning a Fourth of July picnic."

In addition to other things, Tom would wager. He admired Willie for the way she didn't back down with four righteous women in a staring contest with her. He grinned and leaned against a nearby tree. This was more fun than a horse race.

Willie's cheeks were as red as a rose while she visibly struggled to hold her temper in check. Tom thought about kissing the stress from her face, but thought that with the mood she was in, he'd most likely stare down the barrel of her gun instead. Besides, her returning his kiss had been nothing more than an attempt to pull him out of his melancholy. It had worked wonders, and while she might have intended the gesture to be medicinal, in a way, he couldn't help but want more.

"Ladies," he said, stepping forward. "Your husbands have said time and time again not to dabble in things that are a man's concern."

"Our sheriff is a woman, you donkey's rear end." Wilma poked him with her forefinger. "I say we let the women run this town. That would take care of the liquor, the fights, and any other such nonsense men can't live without."

He'd heard of women wanting equal footing as men, but hadn't witnessed it to any degree until Bernard Bloomfield became the mayor. If Tom had had any doubts as to who ran the town, he had none now. Gertie Bloomfield may not hold the title of mayor, but she made the decisions all the same. Lord, protect him from a wife like her.

In fact, the more he spent time with Willie, the more he thought maybe he wanted more of a partner rather than a little lady content with sewing and putting together flower arrangements. It was nice having conversations with a woman who could hold her own. Someday, when she had let go of the notion of being in a dangerous profession, he might actually ponder more on the subject.

*

Bart Johnson pushed away from the sheriff's poor excuse for a barn. Following her around was more fun than visiting the saloon in Billings that held some of the territories greatest beauties. At first, he had considered setting a trap for the lovely lawmaker, but now, with the knowledge the town had its very own group of women intent on making sure nothing bad happened, he could cause enough trouble with that group to keep the sheriff too busy to stick her pretty nose into his whiskey dealings.

He had followed her since early that morning,

learning all kinds of interesting things. The fact she was part Cherokee was knowledge he would keep in his back pocket for the time being. The ace up his sleeve. He rubbed his hands together, relishing the moment he turned the entire town against her.

By the time the ladies group got good and tired of the sheriff's bossiness, Bart could lay the final rock on the wall that would shut the good sheriff up once and for all.

11

After a long debate with herself about whether she should wear calico or leather to the town meeting, Willie decided on her usual sheriff garb. Folks might take her more seriously if she looked the way they were used to seeing her. She sent a prayer heavenward for grace and strapped on her pistol.

"For mercy's sake." Mama shook her head when Willie entered the kitchen. "Why aren't you wearing your blue dress? Don't you care the least about how you look to people?"

"Don't start. If you insist on making me new clothes, you could start with a new leather skirt."

"Go shoot me a deer and I just might." Mama huffed and plopped a bonnet on her head. "Come on young'uns. Let's go watch the town beat up on the sheriff."

Junior's eyes widened. "Why do they want to hurt my ma?"

"It's just an expression, sweetie." Willie ruffled his hair. "I'm sure there will be plenty of different opinions to entertain everyone." Mama was right.

Willie felt as if she would be facing a den of lions alone. Well, not alone, she still believed God was on her side in her new profession. She would do well to remember that when the arrows started flying. Tucking the list of "laws" under her arm, she took Bonnie's hand and led her family to the church.

Tom greeted them when they entered the yard and hoisted Bonnie onto his shoulders. She shrieked with glee. Several heads turned to stare. The man certainly had a way of starting rumors. If he didn't stop acting as if he and Willie were courting, all kinds of false tales could get started. While she was certain he only made such gestures as a token of goodwill, the glares from the single ladies in front of the church told Willie that others thought his actions something else entirely. Head held high, she marched into the church and took a seat in the front.

Once everyone was seated, some standing along the walls because of lack of room, Mayor Bloomfield approached the podium. "Good evening! What a turnout. It must be so everyone can meet our lovely sheriff. Willie Jack, would you stand?"

Willie stood to scattered applause and made a move to sit back down.

"No, please remain standing," the mayor said. "Most of the things on tonight's agenda involve you. Now … " He studied the list in front of him while prickles ran up and down Willie's spine from the numerous stares focused on her back. "Ah, yes. First is the fact that the sheriff has been known to have her children at the jail. This is in violation of town law number twelve that clearly states no children at the jail. Mrs. Sheriff? Please feel free to express your opinion after each of my statements." Was the man's smile pasted to his face?

Willie wiped damp palms on her skirt. "It's no secret that I have children, Mayor, and as the cells were empty, I saw no harm in having them there long enough for my mother to purchase supplies from the mercantile." Seriously? This was important enough to address? This wasn't a town meeting, this was a call the sheriff on the carpet meeting. Mama was right. The townspeople were going to beat her up.

"You were also seen spending time inside Johnson's saloon on," he riffled through his notes, "two occasions. The law strictly states—"

"As sheriff, some of these rules cannot apply to me." Willie faced the townspeople. "While I am acting as sheriff, my gender can play no role in the acts I perform in order to do my job." What had they thought when they'd hired her? That she'd prance up and down the street with Bear and hope no one broke the law? "I stopped illegal gambling and confronted Mr. Johnson as to where he gets his whiskey in an attempt to make sure he's getting it from a legal source. Both situations warranted my entering the saloon." She turned back to the mayor. "This town agreed to give me three months to prove I could handle this job. Now, let me do it."

"Fine. We will make temporary allowances." The mayor nodded. "Now, what do you intend to do about the still you found?"

Darn that Rubert Smith. She should have

known the telegraph operator couldn't keep his mouth shut. "I intend to shut it down."

"What about my chickens?" Mrs Mahoney shouted from the back of the room.

"I found your chickens at the whiskey still. They are alive and well." Willie closed her eyes, regaining control of an escalating temper, then opened them and stepped up to the podium. "If I may, Mayor Bloomfield." She stepped sideways, scooting him away.

"I've said nothing about the still, or the chickens, in order not to alert the still operators. Now that this is out in the open, I will say this once. Shut down the still or I will find you and shut it down myself, locking those responsible behind bars. Good evening." She motioned to her family to follow and marched down the aisle to startled faces on each side of her.

Outside, she took a deep breath in an attempt to rid herself of the antagonistic feelings of the meeting. Taken to task like a wayward school child. She shook her head. No wonder prior sheriffs left after a few months. Well, Willie was as stubborn as they come. She wouldn't go running into the night. She was promised three months, and she intended to hold the town to that promise.

"Willie, wait." Tom rushed out the door and to her side. "I thought there were items you wanted to discuss."

"They aren't going to listen to me." If anything, she'd done nothing more than anger whoever was responsible for the still. She'd all but issued an exact challenge. "I'm not going to waste time explaining myself.”

“I’ve never known you to back down from a fight.”

“You don’t know me well enough to determine that.” His challenging tone spun her around. “You’re a part of this.” She stabbed him in the chest with her forefinger. “You’re on the board. You know some of these rules are ridiculous, yet you’ve done nothing to change them.” She looked around for her family. Mama and the children stood in a cluster of the town’s nosiest citizens, no doubt planning on how the group of women could shut down the whiskey still without Willie’s help. She drew air forcibly through her nose and stomped toward home.

“Sheriff.” Bart leaned against the saloon’s outside wall, his feet crossed at the ankles and a big grin on his face. A rolled cigarette dangled from his lips. “How did the meeting go?”

“Shut up, Bart.” Willie marched past him. Go ahead and laugh it up. She’d figure out a way to knock that grin off his face. She passed the house, calling to Bear on her way, and continued into the woods behind the house, hoping the serenity of nature and the beauty of dusk would calm her frazzled emotions.

She stopped at a small meadow where a deer and its fawn nibbled on the lush grass. Willie sat on a nearby rock and motioned for Bear to stay. Despite the peace of her surroundings, tears welled in her eyes, overflowing to run down her cheeks and soak the collar of her blouse. “Oh, Bear, what am I going to do?”

He nuzzled her hand.

"I've tried so hard to make a good life for Mama and the children, yet I find myself fighting one obstacle after another." Anger at Sam's death, his desertion, brought her sobs to the surface and bursting out of her. The deer bounded across the meadow and out of sight. "Why does life have to be so hard? I don't know if I'm strong enough to manage." She wrapped her arms around the dog's neck and gave the sobs free rein.

*

Everything in Tom wanted to gather Willie into his arms and let her cry on his shoulder, but wisdom held him back. She wasn't hurt and angered only by other people, she lumped him right in there with them. He held back, using the brush as coverage while she cried into her dog's thick fur.

A twig snapped under his boot. Willie leaped to her feet, gun drawn.

Tom groaned and held up his hands. "It's just me."

She swiped her arm across her face. "Following me again. Why can't you mind your own business?'

"Your mother and I were worried when you dashed off and didn't go home." He stepped into the meadow. "What do you want me to do to help you?"

"Nothing." She plopped back to her seat. "I'm going to do my job, wait out the three months, and be sent on my way. There's no reason for you to get involved."

She might as well have shot him in the gut, so

hurtful were her words. He thought, especially after their kiss, that they could at least be close friends. Now, it seemed as if the town meeting had erased any chances of even that. Maybe he should leave her to her thoughts. The more time he spent with her, the more attractive she was to him, and romance was not something he needed, or wanted, in his life right now. He backed into the brush and headed for home, asking God to protect her while she cried in the dark.

"Did you find her?" Winnie stepped off the front porch as Tom turned the corner of her house.

"Yes, but she wants to be left alone."

"That girl carries too much heartache and too much responsibility." Winnie glanced toward the tree line. "I've tried letting her know she doesn't need to shoulder it all alone, but she doesn't hear me." She turned her dark eyes on him. "You stay her friend, Tom Miller, whether she wants you to or not."

"I'm trying."

"No trying about it, you do it." With a swish of her skirts, Winnie went back in the house.

Tom sat on the porch steps. He would give Willie her privacy, but if she didn't return soon, he'd look for her again. She shouldn't be alone in the woods at night, especially after threatening those who owned the still. He picked up a loose twig and drew circles in the dirt at his feet.

Willie's sigh startled him and he rubbed his foot across where he had written her name. Those infernal moccasins, sneaking up on a man like that. "If I would have had a gun, I could have shot you,

Willie."

"Go home, Tom." She climbed the stairs.

"I won't. Not until you talk to me."

Her shoulders slumped. "We can't be friends, Tom. We can't be anything. I don't even want you to be my deputy." She turned, her eyes glimmering in the moonlight. "Someday, you might be forced to make a choice between me and this town. You've lived here a long time. I won't put you in that position."

"That's my decision to make." He stomped to her side. "If you want to keep our relationship on a professional basis, fine. I'll remain your deputy. No more dinners, private conversations, nothing that the job doesn't require. Have it your way. Go through life lonely and afraid." He stormed off the porch. If someone asked him why he was so upset about keeping things professional between him and Willie, he had no idea how he would answer. He saw the wisdom in the decision, but his heart cried for more of her company.

At no time in his life had he wanted a taste of whiskey more than at that moment. He'd heard tell the drink washed away a man's sorrows, and Tom was powerful burdened. Instead, he headed for the parsonage and rapped on the door.

Gloria answered, a smear of flour on her face, and her hair hanging around her shoulders. "Why, Tom, what brings you out at this hour?" She ran her hands down her apron. "I'm finishing up a pie before bed."

"I'm sorry to intrude on your evening, but I wonder whether Mark is available?" Tom rubbed the back of his neck. He shouldn't have come. It was clear the Netzeres were getting ready for bed.

"I'm here." Mark snapped his suspenders into place. "Let's step out onto the porch. Gloria, could you fetch us some coffee?" She nodded and closed the door behind them.

"Is this about the meeting?" Mark waved Tom toward one of the cane back chairs on the porch. "Our sheriff sure has a way with words."

"She's stepping into dangerous territory, and now she's told me to stay away from her." Tom slumped over and dangled his hands between his knees. "We had an argument over her ancestry."

"You didn't." Mark glanced at the window behind him. "Don't let Gloria hear you say that. She'll have the women of this town tar and feather you. We've had this conversation before, Tom. You can't judge one by the actions of a few."

"That ain't all. I kissed her."

"You don't say." Mark grinned. "Did she slap you?"

Tom shook his head. "Nah, she kissed me back, good and hard, too. Aroused feelings in me I'd thought were dead. I know she kissed me out of pity upon hearing what happened to my ma, but still … I'd thought we could at least be friends. Now, she says no. She won't have me choose between the town and her. She plans on shutting the still down on her own."

"That's dangerous."

"Yup, and there's not much I can do about it."

"No, there isn't." Mark turned his chair to face Tom. "I've said this before, but it isn't getting through your thick head. You've got to let God protect Willie. You've offered your help and had it rejected. There's nothing more you can do."

"I don't reckon I can sit back and do nothing."

"Then pray."

Tom peered through the dark at his pastor's face. The man meant well, and was most likely right on all accounts, but he was asking Tom to step outside of who he was. "Maybe Gloria could have her group nose around town and see what they can dig up on the moonshiners. You know, do what nosey women do."

"You aim to keep the sheriff too busy corralling the club to get into trouble." Mark shook his head. "She'll spend all her time herding the women and none looking for the real culprits. The town will run her out at the end of the three months. Tom, she has a little more than two months to prove herself. Do you want her to leave?"

If it meant keeping her safe, he did. But then … he straightened. What if sending her away, put her in the sheriff's position of another town? One that wasn't as concerned for her welfare as he was? He scratched his head. "I've got me some thinking to do."

"I reckon you have." Mark stood. "Go on home and spend some time in prayer. You know where to find me if you need a listening ear. If all else fails, you could ask the woman to marry you."

Tom jerked. "You're wanting me to get shot." He pushed to his feet. "If she doesn't want to be my friend, then she definitely won't want to get hitched." Still, courting her sounded like a good idea. Between him calling on her, and her rebuffing him, and the women's vigilante group nosing around town, Willie ought to be plenty busy. Who knew what could happen at the end of her trial period?

His steps were lighter heading home than they had been on the way to the parsonage. He glanced inside the saloon on his way. Bob Mellon pounded out a melody on the out of tune piano and every table and spot at the polished bar was full. Tom shook his head, thankful he had somewhere to go to work out his troubles other than the saloon.

*

"Next round of drinks are on the house, boys!" Bart Johnson lined up glasses and filled them halfway with his newly purchased whiskey. After that, the customers would clamor for more and he'd substitute with the cheaper moonshine.

Cheers erupted. Good-natured shoving commenced as men crowded closer. It was a good night. The town meeting couldn't have gone any better. He hadn't seen sign of the fools who left their still where it could be found, but Bart would answer the sheriff's dare. He liked a good game of chess as well as the next man or woman.

Once the drinks were poured, he stepped back and thought on his next step. The simple-minded folks who lived in Wild Horse Pass would be easy enough to pit against each other. All he had to do was pay someone here and there to break one of their silly town rules. He'd start off small, so as not to make anyone suspicious, then each exploit would be bigger and better. The sheriff wouldn't know which end was up.

All he had to do was make it to the end of her three months. Once they had another man hired as sheriff, it was easy enough to ply the man with free drinks in order for him to look the other way. Yes, things were going to be just fine. Bart would do anything to make sure of it.

12

Willie glanced up from her desk as Mrs. Mahoney, an elderly man she had yet to meet, and Tom entered her office. Gracious, what could they all want first thing in the morning? It had been two days since the meeting and no one had approached her to even say howdy, and why was Tom clutching a fistful of wildflowers?

"Good morning, folks." She stood and smiled, ignoring the apprehension on Tom's face. "What can I do for you?"

Mrs. Mahoney elbowed her way to the front of the three. "That nosey group of women are tramping all around my property, scaring my chickens, and putting my cow off its milk."

"That ain't nothing." The older man stepped forward. "Some scalawag painted my fence."

Willie stared. She knew what to do about the women, but a painted fence? "That doesn't sound too bad. What did they paint on it?"

"Nothing." He crossed his arms. "It's white. The problem is, I didn't give anyone permission to paint my fence. I prefer the natural look. The thing sticks out like a goat in a pig pen."

"What's your name?"

"Leroy Brown." He glared over a twitching moustache. Every inch of his wiry body quivered with indignation. "I live about a mile down the road. Turn left at the big hickory tree, then continue on until you reach a pile of rocks. Turn right and you'll see my place. Why in tarnation would anyone paint a fence all the way out there without my permission?"

"I honestly have no idea, Mr. Brown, but I promise to look into it." Willie turned to Mrs. Mahoney. "And I also promise to talk to the women about trespassing." Most likely the crazy women had scared the owners of the illegal still into the next county. Once her first two complainers left, she acknowledged Tom.

"These are for you." He thrust the flowers at her, his face as red as the sun when it kissed the top of the mountains. When she didn't reach for the blossoms, he set them on her desk, tipped his hat, and skedaddled like a cat with three dogs chasing after its tail.

What kind of game was he playing? Didn't he listen to a word Willie said? She almost tossed the flowers in the trash, but decided they would brighten the place up. It wasn't the flowers' fault he had picked them. She found an empty can on a shelf and stuck the flowers inside before setting it on the corner of her desk.

"This town has gone plumb loco," she said, reaching for her hat. Bear woofed deep in his throat as if agreeing with her. Now that she had some things to tend to, the melancholy that had plagued her the last few days lifted enough to put a small smile on her face. "One day at a time, uh boy?"

Thankfully, Tom wasn't at the livery when she retrieved Stormy, although she could hear the whoosh of the bellows he used next door at the blacksmith's. The man stayed busy, she would give him that. If he thought the flowers were going to change her mind as to them being friends, or something more, he had better think again.

"Mrs. Sheriff?"

Willie turned. Sally Simpson swayed in the doorway, her pretty face anxious. "What's wrong?" Willie asked. One minute she sat twiddling her thumbs, the next she had more work than she could do in a day.

"Um." Sally swished the hem of her bright pink dress. "I saw Tom Miller taking flowers to the sheriff's office. Do the two of you have an understanding?"

Not the kind Sally thought. "No, why? Are you interested in Tom?"

"I suppose. My pa thinks he would make a fine catch as a husband. He's a mite old for me, but he still looks mighty fine."

Willie grinned. Maybe this young girl could be her way of getting Tom's attention transferred somewhere else. "Let me think on it a bit and see how I can help you."

"Would you?" The girl grinned. "Wow. I didn't know sheriffs played matchmaker."

Heavens to Betsy. Willie shook her head as the girl dashed away. She did seem a mite too young for Tom, but if Willie got a good solid plan in place, Tom would be too busy fending off the young girl's advances to bother Willie with any more courting. In fact, she might just put a bug in the ear of a few other single young ladies that Tom was looking for a wife. She finished saddling her horse and swung into the saddle. Maybe she could sneak out without Tom seeing her.

She guided the horse toward home. She would confront Mama first, then the fence painting incident, then have a look around the Mahoney land. Mama hung laundry over the fence railing when Willie rode into the yard, thus sparing her from having to get off the horse. "Mama!"

Her mother squared her shoulders, thinned her lips, and shuffled toward the horse. "I guess I know why you're here."

"I'm not here as your daughter, but as the sheriff."

"Then you can call me Mrs. Baxter." Mama thrust her fists on her hips.

"What are you women thinking traipsing around Mrs. Mahoney's land? That's trespassing and against the law." Willie folded her arms and rested them on top of the saddle horn. "Well?"

"I have no idea what you're talking about." Mama glanced everywhere but at Willie.

"Don't lie to me."

"Fine." Mama glared, her dark eyes flashing. "We're trying to help. You'll be glad to know we didn't find any still."

"I am glad to hear it." What she didn't like hearing is that the still had moved. Now, she would have to start her search all over. What about Mrs. Mahoney's chickens? Had they been taken along with everything else or eaten to hide the evidence? "Please let me do my job. This group you've joined are making things harder for me. I'll make arrests the next time y'all meddle. I have a full day ahead of me. Don't wait supper. I'll eat when I get back." She pulled the reins to steer Stormy back to the road.

Following Mr. Brown's directions took a bit more thinking. Twice, Willie had to turn around and start over from the hickory tree. Bear kept busy nosing in the brush while Willie walked the horse in circles. Where in the world was the pile of rocks the man had spoken about? As the sun rose high in the sky, she started to believe she'd been sent on a wild goose chase. But, that didn't make any sense. Well, no more than someone being upset because someone painted their fence without permission.

Finally, deciding a small amount of scattered rocks the size of her fist must constitute a pile, she continued on until she came to a small house no bigger than the shack she used to live in. The weathered boards, while seeming sturdy, were as the owner had stated and plain. The newly painted fence around the small yard almost hurt the eyes with its starkness. A small mixed-breed dog touched noses with Bear through the slats. Willie still didn't see what all the uproar was about. A free paint job wasn't exactly a crime.

She dismounted, looped the reins over the fence, and pushed through the swinging gate. It wouldn't hurt to look around for a few minutes.

Despite the lack of attempts to "pretty" up the place, Mr. Brown's small farm was well tended. Three goats frolicked in a pen next to a chicken coop. A milk cow mooed from a small corral. A sow and her piglets grunted from a nearby enclosure. Well maintained and blending in with its surroundings, nothing seemed out of place or suspicious.

Willie took her bottom lip between her teeth. What now? Confess to Mr. Brown that she hadn't a clue as to how to progress? It wasn't as if she could check the shoes of everyone in town to see if she could detect signs of paint. Equally ridiculous would be going to the mercantile and asking about paint purchases.

If the person had destroyed property or painted ill-meaning words or a threat, things might be different. The morning had been nothing but a waste of time. Willie returned to her horse, took her seat in the saddle, and headed toward the Mahoney place.

The same dog as last time she'd visited barked a ferocious warning from the porch. Willie commanded Bear to stay and moved toward the house. She glanced at the chicken coop. Either Mrs. Mahoney had recently purchased more or her previously missing birds were back home. Willie shook her head and knocked on the front door.

"What do you want?" The Mahoney son she had run out of the saloon, answered the door, suspenders hanging around his bony hips and a stained, ripped shirt unbuttoned revealing equally dirty undergarments. Obviously, the sons didn't take their hygiene habits after their mother.

"Is Mrs. Mahoney here?"

"Hey, Ma! That sorry excuse for a sheriff wants to see you." He leered and stepped back.

"Well, what did you find?" Mrs. Mahoney shoved her son out of the way and joined Willie on the porch.

"Your chickens are back."

"Yeah, my boys found them wandering in the woods."

"I've spoken with one of the women who trespassed and warned them that I would arrest the next person to do so. Do you mind if I take a look around?"

She shrugged. "Guess not."

"Much obliged." Willie nodded her thanks and headed toward where she had located the still. She whistled for Bear to join her and parted the thick shrubs. Broken branches and small footprints in the moist dirt announced to anyone looking which way the women's vigilante group had gone. She followed the tracks until she reached the spot where the still had once sat. Nothing, save for a cleared spot in the middle of the clearing, showed that anything had ever been there. Even the falling down lean-to had been removed.

Willie plopped on a fallen tree and removed her hat. The day's temperatures continued to rise, same as Willie's feeling that she'd been duped and sent purposely on a complaint that went nowhere. First, the painted fence, now, the missing still and returned chickens. The second one was easy enough to figure out. Willie would bet her hat the Mahoney boys were the moonshiners. The painted fence still left her stumped.

"Come on, boy." She patted Bear's head. "Let's go see what other games this crazy town wants to play."

*

Tom sat at a window table at the diner and tried not to notice Sally Simpson smiling at him from the other side of the glass. The silly thing looked as if she had a secret bursting to get out. He kept his head down and focused on his roast beef and potatoes.

Willie had left early in the day while he'd been busy shoeing a customer's horse and hadn't returned. Even with the girl staring at him through the window, he couldn't squelch the niggle of worry that poked at his mind. She'd been right surprised when he dropped off the flowers, and one look through the window of the sheriff's office showed she had kept them, but Tom had felt like the biggest goon in the territory by thrusting them at her. In front of other people, too! He should have turned tail and run. He sure hadn't done anything to keep her in town and out of danger. What had he been thinking?

He scowled at Sally, pleased to see her smile fade a bit. Then, he picked up his plate and moved to a table across the room. That simpering look on her face could make a man lose his appetite.

"What's wrong?" Violet Bloomfield refilled his coffee. "The sunlight too strong?"

"Something like that."

"Are you going to the Fourth of July celebration next week?" She smiled down at him, her plump face dimpling.

"Haven't thought about it." He hoped she wasn't out to sink her hooks into him, too.

"If you do, save me a dance, all right?" She trailed her hand across his shoulder as she passed.

What was wrong with the women in this town? He couldn't recall them acting so forward before. He wolfed down the rest of his supper and skedaddled back to the livery. Willie had just finished unsaddling her horse. Good, putting the horse up for the night would give Tom something to do.

"Evening, sheriff," he said.

"Tom." She nodded and went to move past him.

"You've been gone for a good long while."

Her shoulders heaved with her sigh. "That's right. I'm sure the entire town keeps tabs on how much I'm out of my office." She turned those amazing eyes on him. "You were there this morning so you know the ridiculous complaints I received. It took me a while to investigate."

"I could have checked one of them out for you."

"No, thank you. All I'll need a deputy for is if things get rough enough that guns are drawn and I'm outnumbered. Have a good evening." She picked up her pace toward the door.

"Wait." He jogged to her side. "Are you going to the celebration next week? Maybe you would consider going with me."

"I'll be going in an official capacity, nothing else." She grinned. "I know of several young ladies who would be very willing to be escorted by you. If you're interested, I'll give you their names tomorrow." She tipped her hat and left him standing like he had no sense.

How did she know women were clamoring to escort him? He must be doing something wrong. Since he had never courted a woman before he really had no idea how to proceed. First the flowers, now the dance, one left unacknowledged, the other turned down. Sure, he didn't really want a serious courtship, he only wanted to keep Willie busy fending off his advances, but if she wouldn't even bat her eyes or indulge in some minor flirtation, he would be the only one staying busy. Part of that would come from escaping the clutches of the hungry young single women in town.

Maybe he needed to file a complaint of his own. The town rules clearly stated that a woman wasn't to make advances toward a man. But complaining to the sheriff would make him look less a man, wouldn't it? He grabbed the curry brush and set to working on Stormy.

The sparkle in Willie's eyes led him to believe she was up to something he wouldn't like. His mind whirled as he worked. It almost felt as if she knew what he was up to and had decided to play against him. What if Tom's crazy idea of keeping the sheriff busy got him hitched to some silly, lace-wearing girl? He shuddered. He needed a new plan.

"Here's the white wash I borrowed, Mr. Miller." Henry Larson set the pail and brush inside the door. "There ain't much left."

"That's all right. I was glad to lend it to you."

"And I was thankful for the bit of money it brought in. I'm going to spend it on a drink or two. Thanks, again." The young man dashed out and turned toward the saloon.

Too bad he couldn't put his meager earnings toward something more useful, like a home of his own. A man in his twenties shouldn't be living with his older brother and family. Once he finished with the horse, Tom lifted the paint can. The lid fell off, landing on his boot and settling into the stitches. Wonderful. He grabbed a rag and scrubbed off as much as he could before setting everything on a shelf.

He turned down the lantern and headed for the stairs leading to his one room home. Before falling asleep, he would come up with something to keep Willie out of trouble. Something that didn't have anything to do with romance, real or pretend.

*

"Get the job done?" Bart slid a whiskey across the bar to Henry Larson.

"Yes, sir. Looks mighty fine, too." He upended his glass and slammed it down. "Got any more jobs for me?"

"I might. Check with me in the morning. What are you not willing to do for a bit of coin?" Bart dried the inside of a glass, doing his best to act as if his question were innocent, and not as if he were digging for information. The fence painting was nothing more than a nuisance, but after a while, things might have to get a bit more serious.

"I won't kill anybody." He gulped down another drink. "But most anything else is fair game.

Why?"

"Just making conversation."

"You got a problem with our sheriff, don't ya?" Henry shook his head and eyed the bottle of moonshine. "I like her well enough, she don't bother me, but I've heard about the run-in you two had."

"Now, that's where you're wrong, Henry." Bart leaned on the polished wood of the bar. "She's shut down our gambling to the point where we have to do it in secret in the back room. Why, your brother is back there now, complaining about being claustrophobic. Not only that, but she's trying to stop me from getting that moonshine you like so much. I say that means she's bothering you, in a roundabout way."

"I ain't looked at it like that." His brows lowered over booze filmed eyes.

Bart grinned. The boy was landing right where he wanted him. "All I'm aiming to do is keep her busy enough to keep that pretty nose out of our business. So, what do you say? You willing?"

"Yes, sir!" He grabbed another glass.

Bart clapped him on the shoulder. "Drinks for you tonight are on the house. Just remember … we need to keep quiet about this. We don't want anyone else getting in on our fun."

"I won't even tell Oscar."

Sure, he would, which was fine with Bart. Oscar would be willing to do more than his younger brother, especially if whiskey was involved. Yep, things were moving along just fine, and the lovely sheriff hadn't been harmed even a bit.

Bart didn't want her hurt, just occupied and away from him. He would plan something really big for the Fourth of July celebration.

13

With Mama frowning at Willie's choice of wearing the leather again rather than a dress that set off her eyes, Willie strapped on her gun and whip, grabbed her rifle, and then led the family to the cleared area in front of the church. She hoped to enjoy herself, but as the sheriff, it was important that she keep an eye on the festivities and curb any over-zealous celebrating.

"You need to learn to relax." Mama stomped alongside her. "Even the sheriff needs a little fun now and again."

"I have fun." She couldn't remember when, but sometime in the past she had laughed, right?

The churchyard was packed with people, booths, and more food than the townsfolk could eat. Excited chatter filled the air along with joyful screams of children as they raced among the adults. Mama had said the women's group planned horse races, target shootings, fireworks, and other games to celebrate the country's independence. Their busyness at planning the events had kept them out of Willie's hair for at least a day.

Willie had thought of signing up for the shooting, since the winner would receive a credit at the mercantile, but decided it wasn't fair. After outshooting everyone on her first day, it wouldn't be much of a competition.

Mama promised to keep an eye on Bonnie and joined a group of women beside the food tables. Junior dashed off to play with his friends, leaving Willie to patrol a circle around the townspeople. Men were putting together a hasty dance floor. Willie shuddered and headed the opposite direction. She'd make herself scarce when the music started. She'd danced once in her life and that was on her wedding day. She didn't plan to repeat the experience after stepping on Sam's feet and scuffing his new boots.

"Mrs. Sheriff!" Sally and Violet, skirts hiked above their ankles, raced toward her. They skid to a halt and patted their hair into place.

"Did you tell both of us to pursue Tom Miller?" Sally asked.

"Why, you girls aren't afraid of a little competition, are you?" Willie kept walking. "Isn't victory sweeter when it's won by overcoming obstacles?"

"Yes, but—" Violet eyed the other girl's frilly yellow dress. "I suppose I might have an advantage, being older and all. I'm sure Mr. Miller would prefer a more mature woman and not a silly young girl."

Willie grinned. "There's Mr. Miller now, by the horseshoe pit. You two should go say howdy." The girls shrieked and sprinted away, leaving Willie delightfully pleased with her wicked plan. Those two ought to keep Tom out of her business for a while.

She made her way to the steps of the church and took her position on the small landing, propping her rifle against the church wall. From there, she could see most of the going-ons'. She leaned against the pillar, Bear at her feet, and shaded her eyes with her hat.

The two girls converged on Tom like a twister. He stepped back, hands in the air, looking like a cornered cat. He dodged them and made a beeline toward Willie. Try as she might, she couldn't wipe the satisfied grin from her face.

Tom climbed the steps and stopped next to her. He exhaled sharply, sagging against the opposite post. "Something is making this town go loco. It must be something in the water."

"Must be." She ducked her head.

"You think this is funny." He crossed his arms and frowned.

"A bit." She peered at him from under her hat brim. "Relax, Tom, they're only girls. They won't bite you."

"They might. I feel as if they're sizing me up like a prized bull on the auction block. I can't figure out what's gotten into them girls."

"There aren't many eligible bachelors in Wild Horse Pass. Not that would make good husband material anyway." Willie glanced back at the crowd. "You've got Henry Larson, and the Mahoney boys, but only a fool would marry their daughter to one of them. If you want to discourage the girls, you should have gotten hitched a long time ago."

"Are you offering?"

Willie froze and shot him a look that should have made him back off. "I'm not looking to get married again."

"It's a pity, being as pretty as you are." Tom tapped the edge of her hat, and stepped back as if afraid she'd whack him, which she might. "You entering the shooting contest?"

"What? Oh, no, I've decided against it." She couldn't tell whether he was teasing or fishing to find out whether she was also interested in him as husband material. "It wouldn't be fair."

"Mighty big in the britches, aren't you?" Tom cocked his head. "I've entered, and since I never shot against you on that first day, I was hoping you would take up the challenge. Unless, you're scared?"

"Puh-leese. I can out shoot you any day."

"Prove it." Tom marched off the steps and headed to where the targets were set up.

Not being one to turn down a direct challenge, Willie shook her head, grabbed her rifle, and followed. She'd show him who was scared. When she approached the line of participants, a cheer went up.

"Now, we've got ourselves a competition," Mayor Bloomfield shouted. "Gentlemen, and sheriff, take your positions. We will have three rounds. Winner gets a twenty dollar credit at the mercantile. That could be a year of supplies, if rationed right."

Something Willie could definitely use with the frequency Mama visited the mercantile. Not that she blamed her. Money had been scarce since Sam's death, and Mama liked pretty things.

"The three closest to the target will move on to the next round. Oscar Larson, you go first. We already know the sheriff can beat the pants off all of you, so she'll go last." Mayor Bloomfield snapped his suspenders. "Then, Henry, Bart, the pastor, Tom, and Willie Jack. Ready, Oscar?" At the man's nod, the mayor shouted for him to aim and shoot. His shot missed. Most likely because of the whiskey fumes that wafted in Willie's direction.

Tom's shot hit the outside rim of the bull's eye circle. Willie raised her gun, aimed, held her breath, and shot. Her shot landed a hair's breadth from Tom's. He flashed her a dimpled grin which raised her pulse a notch. Heavens the man could pour on the charm. The second round came down to her, Tom, and the pastor whose shot came just outside of theirs.

"I had no idea we had a pastor that could shoot bullets as well as sermons," Tom said, clapping Mark on the back.

"Pays to have many talents here in Montana." Mark grinned.

After the second round, Tom and Willie stood side-by-side. Five cans were lined up on a log about five hundred yards out. "The winner is the one who can shoot down all five," the mayor stated. "Tom, you're first."

Willie's heart threatened to burst free. She needed to win, to keep the respect of the community if nothing else. Since losing in the first round, Bart Johnson had leered in her direction as if daring her to lose. The Larson boys grinned like a couple of drunken donkeys. The three possibly worst people for Willie to lose in front of seemed the most interested in the outcome. Instinct told her they were rooting against her.

Willie closed her eyes, prayed for a steady hand. She shot all five cans, as had Tom. Not wanting to prolong her rival's agony, she blasted a branch off an oak tree fifty feet past where the cans had been set. Cheers and good-natured ribbing filled the air. Tom turned to her with a grin. "Looks like you're the best shot. Congratulations."

"Thank you." Willie tried not to be prideful, but couldn't help the bubbling of satisfaction that came in knowing she'd outshot the town's best. "You want to try your hand at that tree?"

"Nah, that tree hasn't done anything to me. You won fair and square." He clapped her on the shoulder as if she were a buddy of his and joined the group of men heading back to the churchyard.

Mama met Willie as she returned. "That was about the most unladylike display I've ever seen. Men want to know they can do things better than a woman."

"I'm not just a woman, Mama, I'm the sheriff." Willie took her spot on the church steps and set her rifle aside. "Now, you can buy that candy dish you've been eyeing at the mercantile."

"Well, in that case." She grinned and bustled away to join her friends.

Willie smiled and glanced across the crowd,

her gaze colliding with Tom's. My, the man was handsome, and a gracious loser to boot. She couldn't curb her suspicion that the man was attempting to court her, and while she didn't intend to marry again, as she had made more than clear, his attention appealed to her feminine side.

Sally and Violet sashayed past, tossing her a wave as they headed in Tom's direction. He spotted them coming and ducked around the building. Silly man. Those hungry girls would only follow. Willie doubted he would be safe even in the outhouse. They'd probably wait for him to emerge again.

*

"Well, we heard the town had a pretty new sheriff," one of the drovers said. "Looks like we've been gone a mite too long."

Tom folded his hands into fists. While he was doing his best to stay out of the clutches of two certain young women, he'd rather deal with them than a group of men who had been riding the trails too long. "I'd steer clear of her, if I were you. She ain't friendly and knows how to use a gun, and that whip hanging on her hip."

The men laughed. "I'd like a closer look, wouldn't you fellas?" The man speaking grinned and piled a plate full of fried chicken and beans. "I'm Jim Parson, these here chaps have names, but I do most of the talking when we go somewhere. I'm thinking of creating a scuffle just so that sheriff feels a need to come my way."

"I'm the town deputy, and I say it's best if you steer clear of her." Tom took a step closer, narrowing his eyes. His hand hovered over the gun in his belt holster. He'd hoped the cattle drive would have lasted until Willie moved on. Her job, and his job of watching her back, had just grown ten-fold.

From the dance floor, a fiddle tuned. Tom marched to Willie's side and grabbed her arm. "First dance is on me." All the dances if he had a say in the matter.

"I don't dance, besides I'm working." She tried to pull free, only to have him tighten his hold.

"See those men over there? They aim to start some trouble tonight just so they can get a closer look at our female sheriff. I'm keeping you out of trouble."

"This has got to stop, Tom." This time she managed to jerk free. If he was a smart man, he would have taken the opportunity to run. "Let me do my job. If they cause trouble, I'll handle it."

"I don't think you're interested in the kind of trouble they want to start." Tom paled just thinking of the looks in the men's eyes. Willie was tough, for sure, but no match against six men who hadn't seen a beautiful woman in months. "Please, dance with me. What's the harm in them thinking you're my woman?"

Her eyes hardened. "I'm nobody's woman!"

"Just dance with me." Was he that repugnant? He sniffed, trying to decide whether he smelled. Didn't women like dancing?"

"Oh, stop it. You don't stink." Willie took a deep breath. "I'm not a good dancer. You'll regret it."

What was there to regret about swaying on a dance floor with a beautiful woman in his arms? "Let's see, shall we?" He held out his hand.

Her shoulders slumped as she slipped her small hand in his. "Very well, but don't say I didn't warn you. Make sure you turn me once in a while so I can keep an eye on what's happening."

He led her to the dance floor where they were immediately surrounded by couples. Tom steered Willie to the center. While she protested about not having a clear view of the folks not dancing, he kept a firm hold on her waist. Even through the leather she felt soft to the touch. He shoved aside the urge to draw her close as the musicians started a slow song. Instead, he kept her at a respectable distance and waltzed in a circle. Her neck craned to look everywhere but at him. She wasn't kidding about not being able to dance. His poor feet would need a good soaking after her stomping.

"Men are going in and out of the saloon like it's an ice cream party." Willie stumbled, clutching Tom's arms and sending his heart racing. "I think you're right about trouble coming. We should have closed the saloon for the celebration."

Tom agreed, but they'd tried in previous years to no avail. Prior sheriffs had chosen to turn a blind eye to Bart Johnson's place, and as long as the more rowdy of the men could find a good card game, most of them tended to leave other folks alone. He prayed it would be so that evening.

With each day's passing, the danger to Willie escalated. Not all of the former sheriffs had moved on, some were buried in the graveyard behind the church. The last thing he wanted was to see Willie's name on a tombstone.

Raucous laughter and gunshots rang out as festivities at the saloon escalated. Willie pulled free of Tom's hold. "I need to put a stop to that before someone gets hurt, or worse."

He yanked her close. "Don't make me kiss you again."

"Excuse me?" She stiffened.

"I will if that keeps you from going into the saloon." He stared at her lips, remembering the taste and softness of Wilhemina Jackson rather than Willie Jack. He lowered his head.

"Stop." She planted her hands against his chest and shoved. "While I thoroughly enjoyed our one, and only kiss, now is not the time to debate whether you can get away with doing it again. Unhand me or I will plant my heel into the top of your foot."

"You mean more than you already have tonight?" He grinned. Her eyes sparkled under the light of dozens of gas lanterns.

"Sparring with me is wasting my time." She dashed away, pushing through the dancers and heading toward the saloon.

Tom followed at a run. The silly woman was putting herself exactly where the drovers wanted her … within their grasp. He doubted very much whether the town's residents would step into a forbidden building to stop a wayward sheriff from being harmed. The women's vigilante group would have a say about it though, and thus put themselves into danger. Why wouldn't Willie listen to him?

She shoved through the swinging doors, Tom on her heels, and pulled her whip. The drovers were tossing whiskey glasses into the air and using them for target practice. Willie cracked the whip against the next glass thrown, showering the drinkers with shards of glass. "Stop!"

Everyone froze. Then, Jim grinned and sidled toward her. "Hello, Mrs. Sheriff, I've heard a lot about you. Glad to make your acquaintance."

"Can't say I feel the same." Willie re-rolled her whip. "There is no shooting within town limits, especially in a building full of drunken fools. One more stunt like that, and I'll cart the lot of you to jail."

Tom stepped to her side, planted his feet shoulder-width apart, and tried to look as tough as she sounded. Why hadn't he grabbed the deputy badge from the desk? It would have helped him look more official.

Bart Johnson lounged behind the bar, watching the proceedings with interest. He shot Tom a wink as if the whole show was in good fun. The undercurrents of tension between Willie and the drover were anything but. Tom steeled himself to be ready to pull his gun in defense of Willie.

*

The timing of Jim and the other drovers couldn't have come at a better time if Bart had planned it himself. They usually stayed a week or two when passing through and created all kinds of trouble. Things that would keep the sheriff busy and out of his business. Whether Jim made good on his promise of some unsavory acts with the sheriff were none of Jim's concerns. The woman would have to watch herself.

"All right, boys, you heard the sheriff. Break it up and take the party outside." Bart capped the almost empty bottle of moonshine. "It's almost time for fireworks."

"I've something else in mind," Jim said, reaching for the sheriff. She jumped back, leaving him holding part of her sleeve.

Before Bart could blink, she had her pistol aimed between the other man's eyes. "Touch me again. I dare you." A slow smile spread across her face. "Only problem is, I'm just a woman, and we all know women tend to have twitchy trigger fingers, ain't that right? If you move too suddenly, you might startle me, and oops, you've got a third eye."

Jim paled. His eyes glittered with hatred. "You heard the lady, boys, move it outside."

The saloon emptied of all but the sheriff, Tom, Bart, and the angry cowhand. Using one finger, Jim turned the pistol away from his face. "I hear you loud and clear."

"Good. Now go play nice." Willie motioned the gun toward the door. "Your friends are waiting."

Jim marched out, his back stiff. Willie turned to watch him go. Smart woman, not turning her back on the likes of Parson.

Gunshots rang out almost immediately. A woman screamed. Willie and Tom raced for the door.

14

A man lay in the street, his life mixing with the dirt and casting a dark spreading shadow around him. Jim Parson knelt next to the man and glanced at Willie as she rushed to his side, her gun drawn. "Help him, sheriff. He's my brother."

"Tom, fetch Mama. You," Willie pointed at one of the other drovers, "Get someone to help you carry him to that white house at the end of the street. Pastor, would you run and set up the kitchen table so they have a place to lay this poor man?" He nodded and raced away.

Mama wasn't a doctor, but since the town had yet to hire one, she was the next best thing. She'd helped mend many a man when Sam was sheriff of Apple Grove. Willie prayed she would be enough. "What happened?"

Jim Parson stood. "These folks say that fella there shot him down like a varmint." He pointed to one of the other cowboys.

"It was an accident." The man held up his hands and stepped back, his revolver falling into the dirt at his feet. "We was … seeing who had the quickest draw. I thought my gun was unloaded. I thought I shot the last bullet inside the saloon."

Idiot. "You're coming with me. The rest of you folks head back to the party. Don't leave the cleanup to the pastor's wife alone." Willie aimed her pistol at the shooter and motioned for him to walk ahead of her. "You'll be spending time in jail until we get to the bottom of this. Come, Bear." The three of them shuffled toward her office. Mama and Tom dashed past them, a questioning look on Tom's face. He'd have to continue to wonder. Willie would fill him in when she got to the house.

Willie ushered the shooter into a cell and locked the door. "Games and drink don't excuse stupidity, mister. You're in a heap of trouble."

"The name is Luke Sampson, ma'am." He plopped on the edge of the cot and buried his head in his hands. "Barney's my best friend. I hope you can save him." Sobs shook his shoulders. "I didn't mean to kill him, I swear."

"You might want to pray, then." Willie turned and waved for Bear to follow her as she sprinted for the house, saying a few prayers of her own. From what she could see before heading to the jail, the man had been gut shot. His chances weren't good even if they had a regular doctor in town.

She bounded up the porch and rushed to the kitchen. "Willie fetch me the whiskey and cat gut," Mama said. "I'll need to stitch him up."

"Will he live?"

She shrugged. "I got the bullet out, but it's pretty messed up inside. I'll sew up what I can, but his chances aren't good. The pastor's in the parlor praying up a storm as we speak." She wiped her bloody hands with a towel. "Stupid fool. What were these men thinking?"

"The guy in jail said they were playing. He didn't know his gun was loaded." Willie reached above the sink for the medical supplies. "If this man dies, he'll be trialed for manslaughter."

"My brother better live, sheriff." Jim Parson peeled himself off the wall. "If you hadn't been harassing me inside the saloon, this might not have happened outside. I could have prevented it. My men listen to me."

"That's enough." Tom unfolded from a chair. "You attempted to assault the sheriff. No one can be in two places at once. If you had better control of your men, this wouldn't have happened."

"Don't put this on me, blacksmith." Jim stepped forward. Tom did the same. They circled each other like roosters in a pen, chests puffed out, fists clenched.

"That's enough!" Willie put a hand on each of their chests. "We've had enough trouble tonight. Mr. Parson, you're welcome to sleep on the sofa. Tom, go home. Mama and I can handle this."

"If that man is staying, I'm staying." He crossed his arms and glared at Jim. "He can't be trusted."

"Do what you want." Willie handed the supplies to Mama and rolled up her sleeves. "What do you need help with?"

"Just keep the blood out of my way, will you? It's hard to see in there. Try to hold the lantern to light the way." She threaded a needle with the cat gut and plunged her hands back into the man's stomach. She hadn't done more than a couple of stitches before Barney stopped breathing.

"He's gone, Mama." Willie dropped the clean rag she had chosen to staunch the blood with on the table. "There's nothing more to be done."

"No!" Jim lunged at his brother, shaking him. "Wake up, you fool."

Tom held him back. "That won't do any good. I'm sorry."

Jim stared wide-eyed around the room, then dashed out the door. Willie followed with Tom right behind her as Jim raced toward the jail. He kicked in the door and barged inside, gun drawn. Just as Willie stepped inside, a shot rang out. She pulled her gun. "Step away, Jim. Now."

He dropped his gun. "I killed the man that killed my brother. Open the other cell. It looks as if I'm staying." He speared her with eyes as dark as coal. "But I will get even with you and this town if it's the last thing I do."

Keys in hand, Willie skirted around him, her heart in her throat, and waved him into the next cell, locking it after him. "Tom, please fetch me a cot. I'll be spending the night." She should never have left. Even with the new cell doors, if she would have been camped out in the office, this could have been prevented. Sam had slept away from home many nights for just this reason. Her shoulders slumped. Her first real test, and she'd failed.

"I'll stay," Tom said. "It isn't right for a woman to spend the night here."

"But it is right for the sheriff." Willie shook her

head. "Stop looking at me as a woman and start believing in me as the sheriff."

"You actually think I can do that?" He gripped her shoulders. "You're so much woman that a blind man can see how much. You may be the sheriff, but there are things you cannot do."

Her face flushed at the intensity of his gaze. "He's behind bars, Tom. I'm staying. You can't stay with me. What would people say? You need to back down on this." She wanted to be angry at his reference to women's roles, but she couldn't. Not with the way he looked at her, as if she were the most precious thing in his world. Sam had loved her, no doubt there, but he'd never looked on her with the same hunger Tom did. They'd been more like special friends, now that she thought about it. Marriage with Tom would be much more than friendship.

The knowledge saddened her. Here was a man ready to give her his heart and she had to decline. Not only was she not ready for a romantic entanglement but it wasn't possible with her future so uncertain.

He released her and raked his hands through his hair. "I know. Please be careful." He started to say something else, but stormed outside instead.

"Sweet encounters," Jim said from his cell. "I don't need your protection, sheriff. I'll do just fine on my own."

She wiped her eyes before turning to him. She could not let him see her looking weak. "You're a murderer. The vigilante group in this town won't take that lightly."

"Those women?" He laughed so hard, he almost rolled off the cot. "Seriously? You expect me to believe they'll hog tie me and take me out to the Hanging Tree? The same tree they planted flowers around so it wasn't such an eyesore?"

Willie had no idea what the women would do, but she'd make sure they stayed out of the jail. "Go to sleep."

"I'm afraid I won't be able to sleep for fear of those women." He laughed again. "You're a card, sheriff. One of a kind." He rolled in the thin blanket provided and faced the wall, his shoulders still shaking. "Don't worry about me. I'll sleep just fine. There's no remorse over my actions going to keep me awake. I can't say the same about you, though, can I?"

No, he couldn't. Guilt would plague Willie that night. She sat at her desk, propped her feet on the desk, and waited for her cot.

A few moments later, Tom wrestled a cot through the door, tossed a blanket and pillow on top, and planted himself on the bench outside the door. Willie shook her head, but couldn't stop a grin from spreading across her face. The man was as stubborn as the oxen. With Bear at her side, no one would get through the door uninvited. He might as well give up and go home.

She stretched out on the cot, feeling more protected and cherished than she had in a long time.

*

Tom curled up on the hard wood bench outside the sheriff's office and used his hat as a pillow. It didn't do a lot to cushion his head, either. Stubborn

172

woman. She could have been snug at home with her family and let him guard the prisoner sleeping on a cot with a blanket and a pillow. No one would've looked down on her for such a thing. Most likely, folks expected it.

What stuck in Tom's craw the most was how the woman seemed blind to how he felt about her. Either that or she chose to ignore his feelings. If someone would have told him a month ago he would feel this way about a leather-wearing woman, he would have said they'd been drinking too much.

He turned, trying to get comfortable. The voices of those cleaning up from the night's festivities drifted toward him, lulling him into a half sleep. A short time later, fireworks filled the sky with booms of color. He stared at the display, his heart jumping with every explosion. What would it have been like to watch the fireworks with Willie at his side? Would she have allowed him to put his arm around her, maybe hold her hand or even kiss her when the finale was over?

What was the point in dreaming? Willie had made it more than clear she had no interest in him other than as a friend, and barely that.

"What are you doing?" Mark stopped in front of the bench. "We're expecting rain before morning. Got the fireworks done just in time, is my guess."

"I'm guarding the sheriff who is guarding the prisoner who killed the first prisoner." Tom sat up.

"You don't say." Mark peered through the dark window. "We've had quite a lot of excitement tonight. Pity the poor fool who died. Both of them."

He sat next to Tom. Lightning slashed in the distance.

They sat in silence and watched the storm approach. Tom would definitely get wet. A cool breeze kicked up, blowing leaves down the street. Straggling townsfolk hurried home with their empty food dishes and tired children. "I reckon I'm going to need a slicker," he said.

"I'm thinking more along the lines of you needing some sense in that thick head of yours." Mark twisted on the bench. "The prisoner is locked up, and we've seen how well the sheriff can handle herself. Plus, she has that dog beside her. No one in his right mind will bother her with that loving beast. Why do you insist on taking over what God already has a hold of?"

"I can't let her go." He spread his legs and stared at the sidewalk, his fisted hands dangling between his knees. "I've tried. Every time I decide to take a step back, my ma's face rises to the forefront of my mind. If something were to happen to Willie, something I could've prevented, I'll be so damaged I won't be good for anyone."

"Well, I've done my best to counsel you." Mark stood. "This is between you and God, and that woman tossing and turning on the cot inside. Spend some time in prayer, my friend. You might find the answers on your knees." With a nod, Mark headed toward the parsonage.

The first fat drops of rain fell, sending up puffs of dust from the street. It wouldn't be long until the whole street was nothing but a mud bog. Mark was right, but Tom just couldn't let go. He wrapped his arms around his middle in an attempt to ward off the cold. His own brand of stubbornness would most likely result in pneumonia. It would serve him right.

He glanced heavenward. "God, get me out of this mess. My heart knows you're in control, but my head won't forget the past. Heal me of my pain so I can move forward."

"Come inside, you fool." Willie stood in the open doorway. So lost in his thoughts and prayer, Tom hadn't heard her open the door.

"Wouldn't be proper." He shivered as the wind increased.

"You'll catch your death. We won't sleep tonight. Instead, we'll sit with the lights on. Anyone passing by can see straight in the window." Willie stepped back. "I'll make coffee."

With a sigh dredged from his depths, Tom followed her. "It's getting cold."

"The weather's a safe topic." Willie smiled and measured coffee grounds.

Tom took the opportunity to admire her. Having grown used to the leather split skirt and man's hat, he realized the clothing suited her. Sure, she was beautiful in calico, but Willie was far more than a lovely woman in a dress. She was tough, tender, smart, and vulnerable rolled into one leather package.

"Here you go." She handed him a battered mug, pulling him away from his thoughts.

"What happens to Parson now?" He breathed deeply of the fragrant brew. "You'll have to send a telegraph to the Marshall's office to have him escorted somewhere else for trial."

"Which I'll most likely have to attend." Her shoulders slumped. "They may even ask me to escort him."

"Then, I'll go with you."

She laughed. "That will go over well with this nosey town, you and me traveling together for a few days." Her smile faded. "I really do believe God led me to Wild Horse Pass, but I fear there were some things I didn't think through."

"The complications of being a woman?" He concentrated on his coffee, fully expecting another tirade of minding his own business.

"Yes." She sighed.

Tom glanced up to see her blink away tears. A pang shot through him. He wanted to ease her burden but hadn't a clue how to do so without causing her to think he believed her incapable. She was very capable of being the town's sheriff, of that he had no doubt. Still, he worried about the danger. "If you have to take the prisoner to Billings, we'll have a third person go with us."

"Doesn't seem right to ask someone else to make the rough trip on horseback." She sipped her drink. "Maybe the pastor's wife would be willing." She grinned. "She'll be the envy of the vigilante group. Mama will throw a hissy fit, but I need her to stay behind to mind the children." A shadow passed again over her face. "I'm a horrible mother."

Tom set his cup on the desk and moved to her side. Heck with impropriety. He pulled her into his arms and nestled her head under his chin where she fit as perfectly as if God had formed her just for him. "You're a wonderful mother. A lot of women wouldn't be as willing to work as hard as you do to provide them with a good home. Most of them would have married to make things easier."

"Back in Kansas, I was approached by the town madam, the new sheriff, and others to sell myself in order to make a quick dollar. Taking this job was my way out." She shuddered. "Not one man offered marriage, not that I would have accepted, but maybe Sam was the only man who saw me as a virtuous woman. I don't exactly fit into the normal mold of what a woman is expected to do."

Guilt over his earlier treatment of her flooded him. He had come close to thinking marriage was the only answer for a single woman. Willie proved him wrong. Doubly glad she hadn't chosen the easier way of making a living, he tightened his hold. "I'm sorry."

"You've done nothing to be sorry for." She raised her head, putting her lips dangerously close to his. "You stepped in as a friend, something I desperately need, and I've pushed you away."

He didn't feel much like a friend at the moment. He tried to focus on the hiss of the lantern, the bubbling of the coffee pot, anything but how alluring she looked with trembling lips and tear-filled eyes. God, help him. He lowered his head and kissed her in a very 'unfriendly' manner as thunder rolled and lightning slashed.

*

Bart wiped the counter, then turned down the last lit lantern. The storm outside had kept all but one customer away, and Bart had sent him home an hour ago. Even the most die-hard drinkers wouldn't venture out in a storm like the one flooding the street.

Before heading to his room upstairs, he took one last look outside, surprised to see a light burning in the sheriff's window. Couldn't the lovely sheriff sleep on a night such as this one? The idea of her alone appealed to him. He enjoyed the challenge of pitting his wits against someone, and if that someone happened to be a beautiful woman, all the better. He grabbed a bottle of whiskey after donning his slicker. Maybe the sheriff could use a little warming up.

Sloshing through puddles, Bart dashed across the street and onto the opposite sidewalk. Rain poured from store rooftops, splashing his legs under his slicker. Coming out might not have been such a good idea. He shook off the rain like a dog and continued toward the light.

He peered through the window as he reached for the doorknob. Tom Miller and the sheriff stood locked in an embrace, his head bent over hers. It seemed as if the uppity sheriff might not be as moral as she pretended. Bart stored the sight away to be used at a later time. His arsenal against Willie Jack grew every day it seemed. Soon, he would have enough information to have her thrown out of town before the three month trial period was up. Then, he'd make sure the next sheriff was in his pocket. It had worked in the past, it would work again.

He uncapped the whiskey bottle and tilted it to his mouth. The liquid burned to his gut, warming him despite the weather. He took another look inside the window and laughed at the startled look on the sheriff's face as she met his gaze. He had her right where he wanted her.

15

The rest of the night passed with Willie and Tom sitting on opposite sides of the room like two gunfighters waiting for the other to make the first move. She should never have succumbed to pity out of seeing him sitting outside in an approaching storm. Leaving the light on might have worked to protect her virtue had she not given into his kiss. Now, Bart Johnson would tell everyone in town what he had seen and most likely blow the episode into epic proportions.

The light no longer served its purpose as the sun rose over the horizon. Her virtue lay in shreds on the scarred wood floor. She turned down the wick and glanced toward the front window.

"Uh-oh." Willie opened the door.

The women's vigilante group, Mama clutching Bonnie's hand and Gertie Bloomfield holding a rope, stood in the middle of the street. Bonnie wrenched free and dashed toward Willie. She scooped her daughter into her arms, planting a kiss on the end of her up-turned nose.

"Good morning, baby. What has Grandmama

got you up to?"

"Lynching." Bonnie buried her face in Willie's neck.

"Oh, really?" Willie clamped her lips closed and transferred her daughter to her back, wrapping the chubby legs around her waist. "Mama?"

"Don't look like that, Wilhemina. That tree over there has been waiting for such a time as this. We heard that man marched in here bold as brass and shot the other in cold blood."

"Yeah." Gertie stepped forward. "We aim to see that justice is done."

"It will be. Jim Parson deserves a fair trial, same as the next man." Bonnie wrapped her fist in Willie's hair and pretended to ride a pony. Willie flinched under the pain of her hair feeling as if it were being ripped from her skull. "Don't make me arrest you ladies."

Tom moved to her side. "Listen to reason, Mrs. Bloomfield. This isn't a game."

She poked a finger in his chest. "We know that. Now, step aside."

"I'm afraid we can't do that." Willie took one step closer to Tom, their shoulders touching, providing a barrier between the women and the office. "This is your last warning. How will it look if I arrest the wives of the town's leading citizens?" She set Bonnie on the bench. "Stay there, honey." Things looked ugly, and she wouldn't put her baby in danger, regardless of the star pinned to her blouse. Sometimes, a woman was a mother first. "Where's Junior?"

"At home doing his chores." Mama tried to

push her.

Willie planted her feet.

"You can't take us all on, and you won't shoot us." An elbow in Willie's ribs, knocking the breath from her, and Mama was inside, followed immediately by four other women. This couldn't be happening. This was the worst possible thing that could happen to show the town that Willie couldn't keep the law.

Tom barged past her and planted himself in front of Jim's cell.

Willie locked the door from the outside and stared through the window. She couldn't hear what was being said, but from the women's arm gestures and Tom's stony face, it wasn't good. Oh, no. Bonnie waved at her from the chair behind the desk. Could things get any worse?

Apparently so. Gertie slipped past Tom and unlocked the cell. Willie had forgotten about the mayor having a set. Jim barged out, fists flying. He raced to the desk, grabbed Bonnie, and picked up a letter opener from the desktop, holding it across Bonnie's throat.

Willie unlocked the door and darted inside, pulling her pistol. "Let her go."

"Now, Mrs. Sheriff. You wouldn't dare risk shooting this darling child, would you?" He whipped around as Tom moved forward. "Don't think about it, blacksmith. One slip and I'm wearing this baby's blood. Get me a horse."

"Do it, Tom." Willie kept her gun trained on Jim. The man was right. She wouldn't shoot. Not while he held her baby.

Tom raced out the door and across the street. The tension inside the sheriff's office was thick. Willie did her best to keep her attention trained on the man threatening her child, torn between trying to shoot him and wanting to shoot the women responsible for the whole horrible ordeal. Her nerves twitched, making it hard to hold her gun steady. Her baby shrieked in terror, ripping at Willie's heart.

She could do this. She prayed for steadiness, for fortitude, for strength. Her hand steadied. Without a clear shot at Jim, she could do nothing than keep her gaze locked on his. A smirk stretched his lips.

"The horse is outside." Tom leaned against the wall.

"Very good." Jim scooted along the wall and outside. "Now, this is how it's going to go down. I take this beautiful child with me." Willie's heart plummeted. "I'll leave her a mile out of town so long as no one follows me. Whether you find her dead or alive depends on that. You hear me?"

Willie nodded.

"Good." His wolf grin sent shivers down Willie's spine. "Don't worry, Mrs. Sheriff. We'll meet again." He mounted, keeping Bonnie in front of him, and galloped down the street, Bonnie's cries wrenching Willie's soul.

"I've got Stormy saddled and waiting around the corner," Tom said. "Let's go."

"Give him a minute or two." Willie re-holstered her gun. "I won't risk Bonnie."

"I'm so sorry." Mama sobbed into her hands,

her shoulders hunched. "I shouldn't have brought her, but Junior isn't old—"

"I don't want to hear it." Willie turned on her like a rabid animal. "You and your friends could cost me my child! I've told you women numerous times to stay out of it and let me do my job." She rushed to where her horse waited and swung into the saddle.

Tom mounted Nightmare. "You ready?"

Willie nodded. Tears clogged her throat. Fear and anger kept them at bay. "Yah!" She kicked the horse sending it flying down the street. Her heart beat in time with her horse's pounding feet. Please, Lord, let Bonnie be sitting on the side of the road, her chubby little face streaked with dirt and tears. "Mama's coming," she whispered. "Mama's coming."

They found Bonnie sitting on a fallen tree. She looked so small and forlorn. Willie yanked her horse to a stop and slid to the ground. She ran and pulled her baby into her arms. Tom thundered past them, in hot pursuit of Jim.

"I won't leave you again, sweetheart. Ever." Willie smoothed Bonnie's hair away from her face. "From now on, you go where I go." She'd worry about the logistics later. The women who thought it wrong for a sheriff to have her children with her could use the rope they carried and tie themselves to the Hanging Tree. Unless bullets were flying, Willie would no longer let either of her children out of her sight.

She lifted Bonnie onto the saddle, then squeezed up behind her. With a glance in the direction Tom had gone, she turned her horse toward town. Tom had a gun. He'd be fine.

Mama waited on the front porch, Junior at her side. She started toward them until Willie held up her hand. "I love you, Mama, I truly do," Willie said. "But the children will be staying with me from now. You can't have both. It's either them or your new friends. You've chosen your friends."

"But, Willie …"

"No, Mama. Come on, Junior." Willie held out her hand and pulled him up behind her. With one child in front and another in back, she headed for the livery. She dared anyone to complain about them staying with her. In fact, she hoped someone would. Anger bubbled under her skin like a hot spring from underground. All she needed was an outlet to let go of the steam.

Not only that, but an ache settled deep inside at Mama's betrayal. She had counted on her keeping the children safe from harm while Willie worked. Well, Willie could do both. It would be no different than pulling a child on a gunny sack while picking cotton or carrying Bonnie on her back while she hunted. She'd done it before, once or twice before Mama came to live with them, she could do it again.

She left the horse at the livery and trotted her children across the street to her office, glancing down the road for Tom. How far would he go before giving up? What if he caught up with Jim and they fought? What if Tom was injured? No, she couldn't think on that now. "Come on, you two. I've plenty of things to do at work and you can help me."

"Are you mad at Grandma?" Junior asked, slipping his hand into hers. "She didn't mean any harm. Those women talked her into it."

"I'm plenty mad, sweetheart." She stepped through the open door. The ladies had cleaned the place up. Out of guilt, most likely. She pulled a handful of coins from her pocket and handed them to Junior. "Run down to the restaurant and buy three sandwiches and some tea. Can you do that?"

"Yes, ma'am." His chest puffed out with pride. "I surely can." He hitched up his pants and took off at a run.

Willie grabbed a relatively clean rag from her desk and led Bonnie to the pump out back. She let the waiting tears escape while she washed the dirt from her baby's face and neck. "I'm so sorry."

Bonnie patted her cheek. "Don't cry." She wrapped her arms around Willie's neck, making her cry harder.

"Mama's got some thinking to do." She laid her cheek against Bonnie's head. "I don't think I can be sheriff and your Mama. I was loco to think so." She held her daughter out at arm's length and stared into eyes that mirrored her own. "And I won't give you up, so where does that leave me?"

*

"As the sheriff of Wild Horse Pass," Tom said, marching out the back door. "You *can* do both, Willie. I'll help you. Don't let the people of this town down." "They won't care." She straightened and swiped her hand across her face. "I'm half-way through my trial period. They're all counting the days, waiting for me to fail, so they can send me packing."

"Not all of them." He caressed her face. "I want you to stay. Marry me. Let me help you with your family."

Her eyes hardened. "Not you, too. I won't marry just to put a roof over my head." She picked up Bonnie and stomped past him.

"Why not?" Tom followed. "Marriages have been built on less than friendship. We would have a good start to a good life."

She sat Bonnie in a corner. "Did you find Jim?"

"No, but I found the horse I gave him." His shoulders slumped, realizing she'd veer as far away from the subject of marriage as possible. "I gave him a lame horse. He ditched the horse and took off through the woods on foot."

"Then I can track him." She straightened, refusing to meet his gaze. "Can you keep an eye on the children for me?"

"No. I'll be coming with you."

"I have no one else to leave them with. When Bonnie was smaller, I carried her on my back like a papoose. I can't do that anymore." She checked the bullets in her gun and grabbed a rifle from the rack on the wall. "I refuse to leave them with Mama."

He didn't blame her, but letting her go after a dangerous man alone was out of the question. "I'll ask Gloria Netser."

"No. She's part of that group." Willie dropped extra shotgun shells into her pocket.

"She wasn't with them this morning. She's a godly woman, and will do what is right." Tom grabbed the other rifle. "I'm not arguing about this, Willie. I'm going with you."

Junior rushed in carrying sandwiches wrapped in brown paper. "Here's your money back, Mama. The woman wouldn't take it. Said it was the least she could do."

"Give one to your sister. Stay here with Mr. Miller. I'll be right back." She rushed out the door and turned right, leaving Tom to babysit whether he wanted to or not.

"I didn't make it to work today," Junior said. "Too much uproar. You should have heard the women yelling." He bit into his sandwich. "It sounded like a pack of coyotes."

"Don't worry about work." Tom set at the desk and watched the children eat. Maybe he could make the little one some blocks to play with if Willie was going to make a habit of them staying with her. While the little girl was well-behaved, boredom would eventually set in much as it had that morning when she'd been told to sit on the bench outside.

He leaned his elbow on the desk, and rested his head in his hands. What did Willie find so repulsive about him that she wouldn't even entertain the idea of marriage? Under that leather and calico beat the heart of a passionate woman. Life together would be exciting, and if he were honest with himself, he cared for her more than as a friend. Somehow, he needed to convince her of the wisdom in hitching up with him.

"Where's Willie?" Winnie stepped inside, a basket over her arm. "I've brought lunch."

"We got sandwiches from the restaurant,"

Junior said, holding his up. "Mama ran off before eating hers. Do you want it?"

"She doesn't even want my food?" Winnie sagged into a chair by the window, set aside for guests. "I've messed up bad."

"You did what you thought needed doing." Tom rolled his head on his shoulders, trying to loosen the kinks from sitting up all night.

"You don't believe that."

"No, ma'am, I'm sorry, I don't." He speared her a glance. "You and the other ladies were out of line. String a man up? By yourselves?"

"There were enough of us fools to accomplish the feat." Winnie set the basket at her feet. "What do I do now? Willie has never been this mad at me before. I did a stupid thing, and now I have no idea how to fix it."

"Give her some time." Tom stood when Willie and Gloria entered.

Ignoring her mother, Willie kissed each of her children, grabbed the last sandwich, and headed out the door, leaving Tom to follow. At the livery, they mounted up. Tom led her to where he found the horse. They tied the horses' reins to a low-hanging branch and stepped into the cool recesses of the forest. He remembered what she'd said before about walking softly and did his best to step where she stepped and not snap any twigs.

He thought he heard her sniffle a time or two, but since she kept ahead of him, he couldn't guarantee that she cried. It amazed him how she forged ahead with her job while her heart must ache as a mother. Most women would have jumped at the chance to marry in order to make life easier. Not Willie. She'd do what she thought was right until her last breath left her body. It endeared her to him even more.

"Find anything?" He asked.

"No. Shhh. Wait, yes, there's a boot print. He came this way." She put her hand on the butt of her pistol. "Do you smell that?"

"A whiskey still. Guess we know where it moved." It was a bit far for the Mahoney boys. He would have sworn in court that they were the ones supplying the moonshine to Bart. "Do you think Bart has a hand in it?"

"Stop talking." She stood still, looking like an exotic creature of the woods as she sniffed the air and peered into the trees. A slight breeze teased the ends of her hair and the fringe on her skirt. The beads on her moccasins clicked together softly, sounding almost like tree branches hitting against each other. He could stare at her all day and block out the rest of the world.

After a few minutes, she moved forward. They stepped into a clearing much like the one behind the Mahoney place. The setting looked the same. Whiskey ran through copper pipes. Bags of sugar and corn were piled under a lean-to.

"Jim ran through here," Willie said. "But I've lost him. The ground is too rocky, despite last night's rain, for him to leave a print. Who lives around here?"

"No one that I know of." Tom turned in a slow circle. "There're lots of folks, I reckon, that don't make it into town regularly. Maybe we'll find a cabin not too far off."

"Maybe. I'll come back tomorrow. Right now, I need to send a telegram to the Marshall's office and let them know what happened. They'll want to make up some Wanted posters." She brushed past him and headed back the way they'd come.

Tom took one more look around the clearing. Something about the way the supplies were stacked tugged at him. He didn't know many men who would be so neat. The ground had been swept clear of any loose debris, and while the lean-to looked as if a stiff wind would blow it down, it was clean and orderly, too, right down to the empty bottles lined up in a row. He jogged to catch up with Willie.

"I don't think the moonshiners are men."

Willie turned. "What do you mean?"

"Didn't you notice how neat everything was? I don't know many moonshiners that bathe regularly, much less care what their camp looks like."

"You think women are responsible?" She bit her lip, frown lines appearing between her eyes as she thought. "I think you're right. I can't believe I missed it. But who?"

"No idea, but it might help narrow our search some. Those who live on the outskirts and up in the mountains come to town right before the snow hits. We could keep an eye out."

"I may not be here then." She increased her pace toward the horses.

She was right. A few more weeks and Willie and her family might pack up and move on. The thought ripped a hole in Tom's heart. If he had anything to do with it, he'd make sure she stayed.

In the saddle again, they headed back toward town. Willie seemed lost in thought, leaving Tom to dwell on his own thoughts. He sighed. She was most likely right, and the next sheriff would be responsible for shutting down the still. Something that probably wouldn't happen. Until her arrival, no one much cared about the making of illegal liquor.

Gertie and her gang weren't aware before that moonshine was a problem. Maybe their interference alone would make the next sheriff shut it down. Still, the thought of Willie leaving and the quickness of the approaching deadline set upon him an urgency he couldn't shake off. Where once he'd wanted nothing more than for her to go, now he longed for her to stay. Somehow, he'd have to convince the town board that she was the best sheriff they'd ever had, which was the truth, but they wouldn't be able to look past the fact that Jim escaped.

He'd become her full-time deputy whether she wanted him to or not. His blacksmith work could wait until the evenings. It wouldn't be the first time he'd shoed a horse by the light of a lantern. No, if Willie wouldn't marry him in order to stay, he'd help make her the best sheriff she could be. The town would beg on bended knee for her to sign a longer contract.

He guaranteed it. His heart depended on it.

16

Willie grabbed a biscuit from the basket on the table and collected her whip and pistol, ignoring Mama who wrung a dishtowel by the washboard. Willie expected a bit of disobedience to her words from the townsfolk, but not from Mama. Not only was she angry, but her heart held an ache that hadn't subsided since the day before.

The first bite of biscuit stuck in her throat, causing her to reach for a cup of coffee. Now, Tom had proposed marriage. For the first time since arriving in Wild Horse Pass, she considered leaving at the end of the three months whether the town wanted her or not. She couldn't stay in a place that thought of her as weak and unable to do what needed to be done. Nor could she stay in a town that had a group of women that would foolishly endanger the life of anyone, much less a child, for their own misunderstood brand of justice. They had brought Bonnie to a lynching!

What would they do if they knew of Parson's threat against Willie? That was the reason behind Tom's proposal. His fear she couldn't do the job without him by her side.

"Talk to me," Mama said, her voice catching. "I can't stand this tension between us."

"What would you have me say?" Willie forced the biscuit down and reached for a rag to wipe Bonnie's face. She unhooked the belt that held her in her chair and set the little girl on her feet. "See this face?" She turned Bonnie's face toward Mama. "We almost never got to see it smile again." A sob caught in her throat. "That would have killed me faster than if you had put a bullet through my skull."

"I'm sorry." Tears ran down her cheeks. "I wouldn't knowingly put any of my family in danger. It was an accident."

"It was a result of that group of friends you have." She took Bonnie's hand and headed to work. She didn't like fighting with Mama either. The action disrupted her world, clouding the sun, and sapping some of the joy from the day. She swallowed past the lump in her throat and squeezed Bonnie's hand. Gloria Netzer said she'd watch the children whenever Willie needed her which relieved Willie's mind to a great extent. Once Junior returned from working at the livery, she'd take both children over there then set out to find out what she could about the newly erected still.

A new set of sanded blocks sat stacked in the corner where Bonnie played. She squealed and toddled toward them. Willie smiled. Dear Tom. He'd make someone a very good husband and father. It couldn't be her, though. Her future was too uncertain, and there was the issue of her Indian blood. He may act as if he'd gotten past that obstacle, but could someone who had seen their mother brutally murdered by a race ever totally come to terms with it? She couldn't take that chance and risk her heart breaking for a second time.

"Telegram, Mama." Junior burst through the door. "Tom said I could bring it over. It must be important."

"Thank you, son." The telegram stated that a poster had been made with Parson's description. No mention of a Marshall coming to town. At least they believed Willie capable of handling things on her end.

"I've got to get back," Junior said. "Tom is teaching me how to shoe a horse." He dashed away.

Mercy. Junior was too young for such things, but if anyone could keep him safe, other than Willie, it would be Tom. "Well, baby, looks like it will be just you and Mrs. Netzer for now." She hoisted Bonnie onto her hip and set off for the parsonage. Thirty minutes later, she was in the livery to fetch her horse.

Tom looked up from where he explained the shoeing process to a very attentive Junior. "Give us a bit more time, and I can go with you."

"I'm just going to study the area around the new still. I can manage. If I'm not back in an hour, then you can worry and come looking." She planted a kiss on Junior's cheek, which he promptly wiped off with a scowl, and led Stormy from her stall.

The sun hung high overhead, beating on her back with its summer ferocity. She pulled the brim of her hat lower to shade her eyes and rode out of town, relieved that Tom was too occupied to accompany her. She needed the time alone to think about Mama. God's word said not to let the sun go down on your anger, and Willie was in danger of letting it go down two nights in a row without making amends.

Willie might not be one who spoke of scripture often, but she knew where her time in eternity would be spent. She glanced toward heaven. Had she heard God correctly in accepting the position of Sheriff? She thought so. She felt it in her heart she was meant to be in Wild Horse Pass. Then why the unsettled feeling in her soul?

The ride out of town, accompanied by only the occasional snort from her horse, low-throated barks from Bear, and the sound of plodding hooves was a bit lonely without Tom tagging along, but Willie relished the solitude. Despite her unease about a possible ambush similar to the one that had surprised Sam, she occasionally needed the time alone. This morning, it gave her time to pray about Mama and what would happen at the end of the next six weeks.

Would Willie plead her case or let the town decide on their own? She loved the mountains of Montana, and Wild Horse Pass had felt like home from the first night she laid her head on a clean pillow in the room she shared with Mama. But staying presented a mighty big problem. What to do about Tom's proposal of marriage.

The thought of marrying without declarations of love felt too much like the improper suggestions handed to her back in Kansas. Someday, when she wasn't preoccupied, Willie needed to examine her feelings toward Tom. Feelings it didn't take a smart person to know extended beyond friendship.

She reined the horse to a stop at the spot she and Tom had halted the day before. Looping the reins around a low-hanging branch, she snapped her fingers for Bear to follow and headed through the thick trees to where they'd found the still. She doubted she'd find further sign of Jim Parson, but hoped to find out a bit more as to who owned the still.

Same as yesterday, the place was deserted except for the bubbling brew. After listening to make sure no one was around, Willie stepped into the clearing. She was tempted to destroy the glass jugs and pull out the copper pipes, but destroying the still wouldn't get her any closer to finding out who had built it.

She studied the ground. Soft scuffs showed small feet encased in footwear other than boots. In fact, they looked suspiciously like the ones moccasin wearers made. The whiskey makers were crafty. While Willie doubted Indians ran the still, the owners were smart enough to try and hide their footprints. She wasn't working with amateurs.

She ducked and stepped into the lean-to, studying the line of empty jugs and glasses. Not a speck of dirt on any of them. Someone had been there, and recently. It might behoove her to spend the night in the woods and catch them the next time they came to check their still. She'd bring something to mark the jars with, too. Then, she could find out for sure if this was where Bart got his moonshine.

She pulled a three-legged stool into the shadows of the forest and waited. She had a while before she needed to be back and this might enable her to catch a glimpse of the moonshiners. Bear plopped at her feet, raising a small cloud of dust and leaves.

Time ticked by. If Willie didn't return soon, Tom would come looking for her, worry on his handsome face. She'd have a hard time dodging him again. She stood.

A shot rang out.

A bullet grazed her head, knocking her hat from her head and dropping her to her knees. Bear barked, the sound grating against her pounding skull. Willie knelt, stunned for a moment, before reaching for her gun. "I'm the sheriff. Throw down your weapon." She forced the words through the pain. The sound of running feet, heading in the opposite direction, spurred Willie to action.

She pushed against the nearest tree, lumbering to her feet. Blood ran into her eyes, blinding her. She pulled a bandana from around her neck and tied it around her head before grabbing her hat and setting off for her horse. How could she have let her guard down for a second? Had Sam's death taught her nothing?

There'd been no sound, no warning from Bear. Had the moonshiners hid the entire time Willie had searched the area, waiting for an opportunity to shoot? Or had Jim Parson returned? Either way, Willie wasn't stupid enough to hunt the shooter down alone.

The pounding in her head increased. Blood soaked the bandana. Spots danced in front of her eyes. She grasped Bear's collar and ordered him to take her to the horse. The dog licked her hand and pulled her along with him.

The occasional sound of a twig snapping or something brushing against leaves kept Willie tensed in expectation of another bullet. "Hurry, Bear," she whispered.

"You shot the sheriff!"

Willie froze and ducked.

"It was supposed to be a warning shot."

"We're in trouble for sure now."

She couldn't make out whether the speakers were female or soft-spoken men. She kept her pistol firmly grasped in her hand. "Come out of there or I'll shoot."

Someone gasped. "We meant no harm. Go away. We'll shoot you again."

Whether they would or not was a risk Willie didn't want to take. Not in her current situation. She'd be back to track them. With the running back and forth, that shouldn't be too difficult. The only problem was … if she left, they'd pack up the still and leave again. She bit her bottom lip, then turned back to the still. She'd have to sit and wait for Tom.

*

Tom galloped out of town, his heart in his throat. It had been well over an hour by the time he dropped Junior off at the parsonage. His gut told him something had happened. As he raced toward the still on Nightmare's back, he prayed for Willie's safety. He never should have let her go alone. He should have cut his time with her son short. That's what he got for listening to a woman's reasoning. Worry and a cloud of trouble hanging over his head.

It had taken every bit of will-power he possessed to not let on how troubled he was when he dropped off Junior. Questions would have taken up valuable time. He urged Nightmare faster, the horse's hooves thundering against the road. Winnie called out as he flew past her house. He couldn't spare her so much as a wave.

The ride seemed to take an eternity before he stopped beside Willie's saddled horse. Unmindful of silence, he barreled through the trees to where the still stood. Willie sat slumped against a tree, her light blue blouse stained with blood. He rushed and knelt at her side, smoothing her hair from her face. Please don't be dead.

"Hello, Tom," she said without opening her eyes. "I knew you'd come. I couldn't leave. They would have moved the still again."

"You silly, foolish woman." He straightened and searched their surroundings. "We can't stay here."

"No, we can't. My head hurts something fierce." She opened one eye. "You don't happen to have a grease pencil or something in your pocket, do you?"

"What in tarnation do you want with that?" As a matter of fact, he did have one. He carried it to mark tackle.

"Mark those jugs. Then, in a few days, we'll search the saloon for these very ones." She took a deep shuddering breath. "I think I need stitches."

She put a trembling hand to her head. "I can't seem to get the bleeding to stop."

Tom hurried to mark three small pin dots on the bottom of each jug. Then, despite Willie's protests, he swooped her into his arms and cradled her against his chest. "Come on, Bear." He moved as fast as possible in the dense brush to his horse.

He propped Willie against Nightmare, then mounted, swinging her up to ride in his lap. He reached over and grabbed the reins to Stormy and headed back to town, keeping the pace steady in an effort not to jar his precious passenger. She groaned and rested her head back against him. He tightened his grip, loving the feel of her against him while worrying over the severity of her wound. He made soothing sounds to her, much as one would an infant, and prayed her head wound was minor.

When they pulled into the yard of her house, Winnie came sprinting from the garden. "What happened?"

"I'm not sure. I found her this way." Tom slid from the horse, taking Willie in his arms again and carrying her into the house.

"Put her in the first room on the left, bed next to the window. I'll get my medical supplies." Winnie turned left in the house, while Tom went in the opposite direction.

He placed Willie on top of a brightly colored quilt and gently removed the blood soaked bandana from her head. A graze just above her temple, while still bleeding and would require stitches, didn't look life-threatening. But, she had lost a lot of blood. He pulled up a chair and waited for Winnie to instruct him as to what to do next.

"All righty then. Move over, Tom." Winnie bustled in with a tray carrying a bowl of water, rags, and needles. "Iffen you're of a mind to help, you might want to hold her down when I pour this whiskey in the wound. Then, I got to stitch it. If she's conscious, she'll fight us. Stand on the other side of the bed so you're out of my way."

"I can hear you, Mama. I'm not dead." Willie peered at her through one eye. "I'd like to change out of these bloody clothes before you start torturing me."

"Not going to happen. You can change later. I don't want to worry about ruining more of your things." Winnie nodded at Tom, who grabbed Willie's hands, then splashed a small amount of whiskey over the graze.

Willie hissed.

"Take a couple of swigs for the pain." Winnie held the bottle to her lips.

"No. Just sew me up so I can get back to work."

Tom shook his head. While he admired her strength, he despaired at knowing she'd be back in the saddle as soon as the last stitch was tied off. "Let me handle this. Was it Parson?"

"I don't think so. I heard two voices. I think you're right about it being women." She glared at Winnie. "And if you say one word about this conversation, Mama, I'll tie and gag you to the hanging tree." She winced and almost squashed Tom's hand as the needle punctured her skin.

"I've learned my lesson well enough. Hold

still." Winnie pulled the thread through and poked in the needle for another stitch. "We don't want you to have a nasty scar."

"Oh, my God in heaven that hurts." Willie exhaled sharply. "Just make it quick."

Her grip ground Tom's knuckles together. He wouldn't complain. His pain, other than emotional, was nowhere near as sharp as hers. Keeping his gaze on her face, he said. "Focus on me, Willie. It'll be over shortly."

"I swear this hurts more than the bullet. Careful, Mama!"

"I'm trying. If you weren't squirming around like a child, this would go easier."

"I cannot believe you're lecturing me at a time like this. Tom does enough of that every…minute." She pulled in a deep breath "Of … every … day."

"Hey, leave me out of this." He returned Winnie's smile. The woman was a genius at distraction. By annoying Willie, she'd tied off the last stitch, and washed the blood from her hands.

"You can change now." Winnie straightened. "Try not to get shot again. You scared ten years off my life. Other than a little loss of blood, you'll be fine."

Tom helped Willie sit up. "It wasn't pleasant for me, either," she said. She turned her attention to Tom. "We'll wait a couple of days, then visit Bart at the saloon."

His heart leaped at the fact she had included him. "Does that mean you won't head off on your own anymore?"

"Nope. Doesn't mean that at all. It's just that

this crazy town will look better on the fact that me going into the saloon is more proper with you along." She swung her legs over the side of the bed. "I've got your deputy star in my desk drawer. I'd like you to start wearing it. I have a feeling things are going to start hopping around this town, and I can't be everywhere at once."

He would take what he could get, and rather than her try to be everywhere at once, they would both have to. The last thing he wanted was to let her off on her own again. The two of them would be stuck tighter than honey to a bear's lips. Where Willie went, Tom went, and he wouldn't broach any argument on the matter.

17

The town was quiet following the days after Bonnie's abduction and Willie's shooting. Having Mama stitch her up had softened Willie a bit and while she now spoke with her mother, she still didn't leave the children at home without her personal supervision. So, to make things better for everyone, she'd decided to hold office at home. If anyone wanted her, they knew the way. Nothing in the town's laws said the sheriff had to reside at the sheriff's office during daylight hours.

Moccasin covered feet propped on the porch railing, Willie sipped her coffee and stared down Main Street. That early in the morning, few meandered down the sidewalks. Gertie Bloomfield had unlocked and entered the restaurant a few minutes before, but the establishment wouldn't open for at least another hour. The pastor stepped from the parsonage and into the church. Bart locked the saloon and headed around the corner.

Nothing seemed out of place. The town looked every bit the peaceful community advertised in the Kansas newspaper. Willie hadn't expected the town to be crime free; that would have been an unrealistic expectation, but a town in the wilds of Montana that outlawed moonshine but allowed a saloon? She shook her head. Not everything had to make sense, she supposed. It was up to her to enforce said law, and she intended to. Especially now.

She touched the bandage around her head. Things had gotten personal.

"Bye, Ma!" Junior dashed past her, leaping over the steps and landing barefooted on the ground.

"Wait a minute. You can't work bare-foot at the livery."

"Ah, Ma." Junior scuffed his toes in the dirt. "I hate those boots. They make my toes scream."

"Then they'll have to scream for two hours. Get in the house and put them on."

He stomped up the steps and back into the house, returning minutes later, laces flying, and raced down the road before she could stop him again. Willie grinned. Her boy was growing up. What had once been intended as punishment for his ill choice of vandalism had turned into the highlight of his day. He loved working with Tom around the livestock.

Despite the few bumps, she'd managed to make a life here for her family. In less than six weeks, they might have to start all over again. The question would be where? Could she stay in Wild Horse Pass if they turned her down as sheriff? What would she do to make a living? Where would they live? The same questions would need answering no matter where they parked their wagon.

Tom stepped out of the livery, snapping suspenders over his broad shoulders, and stretched. Willie sighed. The biggest question was what to do about Tom? She stared into coffee the same color as his eyes. If she looked to her right, a field of wheat reminded her of his hair. Even Bear's faithfulness brought Tom to mind. Willie was doomed. Whether she chose to stay or go, her heart would be affected.

"How does your head feel?" Mama asked, coming onto the porch. She lifted the edge of Willie's bandage. "It's been almost three days. I think we can take the bandage off. The stitches will have to stay a few more days."

Willie sat still and let her unwind the strip of white cloth. A cool breeze immediately kissed her forehead, dropping the temperature a few degrees. "That feels heavenly."

"It's definitely too hot to wear anything not necessary." Mama sat in the chair next to her and started rocking. "Time is running out, daughter. What are we going to do?"

"I've been thinking along the same lines." First order of business was to shut down the whiskey still. Then, Willie was as lost as the rest of her family. "I don't know. What do you want to do?"

"I want to stay." She motioned around them. "It's got to be one of the prettiest places in the country, I've made friends, it would be a shame to pack up again."

"What if they don't want me to be sheriff? I won't live as a pauper like before, Mama. Not here with these people." Maybe they could move just a bit down the line to another Montana town. One where they weren't known. There was still the problem of making a living, but God would provide something.

"I suppose I could open a seamstress shop. I'm handy with a needle and it brought in money back home."

"Not enough. Besides, the ladies around here tend to buy their clothes either readymade from a catalog or sew them themselves. I don't think this town is large enough for such a venture."

"Then one of us needs to get hitched." Mama pushed her rocker harder. "Since I ain't got one single prospect, it's up to you."

Coffee spewed from Willie's mouth. "I won't marry just to—"

"What?" Mama turned. "To put a roof over your babies' heads? Food in their bellies? There are worse things in this life than marrying a man that looks like Tom Miller. I would've leaped at the opportunity."

"You need to stop meddling in my life." Willie tossed the dregs of her coffee into the bushes. "I understand your concern, but I won't marry without love."

"Love would come, Willie." Mama pointed. "Have you looked at that man?"

Oh, yeah. Willie had looked and then some. She knew the feel of his muscles under her hands, the softness of his lips, the passion of his kiss. Yes, there were worse things, but she wouldn't marry a man because she needed protection. One day, the man would find his true love and resent Willie. She wouldn't let that happen to Tom. She needed to step up her efforts at finding him a wife, so he'd stop messing with her heart, uh, mind. "The subject is closed."

"Fine. Be obstinate about our future. I guess I'll scope out the marriage material come church on Sunday. Maybe I can find a man willing to marry me and take on all of you, too. In fact, I'm going to pray about it this instant." With a swish of her skirts, she banged into the house muttering something about thick-headed daughters.

Bear got to his feet and growled as a farm wagon lumbered into the yard. "Stay." Willie stood, keeping a hand on the dog's head.

A tall, handsome man, his face weathered under a wide-brimmed hat, grey painting his temples, set the wagon brake and climbed to the ground. "You the sheriff?"

"I am." Willie straightened, giving the man a clear look at the gun on her hip.

Mama came back outside. "I didn't expect my prayer to be answered so soon," she whispered.

"Hush." Willie shook her head. "What can I do for you, Mister?"

"Grimes. Theodore Grimes." He held out a hand, then stepped back when Bear took a step forward. "Can you call off your dog, ma'am? I have something I need you to look into."

"Down." Willie motioned for Bear to relax. "What would you like me to do, Mr. Grimes?"

"Well, I'm a pig farmer, rather successful, too." He glanced at Mama, his blue eyes twinkling. "But I've been away settling some things. When I returned, I discovered quite a bit of feed corn gone.

Then, this morning, I discovered a bag of barley missing. I suspect you got moonshiners in the vicinity, sheriff, and they're stealing from me."

Willie would wager a guess as to where his supplies were. Not only were the moonshiners making brew illegally, but substandard quality, too if they used the cheaper feed corn. "I'm aware of the still, and working on finding those responsible so I can close it down. Is it possible for you to lock up your supplies?"

"I reckon, but it's kind of a hassle for me. I'm running the farm pretty much on my own. But," he removed his hat and scratched his head. "Iffen it makes things easier on you, then I'll be mighty happy to help."

His kindness set her back. Mr. Grimes must be the first resident to actually care about whether or not his request made her life easier. Outside of Tom, of course.

"Would you like a glass of lemonade, Mr. Grimes?" Mom tilted her head and fluttered her lashes, looking every bit as flirty as the Simpson girls.

Mr. Grimes's face reddened. "I'd be much obliged." He stepped onto the porch, skirted around Bear, and followed Mama into the house.

She sure didn't waste any time when a handsome man caught her eye. Lemonade, indeed! Mama would fill the man's belly with food, too. Speaking of handsome men, Tom strolled her way, a deputy's star shining from the chest of his blue-plaid shirt, Junior prancing behind.

*

"Theodore's here?" Tom glanced at the wagon. Junior planted a kiss on Willie's cheek then dashed toward the paddock.

"Do you know him?" She smiled as her gaze followed her son.

"He's my uncle. He wasn't due back for a few more days." Tom bounded up the steps and into the house. "Uncle Theo." He grabbed the older man in a hug.

"It's good to see you, boy." Theo clapped him on the back. "That's some looker the town hired, isn't it?"

Tom nodded. "She's better than the ones we've had in the past."

"But?"

He sighed, glancing at Winnie. "She's a woman."

Theo laughed. "So, I've noticed. That leather getup doesn't hide the things God put on women to make us take notice. If she can do the job, there shouldn't be a problem, son. Or could it be the fact these women have Indian blood?" Theo held up his hand. "Don't dispute it, son. The loss of my sister plagues me daily, but I know these fine women had nothing to do with the fact. I'm sure you're smart enough to realize it, too."

Winnie froze, a small plate with a slice of cake on it in her hand. "You don't mind that I'm part Indian?"

"Not at all." Theo grinned. "You caught my eye the minute you stepped on the porch. All I saw was a fine-looking woman I'd like to get to know better."

Winnie's cheeks turned pink.

"Oh, for heaven's sake." Willie squeezed past and grabbed the slice of cake before it could slide to the floor. "Do the two of you want to go on the porch for a bit of privacy?"

"We'd love to." Theo stood, crooked his arm for Winnie to place her hand on his forearm, then led her to the porch.

Tom grinned at Willie. "This leaves us alone in here."

She rolled her eyes. "Not with Bonnie playing house in the corner."

He hadn't noticed the child who stared up at him with a grin and big eyes. "Hello, sweetie."

"Do you want to play daddy?" She asked. "Mama is the mama."

His face heated. He'd love to, but if he said so, he might get shot. He shook his head and sat at the table, his tongue as tied as if someone had lassoed it.

Willie laughed and handed him the cake. "Eat before you fall over."

A slice of chocolate cake taunted him from the plate. With the child sitting in the corner and Willie standing beside him, they looked every bit like a family. Something Tom desired very much, more as each day passed. The knowledge shocked him. Even with his proposal of marriage, he'd forgotten about Willie's Indian blood and realized it didn't matter one whit to him anymore. God had finally healed him of his hatred.

He lifted his eyes and met her gaze. Another offer of marriage teased the tip of his tongue. How many times could he ask her before she walloped him or worse, left town? As she moved to refill her coffee cup, he dug into the cake. Anything to keep his mind off the curve of her hips or the way the fringe on the hem of her skirt swayed when she walked.

He caught Bonnie watching. Almost as if the wide-eyed child could read every thought in his mind and encouraged him. He smiled, earning a dimpled grin in return. It wouldn't be difficult at all to imagine the darling calling him papa.

"Sheriff." Theo called from the porch. "Got someone here to talk with you."

Willie set her just-filled mug on the counter and headed for the porch. Tom shoved in the last bite of cake and followed.

Leroy Brown, face red and hands clenched into fists, stood in the yard. Every inch of his wiry body quivered. "The fence vandals have struck again. This time, they've painted every other slat bright red. My fence looks like a barbershop pole. Now, are you going to do something or do I have to take matters into my own hands?"

"We don't want you doing anything foolish, Mr. Brown." Willie grabbed her hat from a peg just inside the door. "How about I follow you home and take another look around?"

"I reckon that would be fine. I found some footprints and set a feed bucket over them so as the varmints don't mess up the clue."

"Smart thinking." Willie raised an eyebrow at Tom. "Want to come? Maybe you'll see something I missed."

She was seriously asking him to go along? Tom grinned. "You bet. Let me fetch the horses. I'll be right back." He raced down the road.

As he entered the livery, he tripped over a can set in the middle of the aisle. A can of red paint. The can fell, spilling the paint across the dirt floor. He groaned and jumped back, but not before getting some on his boot. Well, it would have to wait. He definitely didn't want Willie waiting, especially the first time she voluntarily invited him along. Not only that, but he hadn't loaned out any red paint, yet here the can sat, right after Mr. Brown complained of another paint job.

He saddled Nightmare and Stormy, leaped onto his saddle, and headed back toward Willie's house. The paint would soak into the ground and he'd dig it up later. Where had the paint come from? He only kept white-wash around the livery. Someone was playing games and he had just gotten caught in the middle.

The moment he entered the yard, Willie took her horse's bridle from him. Her gaze fell on his boot. She leaned closer. "Is that red paint? Is that white?" She dug a fingernail at the dried flecks of white from the last time he'd spilled paint.

"Tom Miller." Leroy stiffened. "Are you playing some kind of game with me? Why would you paint my fence?

"No." Tom shook his head. "I tripped over the can in my haste and knocked it over."

"I can't believe you would harass Mr. Brown in order to spend time with me." Disappointment spread over Willie's face. "It's unheard of."

"It isn't my paint." How could they honestly believe he'd do something so irresponsible as spend time he didn't have playing tricks on someone. "You have to believe me, Willie. What reason would I have? Wait. I loaned the white paint to the youngest Larson boy. He said he had a paying job and needed it."

She narrowed her eyes. "I guess we'll need to pay a visit to Mr. Larson. Hopefully, he can back up your story." She faced Leroy. "I think we'll have your culprit within a few hours."

She seriously didn't believe him? Of course, with paint all over his boot, he might have a hard time believing himself innocent, too. But Willie knew him. She wasn't thinking clearly. How could she not trust him?

*Bart stood in the doorway of the saloon, Jim peering over his shoulder. "Looks like a ruckus at the sheriff's place," Jim said. "Your idea is working."

"Of course it is. I'm not stupid." He rolled a cigar between his fingers, thankful his shipment had finally arrived. It took too darn long for the finer things in life to show up in Wild Horse Pass. This time, he'd ordered enough for half the year for himself and a few extras to sell for a good price. Once the Hickman sisters delivered the next batch of moonshine, he'd be fully stocked for the next round of cowboys to ride through.

He grinned. "Things are going to really shake up around here, Jim. You keep on hiding out until the time is right, then you'll have your chance at the pretty sheriff."

"I ain't a patient man, Bart. My blood boils every time I see her." He laughed. "In more ways than one."

Having Jim Parson develop an itch for the sheriff fell right into Bart's plans. There was nothing better at getting a woman to stop nosing around than a traumatizing event. He stuck the cigar between his lips and struck a match on the bottom of his shoe. An event such as the one involving her daughter. If he thought hard enough, he could come up with a similar idea that would keep Willie out of town for several days.

18

Was Tom so addle-brained about proposing to Willie that he didn't put the painted fence and loaned paint together? A true sheriff, or deputy for that matter, did not let their personal feelings cloud their judgment when there was a job to do. She cut Tom a sideways glance. He kept glancing at his shoe, his face creased in thought.

Did he think the spots would go away? Of course, she didn't truly believe he was responsible for the paint on the fence. It only annoyed her that he hadn't immediately put the pieces together.

The Larson boys lived an hour's ride up the mountain. Willie stopped her horse a few yards from the log cabin. A woman so thin a strong breeze would blow her away stepped onto the porch and shaded her eyes. A toddler boy clung to her faded calico skirt. While Willie judged her to be around her age, worry lines made the woman appear older. She slid from her horse, motioning for Tom to stay put for a second.

"Good morning, ma'am." Willie tipped her hat. "Is Henry around?"

"He ain't been home for days. Neither has my

husband. I'm running low on food, so if you see those two no-good scoundrels, tell them to high-tail it home."

Tom passed Willie, his hand in his pockets. "Here, ma'am. Take this." He handed her a fistful of coins. "Pay me back once your men come home or keep them, whichever you prefer. I suggest you purchase what you need and not tell them about the money."

Tears welled in the woman's eyes. Willie choked back emotion. From the looks of things, Mrs. Larson would never be able to pay back the loan, and Tom most likely knew that. Yet, he emptied his pockets anyway.

"Do you have a way into town?" He asked.

"I've a buckboard that will do. Thank you."

"Mind if I take a look at it?"

She motioned toward the back of the house. Tom glanced Willie's way, then left.

"You're that new sheriff." Mrs. Larson placed the child on her hip and moved toward Willie. "What's it like sending convention to the four winds? I bet the men put up a fight when you showed up." She glanced around the dirt yard. "I've always wanted to know what I could do if given the opportunity. Even thought of joining that woman's vigilante group, but with the young'uns … well, it ain't feasible."

"I'm trying to shut that group down." Willie almost told her of the fiasco with Bonnie, but held her tongue. She could find a friend in Mrs. Larson, if not for the woman's husband and brother-in-law. She sensed a kindred spirit. She prayed Tom's coins would be enough to ease the woman's burden a bit. "I did meet up with a fair amount of opposition. I'm only here on a trial basis."

"Well, you show that town a thing or two. Us women can do just about anything a man can do except use the necessary standing up. Guess we could do that, too, iffen we had a mind to." Mrs. Larson sighed. "I keep this place up mostly by myself. Ain't doing too bad. Just goes to show how strong our so-called weaker gender really is."

"You're right, ma'am. It looks fine to me." Willie grinned.

"Wagon had a loose wheel," Tom said, joining them. He wiped his hands on the thighs of his britches. "But it's fixed now."

"Next time you're in town," Willie said. "Stop by and share a glass of lemonade. The little ones, too. I've a daughter who would love some friends to play with."

"I'll do that. Call me Alice. I reckon I'll make it that-a-way in a day or two." She smiled, nodded, and headed back for the house.

A bit of kindness often went a long way. "That was good of you. To give her money."

Tom shrugged. "It isn't her fault her husband gambles or drinks away the small amount he earns. Once in a while, I've seen Alice in town selling eggs or butter in order to feed her children. I wanted to help."

She placed a hand on his arm. The heat from his skin seeped through his shirt and into her palm. She fixed her gaze on his eyes. "You're a good man, Tom Miller."

"Just not good enough for you to marry." He tucked a loose strand of hair behind her ear, brushing against her stitches and sending her heart thundering. His eyes softened, stealing her breath.

"You're more than good enough." She ducked her head, hiding under the brim of her hat. "I can't make commitments right now. I have a job to do and an uncertain future ahead of me." She forced the words past her tear-filled throat, knowing he was smart enough to see her reasoning. He had to. She refused to marry a man because she felt she had nowhere else to turn. If she married, it would be amidst declarations of love and passionate kisses.

She turned and planted her foot in the stirrup, swinging into the saddle. Avoiding his gaze, thus sparing her heart from the tender glances he cast her way, she turned Stormy down the mountain.

"What do you want, Willie?" Tom asked, catching up with her. "What do *you* really want?"

She cut him a sideways glance, not sure how to answer. Could she voice the things she wanted? Her answer would give him more ammunition in regards to the reasons she should accept his proposal. Still, honesty seemed best. "I want a place to belong." She exhaled deeply. She hadn't belonged anywhere since Sam's death. "Guess I won't find that until I figure out who I am."

"I know who you are." He moved his horse closer and rested a hand over hers resting on the pommel. "You're a mother, a daughter, a widow, a fine sheriff, a beautiful woman, and a daughter of the King. You are all these things and more."

His hand, rough and calloused from hard work,

enveloped hers, making her feel small and protected. His words washed over her like balm on an open wound. She *was* all those things, so why did she feel so unsettled? Why was she constantly searching for something else? The list of her attributes should be enough. Still, Willie wanted more. Only, she didn't know what that "more" was. She slipped her hand from under his and nudged Stormy away from Nightmare. Until she knew what it was she searched for, she couldn't encourage Tom or accept his advances.

"I need to pick up the children from Gloria," she said, keeping her face hidden under the brim of her hat. "I want to check the saloon for the marked jugs and for the whereabouts of the Larson men." She sighed. "I'll have to trust Mama to keep an eye on my children. Gloria shouldn't have to watch them all day."

"I don't think you have to worry about her longing to make friends to interfere with their safety again."

"I hope so." They rode side-by-side down Main Street toward the parsonage.

Bart Johnson lounged outside his saloon, puffing on a cigar. Willie curled her lip and kept riding. One day, soon she hoped, she'd take the man down a peg or two.

*

Tom met Bart's stare with a stern one of his own. The man knew something, was up to something, if Tom wagered a guess, it had something to do with Willie. He suspected from the rigid set of her shoulders, that Willie thought the same.

When they arrived at the parsonage, Willie's children raced to greet her. She swung Bonnie onto the saddle in front of her, while Tom did the same for Junior. Again, he was reminded of how much like a family they must look to others. He wanted to propose again, for the sake of her children, if not for his heart, but in doing so, he feared he'd push her so far away he would never be able to close the distance.

He followed her to her house where she left the children with her mother. Winnie held the little ones close and cried, vowing to never let them out of her sight again. From the look on Willie's face, she struggled with the same notion. Didn't she know that if she were to marry Tom she would never have to let them go again? The town would hire another sheriff, and Willie would be free to be a mother.

"Stop thinking along those lines." Willie turned her horse toward the road. "I can read your mind as if you'd spoken the words out loud. I love my children more than my own life, but being sheriff is something I have to do."

"Why?"

"We've gone over this."

"Help me understand."

She reined her horse to a stop. "You are the most persistent man I've ever met."

"You're the most stubborn woman I've ever met." He grinned, trying to loosen her defenses. For several seconds, he thought his attempt at humor wouldn't work, then a slow smile graced her face.

She glanced toward the saloon, then in the

opposite direction. "Let's find a place to talk."

"I know just the spot." He led her past her house and into the forest where a brook babbled over rocks and the sun lit up a small clearing. He used to come there often as a newcomer to Wild Horse Pass. God often spoke to him there, healing his spiritual wounds and helping him think. He hoped it would have the same effect on Willie.

They dismounted, letting the reins loose on the ground. Tom took Willie by the elbow and led her to a fallen tree that had heard his heartaches and dreams more than once.

"This is a beautiful place." She removed her hat and shook her hair free.

"Better than a church, almost." He sat beside her, placing his hat on his knee.

"Are you going to preach to me?" She tilted her head, a smile teasing the corners of her mouth.

"No." He took a deep breath and stared across the creek. "I reckon you understand why I act the way I do, especially after hearing about my ma."

"The Indians."

"Not really that, anymore. I've let that go." He entwined his fingers with hers, expecting her to pull away. His heart leaped when she didn't. "I've never thought it Ma's place to till the field. I was busy with feeding the stock, Pa was huntin' some wayward livestock, and once I'd finished, I intended to take Ma's place. Except—"

"You were too late."

"Yeah." He blinked back the tears prickling the back of his eyes. "I swore right then and there, as I hid like a coward, that I would never sit back and let a woman do a man's job without stepping in and putting a stop to it." He cut her a sideways glance, a bit unnerved at how intently her blue eyes were focused on his face. "After meeting you, I know that the lines between men and women's roles are blurred, but I can't let go of the need to protect what I deem the weaker gender."

"If I weren't the sheriff, I never would have had the opportunity to outshoot you. The contest set Mama up with the supplies she needs to run my house."

"True, but that isn't the reason you're here, is it?"

She shook her head. "No. I rode along with my Sam on most of his duties and never felt an ounce of fear. Why should I? I could take care of myself. Then, on a normal drive home from church, we were ambushed. He died in my arms. I never found out who shot him. Some folks said it was a hunter's wayward bullet. Maybe so. Still … " She shook her head. "If it were only me, I could have scraped out a living from a rocky patch of soil and lived off hunting and trapping, but I have a family to feed. In Kansas, the women work the fields right alongside the men. No one thought twice about me escorting Sam while he kept the peace. Not like here." She scuffed her moccasin in the leaves at her feet.

"Even now, no matter how brave of a face I put on, when I ride down a lonely road, I expect a bullet to find me." She raised shimmering eyes. The sun's rays through the tree branches kissed her dark hair with hints of blue. "Seems an odd fear for a sheriff to have, doesn't it?"

"You hide that fear well." One more reason for him to escort her when she left the town limits.

"Being sheriff is all I know to do, other than hunt or farm. I wasn't made to sit at home and cook and sew. Alice Larson farms that place alone from what I could tell. Does that bother your reasoning of men and women roles? Times are changing, Tom." She slid her hand from his and picked up a rock. With a flick of her wrist, she sent it skimming across the water. "Being sheriff now will help me conquer the fear that set upon me over two years ago.

"Thanks for explaining why you act as you do." She stood. "But, I am the sheriff for a month longer, if nothing else, and there's work to do."

He understood her perfectly. Even as a wife, she wouldn't be content with the traditional role of a woman. Tom pushed to his feet. Could he marry a woman who couldn't be content keeping house? Not that she had accepted his proposal, but were the majority of women starting to think as she did? If so, maybe bachelorhood was in Tom's future more than marriage.

They rode into town and dropped the horses off at the livery. With Willie's declaration of paying Bart Johnson a visit, Tom decided removing the saddles and brushing down the horses would have to wait. He fed Nightmare and Stormy a sugar cube from a can he kept next to the stalls and hurried after Willie.

Sally Simpson and Violet Bloomfield blocked his path. He eyed Willie approaching the saloon and tried stepping around them.

"I brought you home baked cookies." Sally held out a plate.

"I brought you an apple pie." Violet grinned. "Which is your favorite?"

"I like them both. Excuse me." He stepped to the side, they followed. What had gotten into them?

"Try one of my cookies," Sally said. "You won't regret it."

"I'm sure I wouldn't." Except for the fact taking even one bite would encourage her. "I've work to do. Just set the plates on that shelf." He set his hands on her shoulders and moved her to the side enough for him to pass.

"He caressed me," she sang to the other girl.

Tom groaned and increased his pace, barging into the saloon on Willie's heels. They might as well carve their names in one of the tables as often as they stepped through the doors of the establishment. He glanced back to see Sally and Violet peering through the swinging doors, eyes wide, hands still clutching their baked goods.

"Willie?"

"For goodness sakes." She held up a finger for Bart to stay behind the counter, then turned to address the girls. "Out. Right now. What would your mas say?"

The girls squealed and skedaddled. With Tom's luck, they'd be waiting for him at the livery when he returned. He really needed to speak with their mothers about their forward behavior.

"Any new shipments of moonshine?" Willie bellied up to the bar and rested her elbows on the counter.

"You aiming on buying a drink, sheriff?" Bart grinned, wiping a glass. "We're closed, but for you I could make an exception."

"Nope, just want to take a look at the jugs."

Footsteps sounded overhead. Tom glanced at the ceiling. He'd suspected Bart rented out rooms meant for working girls. He also suspected the footsteps belonged to one, or both, of the Larson men. "Tell the Larsons that there's a hungry family waiting for them at home."

Bart sneered. "I will iffen I see them."

Willie moved around the counter. Bart blocked her path. "Mind if I ask why you're nosing around again?"

"You can ask, but I won't tell you." She reached under the counter, grabbed a jug, and handed it to Tom while grabbing another for herself.

Tom turned the jug over. Right in the center were three black dots. "Got it."

"I'm closing you down, Bart." Willie replaced her jug. "These are from illegally brewed moonshine. Now, I reckon I knew that, seeing as how they aren't in fancy bottles like your whiskey, but now I can prove it."

*

"You can't prove a thing." Bart tossed the rag he was using on the counter and reached for his pistol. "You can't shut me down. This is my livelihood. I've done nothing wrong." He aimed the pistol at the sheriff, only to find Tom pointing another at his head.

"If you close me down here, I'll just rebuild

one outside of town limits where you have no jurisdiction," he said.

"I have jurisdiction. Only thing is, you'll then be outside of town limits and certain laws will no longer apply, but most of them will."

"Folks won't want to ride way out there. I'll lose business."

Tom cocked his gun. "This isn't getting us anywhere. You shoot the sheriff, I shoot you, I walk away unscathed and burn this place to the ground."

Bart considered his options. He knew Tom wouldn't hesitate to shoot if another person was harmed, especially a woman. Now, if Bart left peaceful like, he could open up a new saloon and even hire pretty gals to serve the customers. While he hated being put on the spot, he should have thought of moving a long time ago. He slipped his pistol into the waistband of his pants. "The two of you won't get away with this. The men will uprise—"

"We all know who runs this town," Willie said, drawing her gun, "and it isn't the men."

True. That nosey woman's group made the rules, often changing them to suit their needs at the time. Bart needed to shut the whole bunch of them up. "I believe you are correct." He crossed his arms. "Seems to me like you're slacking on your job allowing those women to rule the place."

"They haven't done anything wrong." Willie lowered her gun. "Who are the moonshiners?"

"Now, if I tell you that, I don't have any cheap liquor to serve my customers. Not all of them can afford the finer drink." Bart shook his head. "Nah, you'll have to find that out on your own."

"Bart Johnson, I'm placing you under arrest for the purchase of illegal alcohol." Willie motioned for him to proceed ahead of her.

"I reckon I can make bail."

"Eventually, even you will run out of bail money." She grinned. "Tom, please run off those upstairs and board up the doors to this place."

Bart shoved through the swinging doors. He'd make her pay in ways she'd never imagined. He looked forward to seeing her fall.

19

As he'd said, Bart posted bail with no problem. Willie escorted him to the town boundary and watched him ride away. Good riddance. Of course, if he made good on his threat of setting up a saloon somewhere else, she may have other troubles to deal with but each day had enough worries of its own. First, she'd find the moonshiners, then worry more about Bart.

The town church bell rang, signaling the start of yet another town meeting. Willie sighed. One more month and the town would decide her and her family's future. She turned and headed with heavy steps to the church.

Mama and the children, with Theo beside them, were already seated in the front row. Heads turned to stare as Willie made her way down the aisle to join them. Mayor Bloomfield stood at the pulpit, his never-ending grin plastered on his face. Poor Tom sat squashed between Sally and Violet in the seats behind Willie's family. She slid onto the pew, hiding her grin.

"Now that the sheriff is here," the mayor said.

"We can begin. First on the agenda is …" he ruffled through papers. "Ah, yes. We received an anonymous tip that the sheriff is in fact an Indian."

Shocked gasps rang through the church. Tears coursed down Mama's cheeks. She ducked her head.

Willie clasped her hands together and stood. The sooner the matter was addressed, the sooner Mama could lift her head up again. "Yes, I am one quarter Cherokee and the rest Scottish. I fail to see how this has any bearing on town concerns."

"This person who made the accusation fears it may cloud your judgment if some of … your people were to cause trouble." The mayor's smile faded. "Would the person who filed the complaint please stand?"

Willie faced the crowd. No one stood. So, either the person didn't want to face her or they weren't present. Who outside of those closest to her knew of her heritage?

Theo stood. "I've been a long standing member of this community and I don't see where it matters a hill of beans what race these women are. There ain't a one of us here that doesn't carry something in their veins that could cause disapproval somewhere."

"I agree." Gloria Netser also stood. "God sees the inside of a person, their heart. The matter presented before this community should be whether or not the sheriff is doing the job she was hired to do. I say she's so doing admirably."

The women's vigilante group surged to their feet with cries of "Hear, hear!"

Willie swallowed back tears. Not too long ago, these very women had rallied against her, now they stood in staunch support.

Several men bolted to their feet with cries of their own saying Indians can't be trusted. Tom sat with head down as if he were praying. Why wouldn't he come to her defense? Willie bit her bottom lip. Was he the one who told of her Indian blood? Surely not. He'd told her it no longer mattered to him.

He started to stand, only to be pulled back down by Violet. The lovely young girl whispered something in his ear. Had Willie's plan of keeping Tom occupied backfired? Did his loyalties lie with someone else? Her heart landed in her stomach with enough force she wrapped her arms around her waist. Then, not wanting to show weakness, she balled her fists at her sides and squared her shoulders.

The mayor shouted for order. "One at a time, please!"

Willie cracked her whip. A woman screamed, then the room quieted. She took a deep breath. "Yes, I'm Indian, I'm Scottish, I'm a woman. I'm a widow and a mother. I'm also your sheriff for another month. I am, as many of you, many things." She took her time rolling her whip and hanging it back on her belt. "I don't know, nor do I care, who thought it was important enough to bring up this topic at the meeting. My suspicion is that someone wants to create discord among the town's citizens at my expense. We cannot let that happen." She sniffed. Was that smoke?

Yes. Tendrils of grey smoke drifted under the choir room door to her right and another under the front door. She eyed the windows just as flames licked over the sill to her right. Dread coursed through her.

"Fire!" Someone shouted.

The crowd stampeded for the front door.

"Stop!" Tom fired a shot over their heads. "You fools. Can't you see the front of the church is on fire?"

"So is the back." Willie picked up a potted plant and threw it through a window on her left. "Theo, take care of my family."

He nodded, tossing Bonnie out the window and turning to Junior.

Willie smashed another window and continued to the next two. The crowd converged against her, smashing her against the wall, knocking the breath from her. Her arm scraped across the jagged edge of the windowsill as she knocked out the last of the glass ripping the flesh on her arm. She struggled to push free of the horde.

Smoke filled the room, adding to the panic. She pulled her bandana over her nose and mouth and helped lift an elderly woman through the window. "Stand back!" If they kept up their crazed behavior, people would die and not from the fire.

Terror, stark and burning like the flames licking the walls of the church clogged her throat. A quick glance out the window showed Mama and the children standing at the far edge of the yard. Theo stood outside the window, helping those who crawled through land on their feet. Still, the throng continued to stampede. The smoke increased. Tears streamed from Willie's stinging eyes, blurring her vision. Despite her discomfort she struggled to help the town residents through the windows.

A large man barreled into her, knocking her against the wall and to the ground. She struggled to regain her footing, only to fall again. She struck her head on the edge of a pew and laid prostrate on the floor. *God, don't let me die here.*

On her hands and knees, she crawled through the legs of the panicky townspeople until she was clear. Unsteady, her head pounding, she pushed off the solid wood seat and got to her feet.

Flames now licked at the entire right side of the church. Pastor Netzer struggled to revive a fallen woman. Willie staggered to his side. "You have to go."

"I can't. She's unconscious." His soot-covered face was creased with worry.

"I'll help you." Willie forced back the pain and helped lift the woman to her feet. Together, they dragged her to a window and handed her into Theo's hands. "You go," she told the pastor. "I'll be right behind you." As soon as she did one last check to make sure no one was left behind. The moment the pastor dropped to the ground, she dashed down the aisle, one hand held tight against her bleeding head.

The roof groaned. She screamed and dove out of the way of a falling beam.

"Willie!" Tom grabbed her around her waist. "What in tarnation are you still doing in here?"

"Looking for people!"

"Everyone but us is out."

Heat seared her skin as the back wall caught. She glanced around them, wishing the church had built a baptismal. Anything they could use to keep the flames at bay. "We're trapped!"

"No, we're not." He pulled her along behind him as he made his way to the one window not covered with fire. "Up and out, Willie."

"You first."

"No." He cupped her face. "If I go first, you'll dawdle, hoping to find someone left behind. It will be too late. I can't lose you." He winced as a burning ember fell on his back.

Without a second thought, she dived through the window. If she waited, Tom would be burned alive. "Come on."

He nodded and followed her, hitting the ground and rolling. He scrambled to his feet and grabbed her hand, dashing away from the building as with one mighty groan, the roof fell. Amber sparks drifted to the sky like fireflies at dusk.

Willie sagged to the ground and ripped off her bandana. Coughs ripped at her throat. Someone brought her a dipper of cool water. She downed it, soothing her parched throat. "Did everyone get out?"

"Thanks to you." The mayor squatted next to her. "I'll fight to keep you here after the trial period, Mrs. Sheriff, but I can't guarantee what the majority will want. Your bravery tonight will go a long way in your favor."

"Enough jaw flapping." Mama pushed him out of the way and fell to her knees beside Willie. "You scared ten years off me, and I might not have that many left. You're bleeding."

"Just a knock on the head." Willie untied her bandana and held it to her head.

"Don't use that, it's filthy. You aren't only bleeding from your head. Your arm will need stitches. Won't be too long before you resemble a patchwork doll." Mama pulled a handkerchief from her pocket and handed it to her, then ripped a piece of her petticoat to tie around Willie's arm. "We need to get you home. Has it occurred to you, with the knocks on the head you've been getting lately, that someone might be trying to tell you something?"

"Possibly, but I can't leave yet." Willie got to her feet. "This fire didn't start by accident, Mama. Not at this time of the year. Have Theo escort you and the young'uns home. I'll be there directly."

Tom mingled among the residents. Willie called his name and waited until he moved to her side. "Let's see whether we can figure out how this fire started."

"I know exactly how it started." He pulled a cigar from his pocket. "I found this on the porch along with the strong smell of kerosene."

"Bart Johnson."

"That's what I figure. Not many around here that can afford expensive cigars." Tom kicked at a rock. Anger radiated from him in waves. "Luckily, no one was killed."

"It's also a good thing the church sets off by itself aways." Willie glanced down Main Street. With no wind, they shouldn't have to worry about any other buildings catching fire. She pressed the cloth harder to her head, biting back a hiss at the pain.

"You need to get home. Let me take you. I'll look to this when I get back." Tom motioned to the smoldering building. "Me and some of the men will douse what we can with water and watch the rest to make sure it doesn't spread."

"You saved my life, Tom." She put a hand on his chest. Every heart beat against her palm a blessing and a reassurance that he still lived despite the fact she had lost sight of him almost immediately. "Thank you."

*

Tom left Willie to be tended by her mother before going in search of the mayor. He found him and the pastor gazing upon what was left of the church, which was nothing more than a pile of glowing timbers.

"It's a total loss," Mark said.

"A crying shame," the mayor agreed. "I suppose we can move church to the saloon. With it shut down, there's no point in it sitting empty."

"Speaking of the saloon," Tom said. "The sheriff and I think Bart is to blame for the fire." He showed them the cigar. "I saw him smoking one of these the other day and found this right where y'all are standing."

The mayor took the cigar, expelling a heavy breath. "Yeah, Bart loves these things. Why would he burn down the church?"

"Retaliation against the sheriff, perhaps?" Tom shrugged.

"Then why not shoot her on her way home from somewhere? Why jeopardize the entire town?"

"Maybe it wasn't Bart," Mark stated. "What if someone wants us to believe it was him? Who else has a grudge against the town?"

"Jim Parson," Tom and the mayor said in unison.

Tom took the cigar back from the mayor and slipped it into his pocket. Jim or Bart? Either one had something against Willie. Fortunately, no one had died in the fire. If they had, the culprit could have used that against Willie in an attempt to convince the town that she had failed. He glanced toward her house in time to see her step from the porch. With the light of a full moon, he could make out the white of a fresh bandage around her head. Couldn't she rest for one night?

He met her at the edge of the churchyard. The fringe of her skirt was charred, several of the fringes missing. Several inches of hair on one side was burned, leaving the inky cascade in a ragged line. She'd come so close to perishing at the sake of others. Wilhemina Jackson was the bravest, most caring woman he'd had the fortune of meeting. He took the unsinged hair in his hand, letting it fall like water through his fingers. "You'll need to cut this off to match the rest."

"I know." Her breath hitched. "It's only hair. It will grow back." She lightly touched his arm. "You need Mama to take a look at that burn."

"I will." He let her silky hair fall down her back and turned his attention to the other two men. "The best we can figure is that the fire was started by Jim Parson or Bart Johnson, both of whom have a beef with you."

She nodded. "Now, we need to prove it. The cigar is a good start, but not good enough. What we need is a witness … or a confession."

"I doubt we'll find either." Tom glanced toward the saloon. "Church will be held here in the meantime. I reckon it won't be too hard to put up a regular door to keep out those looking for a drink."

"I'll get the women's group to clear out the whiskey," Mayor Bloomfield said. "That ought to keep them busy for at least a day."

Tom agreed. The women would have the former saloon looking nothing like what its intended purpose had originally been. Keeping them busy would keep them from digging into the cause of the fire and setting out to exact their own brand of justice.

Willie studied the area around them, kicking at fallen boards. "Here's a print."

"Could be from anybody," the mayor said.

She shook her head. "I don't think so. It's in an area where no one climbed from a window. Look." She pointed and moved toward the tree line. "The prints are far apart as if the person ran away from the church. Those in the meeting moved in the other direction, not toward the forest."

Tom matched his pace to the prints. "The man's leg span was pretty equal to mine." Which cinched tighter the fact it was Bart or Jim.

Both of them met Tom eye-to-eye when facing him, and both were dangerous men. As if one of them were watching at that moment, which might actually be the case, Tom hurried back to Willie's side. He might not be able to know from which direction a bullet would come, but being near her, protecting her, helped him not feel so worthless as a protector.

"No sense standing around here," Mayor Bloomfield said. "I'm heading home to the wife. Let me know what you find out in the light of day, sheriff." He clapped Mark on the shoulder. "At least the parsonage is still standing."

"Yes, sir." Mark glanced toward his home. "My wife is waiting on the porch. I'll spend some time in prayer for this town tonight and in thanksgiving that lives were spared." He strolled across the lawn to where Gloria waited. The mayor set off down Main Street, leaving Tom and Willie alone.

Tom scanned the trees. "Let me take you home." He kept a sharp eye between the buildings, jumping at shadows, as they traversed down the middle of the street. A cat darted from behind the diner, almost sending Tom out of his boots.

"Relax," Willie said, a laugh in her voice. "I think the trouble is over for the night."

"I'd feel better sleeping on your couch if you don't mind."

Her steps faltered. "I think this time I'll let you." She turned to him, her eyes sparkling in the moonlight. "For the first time since accepting this job, I can say I am truly afraid."

He wrapped his arms around her, nestling her head under his chin. She smelled of smoke and charred wood. It was the most wonderful smell in the world since she stood on two feet, her arms around his waist, and still breathed.

"Not for me," she continued, "but for my family. They could have been injured or killed tonight. All because I stood up for the law of the town."

"Something someone should have done a long time ago." He closed his eyes and prayed for her safety and for peace so she could rest. "The sheriffs before you were bought with whiskey or run off by meddling women. You've stood firm for what you believe is right."

"And endangered everyone I care about."

"Are you going to quit?"

"Not for one second. I'm a stubborn Scot, remember?"

*

"It's done." Parson emerged from the trees to where Bart hunkered over a fire.

"Anyone dead?" Bart broke a small branch in two and fed it to the flames.

"Not that I know of. Almost finished off the sheriff and the blacksmith as they stayed to help folks, but they got out." Parson poured a mug of coffee from a tin pitcher. "I reckon we told the sheriff to watch her back loud and clear." He gulped his drink, wiped the back of his hand across his mouth, and laughed. "I can't wait to see what's next."

Bart joined in his laughter. "What's next will riot the fireworks on the Fourth of July."

20

"**I don't think** I can repair those," Mama said when Willie handed her the leather clothing from the fire. "Too many scorched marks and cinder holes. I can modify your brown skirt into a split one."

"All right." Her spare leather would work for hunting or tracking. While in town, she'd wear the brown skirt. The women of Wild Horse Pass shared Mama's sentiment in regards to her leather anyway. After the way they'd stood up for her at the town meeting, she could appease them by wearing something more … acceptable.

"Not like you have much of a choice, anyway." Mama tossed her clothes in a burlap bag with quilting scraps. "I haven't gotten the blood out of your other leather skirt."

Willie sighed and slipped into her more feminine skirt and a yellow blouse. She tied her now shoulder-length hair back with a strip of leather and grabbed her gun holster. At least the split skirt still allowed her to wear her gun and whip on her hip.

"I'm headed to the telegraph office," Willie said. "Then, I'll meet you at the saloon."

"Church."

"What?" Willie frowned.

"It's the church now."

How could she have forgotten? Maybe hitting her head had lingering effects. Many more stitches and she'd never be able to hide the scars under her hair. She set her hat gingerly on her head, headed to the kitchen to kiss her children goodbye, and then marched down the street with Bear at her side.

Already, the infamous women's group, armed with brooms and buckets, were converging on the former saloon. They raised hands in greeting, paused at the swinging doors, then as one, squared their shoulders and went inside. Willie chuckled. Old habits were hard to break. She doubted whether any of them had ever set foot inside the establishment before today.

As she reached to open the door to the telegraph office, a buckboard rattled down the street driven by two of the tiniest, oldest women, Willie had ever seen. She watched them stop and stare at the saloon, then turn their wagon around in the yard of the burned church. One of them flashed Willie a toothless grin as they passed by again.

She nodded, commanded Bear to stay on the sidewalk, and pushed into the telegraph office. "Morning, Mr. Smith."

"Sheriff." The wiry man peered over his spectacles. "Another telegram?"

"Unfortunately." Willie handed him the note she had written that morning informing the

Marshall's office about the burning of the church. Any more unfortunate incidents in town and she might see help coming riding into town. She wasn't sure how she felt about that. While her primary concern was the safety of the town's residents, she didn't want to be looked upon as a failure.

"No reason for the long face, sheriff." Mr. Smith grinned, a gesture that shriveled his face up like a plum left in the sun too long. "You're doing a fine job. You're accessible, you aren't willing to not get your hands dirty, and you care about saving the townsfolk before yourself."

"Thank you. That means a lot to me." Her heart swelled. Oh, how she loved this town. She handed him a coin and stepped back into the morning sunshine. The rank odor of burned wood hung over the town like a shroud. She wrinkled her nose and headed for the saloon, uh, church. Tom and a handful of other men started removing the scorched pile of debris that was once the town's place of worship.

Loud voices greeted her at the door of the saloon. Willie stepped inside.

"You cannot stay here!" Gertie Bloomfield brandished a broom at a short man with a bulbous nose who guarded the saloon piano as if it were a pot of gold.

Arms outstretched, legs planted shoulder width apart, he glared at the women. "Rules state no women allowed. Get out!"

"That no longer applies." Mama stepped forward. "This is a church now."

"Over my dead body!"

Willie moved to the front of the group to stop that very thing from happening. "What's going on?"

"Bob Mellon refuses to step aside and let us clean this den of iniquity," Wilma Coffee said. "Gloria tried to talk sensibly to him, but even a preacher's wife can't get sense through his thick skull. We can't hold church here until the place is clean and prayed over." She leaned inches from his face. "That includes you!"

"Make me. I bathe twice a year. Easter and Christmas. That's been good enough my whole life and I ain't aiming to change."

Willie bit her bottom lip to keep from smiling. "Mr. Mellon, I don't think that's exactly what these women are implying."

"Of course it is," Mama said. "The man smells to high heaven."

"Junior, take your sister outside and play on the sidewalk." Her son did as he was told. Willie shook her head at Mama bringing them to the saloon, then realized it was no longer going to be used for that purpose. There was nothing wrong with taking children along while you cleaned a church.

"Mr. Mellon." Willie held out her hand as she would to a stray dog. She needed the man to feel as if he were among friends and not women bent on running him off. "We aren't going to hurt you or your piano. I propose you become the church's piano player."

"Mrs. Sheriff!" Gertie Bloomfield thrust her fists on her hips. "I'm the organ player."

"Can't we have both?" Willie cocked her head. "Why, Gertie, you could be solely responsible for bringing this lost lamb into the fold. Imagine the beauty of the piano and organ melding together." She ignored the sputterings of Mr. Mellon. All she wanted to accomplish at the moment was peace so the work could be done.

Gertie crossed her arms. "I suppose that would work."

Willie turned to Mr. Mellon. "Are you a church-going man?"

"Ain't been since my ma forced me to as a young'un."

"Then it's time you start again. The piano will stay. Please help these ladies cart the liquor outside." Willie marched past and headed up the stairs.

A second story landing overlooked the floor below. Along the far wall were four closed doors. At the end of the landing was another set of stairs winding to a smaller third floor. Evidence of Bart's financial success, despite the lack of working girls, showed in polished wood and brass light fixtures.

Willie opened the first door. A single cot and small bureau filled the space. The other second story rooms were the same. She headed to the third floor where three bedrooms held cots with rumpled bedclothes. Two had dirty laundry strewn on the floor. The last room held a battered hat and scuffed boots. She'd guess the Larson boys had stayed a few nights under the saloon roof. But who was the third man and where were they all now?

Bear barked shrilly from outside.

"Where in Sam's hill is Bart?" A shrill gravelly voice carried from the bottom floor.

"Mrs. Sheriff?" Gertie called. "You'd best come on down. We've got trouble."

A gunshot rang out. Plaster fell from the ceiling and rained down on those below. Wilma Coffee screamed. Bear barked harder.

Willie glanced over the railing in time to see Mama grab a shotgun from under the bar and point it at the two elderly women who had earlier been driving a wagon. Willie increased her pace, taking the steps two at a time.

Once she'd reached the bottom floor, she withdrew her pistol. "Ladies, I suggest you put down the rifle."

"Ain't gonna do it." The sprightly little thing aimed the rifle at Willie. "We're the Hickman sisters, I'm Verna and she's Vera. Bart owes us a passel of money for our moonshine. If you're the new owner, I reckon you owe us now."

"I am not the new owner. I'm the sheriff." Willie kept her pistol aimed on Verna.

"Nonsense. Ain't never been a woman sheriff around here. What do you think, Vera?"

"I think we keep these folks right here until we get to the bottom of things."

"In the name of Pete." Willie gritted her teeth. "There's a woman sheriff now, and she's getting mighty fed up with this nonsense. Drop your gun."

So these two characters owned the moonshine still. Willie would never have guessed in a lifetime of Sundays that two women older than Methuselah were capable of running moonshine or holding a group of people hostage.

"Drop yours first," Verna said, "or the little old

man gets the first bullet."

Mr. Mellon ducked behind the piano.

"Oh, for heaven's sake. Forgive me, Lord." Gloria cast a glance heavenward before stepping up behind Verna. She whacked her over the head with a whiskey bottle and turned the jagged, dripping edges toward Vera.

Willie kicked the fallen woman's gun to the side. How could she ever have doubted the women vigilantes from holding their own? "Mama, see if you can find some rope."

Mama propped the rifle she'd found against the wall and dug under the bar, coming up several minutes later with a roll of twine. "This will work."

Life in Wild Horse Pass was definitely not boring. Willie cut strips of the twine and tied the Hickman sisters' hands behind their backs then hauled Verna to her feet. "Let's go, ladies." She marched them across the street and into the jail.

"We got to stay together," Vera said. "We've spent every day of our lives together."

"Makes no difference to me." Willie locked them together in a cell, noting they both wore boots worn smooth on the soles. "I'm afraid Bart has left town, and can't pay you what he owes. You also need to know I'm closing down your still once and for all. Not to mention the fact I believe one of you took a shot at me a while back."

"That was an accident," Verna said. "We meant to scare you off. Didn't know you was the sheriff. Now, you might as well take food out of our mouths."

Willie sighed. "I'm guessing you two have

enough coins set aside to take care of yourselves for a good long while. There's always been money in illegal liquor. Hopefully, you set some by for such a time as this." She slipped the cell key into a hidden pocket of her skirt and headed back to the saloon slash church. The mysterious moonshiners were locked up. Now, all she needed to do was find Jim Parson.

*

Tom hefted a scorched beam into the back of a wagon. Very little could be salvaged from the burned church, but Theo thought he could put the charred chunks of wood to good use along his fence line.

He glanced toward the saloon, it would take him a while before he thought of it as anything else, in time to see Willie marching two old ladies to jail. He itched to run see what had transpired, but work waited for him here and he'd given his word. He tossed a two-foot piece of the podium onto the wagon.

Bibles lay among the ashes, their pages charred, covers burned, most of them unrecognizable. The large cross that had once hung on the wall behind the podium was no longer distinguishable from any of the other debris. The glass windows, the church's pride, were no more. Tom tightened the bandana around his nose and mouth and kept working.

Soon, his once blue shirt was as black as the soot. His arms covered with black grit. He hated to see what his face looked like with ash and sweat. Since he wore the bandana, he probably resembled a raccoon.

Gloria passed on her way to the parsonage, returning moments later with a bucket and a dipper. She served her husband first, then approached Tom. He filled the dipper and quenched the dryness in his throat with cool well water.

"Much obliged," Tom said.

"We're so busy over there, we almost forgot about you men."

"Who did Willie cart off?"

"Two women willing to risk a gunfight to get the money Bart owed them for their moonshine." She waved Theo over to get a drink.

"Those were the moonshiners?" Tom chuckled.

"Funny, isn't it?" Gloria shrugged. "They actually drew their gun on Willie, but within seconds every one of us had something trained on them. I finally had enough of the standoff and hit one of them over the head with a whiskey bottle, may God forgive me."

"I would have liked to have seen that."

She grinned. "The day isn't over yet." She turned to greet Theo, leaving Tom to return to his dirty job.

They finally had anything big enough to pick up piled in the back of the wagon. While Theo drove to his land, Tom headed to the blacksmith side of the livery. He closed the door, leaving a few inches open to allow light to come in and immediately removed his shirt. Bare-chested, he approached the water barrel he used to cool his iron. He grabbed a scrap of flannel and scrubbed every piece of exposed skin he could reach.

"Oh."

He lowered the flannel from his face. Willie stood wide-eyed in the door. At first, she looked as if she might bolt, then thought better of it and took slow steps in his direction. His heart rate accelerated. His gaze stayed glued to hers. Her lips parted slightly, her chest rising and falling with quickened breaths as she approached him with curiosity. He felt if he moved she would bolt like a skittish horse.

She approached close enough to place a hand on his chest. His nerves rippled at her touch. "You have a scar." Her whispered words tickled his skin as she traced the small puckered circle below his clavicle. "It's a bullet wound."

Unable to speak, he nodded. He wanted to grab her in his arms, march to the parsonage to get married, then carry her upstairs to his room. Since she'd made it clear how she felt about marriage to him, he could do nothing but stand still under her administrations. Improper or not, he couldn't have moved if the building was falling around his ears.

"How did you get it?" When she continued to caress the scar, he placed his hand over hers.

"A hunting accident." He swallowed past the desert in his throat as she brushed her free hand across the burn on his other arm. Being in such close proximity with a shirtless man might not be a totally new experience for her, having been married before, but Tom found it strongly intimate. With a force of will he hadn't known he possessed, he stepped back and grabbed his shirt.

The gesture seemed to break whatever spell

had come over her, and Willie took a deep breath. "The moonshiners are in jail." She twirled the flannel in the barrel of water.

"Gloria told me." His fingers shook as he fastened the buttons on his shirt.

"The only thing to do in the month I have left is find Jim Parson." She wrung out the rag and wiped a spot on Tom's cheek. "You missed. The Marshall's office responded to my telegram saying to contact them if he poses a threat to the town that I can't handle." She gave a sad smile. "Since I've lost him, I'm not sure whether that is the case or not."

The only threat Tom knew of was Willie's threat to his heart. He took her hands in his. "Do I affect you the same way you do me?" He searched her eyes, clouded now by confusion and what he hoped was desire. "Do I make you lose all reason? Cause your heart to pound so hard you fear it will sprout wings and fly from your chest? Do you lose sleep thinking of me?" He tugged her closer, his voice lowering. "Do you think of the kisses we've shared?"

Her eyes shimmered. "I think of you every waking moment. You're in my dreams."

"Then marry me."

"I can't." She placed her fingers over his lips. "I won't lose another man I … I can't lose anyone else to a bullet."

Had she almost said she loved him? "I don't understand." He released her, turning away. "I'm your deputy. There's a chance I'll die in the same manner as your husband. You could die the same way. I'm willing to take the chance now." When she didn't respond, he turned, only to find her gone and the back livery door open.

He lowered to an upended barrel and buried his face in his hands. He could see her want and loneliness every time he looked into her face. Why her strict reluctance to allow herself to dwell in the fact he loved her and wanted to take care of her? He would even overlook the fact she was a woman in a dangerous profession as long as he could be by her side every minute. If the town chose to send her away in a month, he'd go with her. Why couldn't she see that? What would it take for her to understand?

"Mr. Miller?"

He glanced up to see Sally swinging her skirts from side-to-side. "I was wondering whether you would step out with me tonight? We could stroll up and down Main Street."

"I appreciate the offer, but I'm headed to bed."

She stepped closer. "But, you took the cookies, Tom. You said I could leave them and that's the same thing, ain't it?" She fingered one of his buttons. "That was as good as asking me to be your girl."

"Violet also left her pie. Does that mean I'm stepping out with both of you?" He placed his hands on her shoulders and moved her back.

"Does it?" Her voice hardened. "Are you trifling with our affections?"

What had happened to the sweet young thing that trailed after him? She'd turned into something cold and hard. A trickle of unease skittered up his spine. While he'd given her no encouragement, she believed he'd expressed an interest in her. How could he convince her otherwise without things turning ugly?

She threw her arms around his neck and pressed her lips against his. Untangling her was like wrestling a bag of snakes. "Stop it, Sally."

"You have to marry me now," she said with a simpering smile. "You've taken liberties."

"You're acting like no more than an addle-brained child."

Her eyes widened. "I've seen the way you look at the sheriff. I watched as she fondled your bare chest. You watch and see what I can do with this information." With a swish of pink calico, she dashed back to the street.

Tom shook his head and noticed Willie standing in the shadows beside Stormy's stall.

21

This was all her fault. Willie hadn't imagined for a second that Tom might be put in a precarious position because of her wanting to keep him from proposing to her again. Her gaze clashed with his startled one. "I'm so sorry."

"This isn't what it looks like." His words mingled with hers, spoken at the same time. "Wait." He frowned. "Why are you sorry?"

He was going to be angry with her, hurt, and a ton of other emotions. Tears stung her eyes. "I encouraged Sally and Violet to ply you with their attentions."

"Whatever for?" He slumped on an overturned barrel. He looked as dejected as she feared he would.

Tears sprang to her eyes. "I thought one of them might be a better fit for you."

He buried his head in his hands. "Do you know what you've done?" He raised his head. "I'll be forced to marry now. It's my word against hers."

"I'm a witness to what happened." She stepped forward and placed a hand on his shoulder. He shrugged her off.

"It won't matter." He lunged to his feet. "What do you want from me, Willie? You come in here while I'm bathing, touch me, while all the time you've been plotting to marry me off to someone else." He gripped her shoulders. "Do you honestly think I want to be married to one of those silly girls? I want a woman, Wilhemina Jackson. I want a woman like you, not a girl in ribbons and bows." He released her and ran his hands through his hair. The ends stuck up like ripe wheat.

Her heart soared. While she hadn't heard the declaration of love her heart craved, she'd gotten the next best thing. Tom wanted to marry her, not because he wanted to protect her, but because he wanted to be with her. How things had changed since her first day in Wild Horse Pass. Maybe she could stay in the town she'd grown to love. Not as sheriff, unless things moved in her favor, but as the wife of the town's beloved blacksmith. She would belong because she was married to Tom.

While it might not be exactly what she wanted, it would begin to heal the hole in her heart. She'd work beside him, running the livery side of his business while he continued to form iron into things of beauty.

"I can't believe you find marrying me so repugnant, you would throw young girls in my path." Tom shook his head.

"I don't find the idea repugnant. I find it the opposite in fact. God is at work in me, Tom, and—."

"Tom Miller!" Frank Simpson's voice rang out

from the street.

Tom cast such an agonizing glance at Willie that she felt as if he'd punched her in the gut. With a slow shake of his head, and a slump to his shoulders, he stepped outside. Willie shuffled after him.

Frank stood on the sidewalk, Sally beside him. The girl's face was stained with recent tears, and while some still escaped her pale blue eyes, there was a hardened glint in them that set Willie's nerves on edge.

"See, Papa," Sally pointed. "He's gone straight from my arms to hers. He's playing all the single girls in town against each other."

"Hogwash!" Tom straightened. "Your daughter threw herself at me right before she threatened to cause me trouble. If anyone is at fault here, it's her and her forward behavior."

"Forward behavior?!" Frank sputtered. "Why, I never thought an upstanding member of our community was capable of such crass actions with an innocent child. I demand you make things right."

A crowd quickly grew around them, forming a semi-circle in the street. Curious faces quickly turned indignant as the onlookers whispered among themselves.

Willie stepped forward. "As your sheriff, I insist all of you head home and back to work. This does not concern you."

"Whatever goes on in this town concerns every one of us," Mayor Bloomfield called out. "It's clearly stated—"

"I'm well aware of what the town's bylaws

state, and it also is quite clearly against anything resembling an unruly crowd. Go home."

"You're no better than he is," Frank said, coming to stand nose-to-nose with her. "We didn't bring it up at the meeting because of the fire, but you were clearly seen acting improperly in your office with Tom Miller. The town was clearly remiss in hiring you, even on a temporary basis."

"Now, see here." Tom stepped to Willie's side. "This is between me, you, and Sally. Leave the sheriff out of it."

"Why, so you can kiss her without your shirt on again?" Sally faced the outraged crowd. Gasps punctuated her words. "That's right. I saw them with my own eyes. She caressed his bare chest moments before Tom Miller kissed me." She put hands on her hips. "I bet this town didn't know what a Casanova we had for a blacksmith."

"I insist you marry my daughter and make this right!" Frank jabbed a finger in Tom's chest. "There will be a wedding tonight folks, mark my words."

Willie squared her shoulders. "Yes, there will." She held up a hand at Tom's puzzled look, then slipped her arm through his. "Sally didn't witness a mere kiss between Tom and I, she witnessed me accepting his proposal of marriage." She kept a firm grip on his arm as he tried to pull free. "It was her own anger at feeling slighted that caused her to throw herself at Tom, not the other way round."

"No, Papa." Sally stomped her foot. "She's lying."

"Oh, please." Violet pushed through the crowd. "You've been throwing yourself at Tom for weeks."

"No more so than you!"

The two squared off like cats.

"Enough!" Mayor Bloomfield bellowed. "No offense, Frank, but the entire town knows how wayward your oldest daughter is. Yes, there will be a wedding tonight, but it will be between Tom and the sheriff. Once our most eligible bachelor is married, there won't be any more of these types of shenanigans. It will be best for everyone. We'll see you in front of the saloon at five o'clock." With a tip of his hat and a wave of his hand, the town residents dispersed.

Tom faced Willie. "What are you doing? There's no way out now."

"I know." She forced a smile. "This isn't how you thought your wedding would go, but don't you see? It's the best solution. We're such close friends, and now—"

"Friends," he spit out. "I don't want to marry a friend."

"That isn't what I meant. You've proposed to me enough times, I thought—"

"You thought that after multiple rejections I'd jump at the chance." He grabbed her arm and dragged her into the privacy of the livery. "You're right. This isn't how I wanted things to happen. Go home, Willie. You have a wedding outfit to put together."

Her mouth fell open. She'd thought he would be pleased at how she'd saved him from Sally's clutches. "You can always back out. Sally will be more than happy to step into my place."

"I don't want Sally!" He forced out through

clenched teeth. "But I don't want you either if it means you're marrying me out of some misguided sense of guilt."

Maybe she'd felt a smidgeon of guilt at first, but no longer. Yes, she'd offered marriage as a way to save him from a greedy girl's talons, but now she found she didn't regret the offer one little bit. In fact, marriage to Tom would be wonderful, whether they experienced a romantic love or not. Willie was a widowed mother. A marriage based on respect and friendship was good enough for her, now that she looked at things with an open heart and an open mind.

To her further surprise, she realized she loved him. The emotion had been building for weeks. Now, it rose up in all its glory and lifted her heart. "I love you, Tom. I can admit that now."

"Platonic love." He shook his head. "Well, I've proposed enough times. As I'd said before, marriages were built on much less. I'll see you this evening."

Dismissed, tears burning the backs of her eyes, Willie headed home to alert Mama that she'd be getting married. Where would they live? She shared a room with her mother. Maybe Mama could sleep with the children until further arrangements were made. Her face heated at the thought of what came after the vows.

Not that she was a stranger to the physical act of marriage, but with Sam, they'd been two starry-eyed young people experiencing the newness together. This time, it would be two passionate adults coming together. Her heart rate accelerated.

She prayed Tom wouldn't regret the decision she'd forced him to make. Hopefully, he wouldn't regret not finding the love of his life and settling for a woman who defied convention at every turn.

"Mama, I'm getting married," she said, pushing through her front door.

"Excuse me?" Mama straightened, a cake in her hand.

"It's a very long story." Willie hung her hat on a peg sticking out from the wall. "But, Tom and I will be wed at five o'clock today." She filled her mother in on the morning's happenings.

"Mercy." Mama set the cake on the table and fell into a chair. "You do beat all. I reckon I'll press your new blue dress."

Willie nodded, taking a seat at the table. "I never thought I'd marry again, especially a shotgun wedding." She flicked a cake crumb onto the floor. "At least it looks as if we'll be staying in Wild Horse Pass." With the end of her sheriff days approaching like a freight train, she'd have to keep an eye out for another place to live. Wait. That was no longer a decision she could make on her own. She'd have to discuss it with Tom. Relinquishing head of the household would be difficult.

She pushed to her feet. "I'd better bathe. I'd like to put my hair in curls for the event."

"I'll send Junior out to pick flowers for your bouquet." Mama clapped her hands. "Right after I run to town and let the ladies know to cook up a feast."

"I'd rather we kept the celebration small."

"Nope. If this town wants a wedding, we'll

give them one."

*

Tom grabbed his best clothes, a towel, and a bar of soap and headed out of town to the nearest creek. No sponge bath for his wedding day. He scoffed. Why couldn't Willie have said yes the first time he proposed? They ended up right where they would have been, except the townfolks wouldn't be wearing scowls.

He didn't believe Willie's declaration of love for a minute. Sure, she'd gotten him out of a sticky situation. He would have left town rather than marry that silly girl, Sally, but he wished things could have been different, is all.

Uncle Theo would stand up as a witness easy enough. Most likely Winnie would as well. Those were the two that should actually be getting hitched that day. Sparks flew every time they glanced each other's way.

Arriving at the creek, he draped his best clothes across a bush and dropped his dirty ones to the ground before stepping into the frigid water of a fast flowing creek. He couldn't fault Willie for her deceit of turning the girls' attentions on him. After all, he'd originally courted her for the sole purpose of keeping her too busy to get into danger. That had backfired in more ways than one. He might have kept her a bit occupied, but his heart had suffered as he'd fallen into a love that wasn't reciprocated.

Not that Willie wouldn't be a good wife. Other than her strong will to do things her way, she'd make a wonderful companion, and the act between a man and a woman would set the sheets on fire if her kisses were any indication of the passion inside her. Those thoughts made him grateful for the cold water.

He soaped up, rinsed off, and sat on a large boulder to air dry, taking the time to spend some time conversing with his God. While Tom and Willie might not be getting married with romance, Tom intended to be a godly head of household and a good husband to Willie. In order to do that, he needed time spent with His Heavenly Father.

Dry and at peace, he dressed and headed back to the livery. Most of the folks he passed snickered behind their hands or turned their faces. Except for the women's group. What in tarnation had they done to the saloon?

The outside of the building was draped with fabric, burlap, and flowers. A hastily erected arch stood in front of the swinging doors. Tables and chairs were being set up in the vacant lot where the church used to stand, complete with a dance floor. The women had worked quickly in the time he had been gone. Instead of a wedding, they were providing a circus.

He rushed upstairs to his room before anyone could accost him and watched the proceedings through his window. The closer time ticked to five o'clock, the faster his heart raced. Was Willie feeling the same? Was she apprehensive or excited that this was happening?

Mark, Gloria at his side, stood under the arch and surveyed the street. Uncle Theo sat in front of the sheriff's office, no doubt chuckling about all that had happened.

Why were people going to so much trouble for a wedding practically happening at gunpoint? Tom struggled to regulate his breathing. He stepped back and sat heavily on the edge of his cot.

The rumble of a wagon sounded outside his window. A glance at the clock on his wall showed it was most likely Willie arriving at the "church". He remained seated, not wanting to see her until it was time. What if she'd changed her mind and someone had yet to make their way to his room to tell him? No, Willie was a woman of her word. She would be there.

He headed out to the street. The early evening sun still beat with summer ferocity, making him wish for his hat. He squinted against the glare and headed for the former saloon. The townsfolk congregated in the middle of the street.

Bonnie peeked out of the saloon doors, flowers clutched in her chubby fist. Junior peered out, grinned and waved, then pulled his sister back inside. Tom's spirits immediately lifted. Not only was he gaining a wife that day, but a family as well. A son to teach to hunt and fish, and a beautiful little girl to call him Papa.

Steps lighter, heart dancing, he headed for the arch. "Evening, Mark."

"Tom." The pastor's eyes twinkled. "This was quite the surprise."

"Well, something that should have been private ended up being anything but, and now here we stand."

"Yep." Mark nodded. "Here you stand. God definitely has a sense of humor."

Tom laughed. "That He does."

"You're getting a good woman." Mark turned serious. "I hope you realize that, despite the circumstances."

"I'll be a good husband. You know I already have feelings for her."

"Lust is not enough to make a good marriage. Looks fade and bodies soften. Can you stick by her when she's ill or temperamental? What if you run across hostile Indians? Will you be able to forget that Willie carries that blood?"

"Don't fret. I'll take my vows seriously." Tom checked to make sure his nut brown shirt was tucked into his tan pants.

"I hope so."

"I will." Tom scowled. "You should know me well enough. There are worse things than being married to Wilhemina."

"What if she wants to remain the sheriff?"

"If the town allows her to, then I'll work alongside her. I'm not worried about that anymore." Tom narrowed his eyes as Frank Simpson, followed by his wife and daughters approached. Sally sniffed and dabbed her eyes with a lace trimmed handkerchief. Tom snorted and turned his back on her as Bob Mellon banged out the wedding march on the saloon's old piano.

The doors swung open and Junior, his arm linked with his sister's, stepped through the arch. A couple of young boys held the doors open and Willie appeared in the doorway, a vision in a dress that matched her eyes. Instead of her usual cascade of ebony tresses, curls tumbled over her shoulders.

Small pink flowers were pinned here and there.

She gave him a shaky smile and stepped to his side offering her his hand. He lost focus of her face as tears filled his eyes. He'd make sure she fell in love with him. He'd work on it until the day he died.

"Dearly Beloved," Mark began. "We are gathered here together …"

Tom yanked his attention away from Willie's face and tried to concentrate on what the pastor was saying. "I don't have a ring," he whispered.

"That's all right," Mark smiled. "That can come later."

"No." Tom shook his head. "I want to do this right."

Willie paled.

"Here, son." Theo pulled a gold band with a tiny diamond in the center from his pocket. "This was your Ma's. I took it from her hand the day we buried her." He dropped the ring into Tom's hand. "Pastor, you may proceed."

Mark nodded. "Repeat after me. With this ring,"

"With this—"

A gunshot rang out, followed by the thundering of hooves. Tom stepped in front of Willie, who shoved her children back into the saloon. Tom reached for his gun, only to remember he hadn't worn it. Not to his wedding. Willie didn't appear to have hers either.

Jim Parson, a six-shooter in each hand, charged down the street, stopping in front of them. "Well, now, I guess I made it in the lick of time." He cocked his head. "Pastor, I oppose this marriage, seeing as how I'm taking the bride with me. Her and her daughter. Son, too, iffen the sheriff doesn't cooperate."

"My children aren't going anywhere with you." Willie stepped forward.

"Let's see whether I can convince you." He turned the gun on Tom.

The bullet took him high in the shoulder, spinning him and dropping him to the ground. "Someone fetch me a gun," he ground out against the pain.

"Fetch a horse and your little one, sheriff or I'll start shooting these fine folks one by one until I get to your young'uns. But first, I think I'll finish off the blacksmith."

"No." Willie stepped in front of Tom. "I'll come, but please leave my daughter." "Can't do that. She's good insurance to make sure you cooperate. Now, I ain't got all day."

"Willie, no." Tom reached for her, grabbing her hand. Before she could step back, he dropped a small knife into her palm.

She slipped the knife into a hidden pocket in her dress. "I'll be back. I promise." She bent and planted a soft kiss on his lips then waved Bonnie forward. Mama always complained on how much extra work Willie caused when she insisted on hidden pockets in her skirts and dresses. This time, the extra work was worth it.

Tom could do nothing but lay in the street and bleed while the woman he loved rode away with a killer.

22

"Sorry to upset your wedding." Parson laughed, the sound grating across Willie's nerves.

She tightened her hold on Bonnie, who rode in front of her, and chose not to respond to the man's attempt to goad her. She needed to keep her wits about her, find a place to leave Bonnie that would allow those who would follow them to find her. And they would follow her.

How badly was Tom wounded? She glanced at the sliver of a sun visible over the horizon. Mama would bandage him and Tom and Theo, possibly others, would thunder after them as if the hounds of hell had taken Willie. She glanced at Parson. Maybe that was a pretty correct assumption.

Her captor kept one gun trained on her and one eye on the road. When he got close enough to jeer, whiskey fumes wafted over her. She tried not to wrinkle her nose or show emotion whatsoever, but every time Bonnie whimpered, Willie's heart broke a little more.

Parson was correct in knowing that Willie would not have cooperated if she didn't have to worry about her daughter. Now, she couldn't fight him for fear of Bonnie's safety, nor did she have a weapon.

A shadow in the trees caught her attention. She bit back a smile. Bear kept pace with their fast trot. He would keep her baby safe once they stopped and she could convince Parson to leave Bonnie behind.

Darkness enveloped them by the time Parson called a stop to their race away from town. "Hide the horses in the bushes. We'll catch a couple of hours rest then move on again."

Willie slid from the horse, keeping a firm grip on Bonnie, and led Stormy into the shadows, all the while glancing around for something she could use as a weapon. Even a thick stick would be better than nothing. Paired with the knife Tom had slipped into her hand, she might have a chance to survive.

"My daughter needs to use the necessary," Willie called over her shoulder.

"As long as you stay within my sight." Parson lit a cigar, took a few puffs, then blew a silver haze into the air.

Willie sat Bonnie on a log. "You wait here for Bear, understand?" She whispered. "Then you hold onto him real tight and he'll take you home."

Bonnie nodded, her features hidden by the dark.

"Now, Mama wants to play a game. I'm going to call out for you, but you stay very quiet, all right? Don't answer back. We want to see whether the bad man can find you." Tears clogged her throat. "I bet he can't, because you're a good hider." Bear nuzzled her hand. "Stay, Bear. Watch."

Bonnie nodded.

"Okay, let's play now." She pressed her lips to her baby's forehead, then straightened and headed away from her, leaving Bonnie in God's hands and in the paws of a faithful friend. "Bonnie? Come out, sweetheart."

"What's wrong?" Parson pushed away from the tree he'd reclined on. "How could you lose her?"

"She likes to play hide-and-seek." Willie forced herself to look worried, rather than determined. "I only turned my back for a second."

He shook his head and stubbed out his cigar on the tree trunk. "I don't have time to look for her. Let's go."

"You said we were resting for a while."

"I changed my mind. Mount up."

Willie squared her shoulders. "Where are we going?" She glanced around as if looking for Bonnie. "I can't leave her. Bonnie!"

"It doesn't matter where we're going." He leered and moved toward her. He pinched her face between his fingers. "But you and I will have a chance to get to know each other better. You can count on that." He patted her cheek roughly and drew his gun. Aiming it at her, he said, "Back on your horse."

Her fingers itched for the knife in her pocket. She was almost as good at throwing knives as she was at shooting. Her lip curled, imagining him with the blade quivering between his eyes. She focused on revenge rather than fear for her daughter and climbed back onto Stormy's saddle.

There was no mistaking the gleam in Parson's

eyes. Willie needed to get away before they reached their destination. She was strong, but he was a roughened cowhand. The odds were against her in strength. She would have to use her wits.

She glanced once more to where Bonnie and Bear hid, then kicked her horse into movement. *God, see that they make it home safe*. Leaving her child with a dog might very well be the craziest idea she'd ever come up with, but it seemed better than the alternative … taking her to an unknown destination with a mad man intent on immoral actions.

"Now, isn't this nice?" Parson grinned. "The two of us, riding down an isolated road at night. I'm tempted to stop and have a little fun right now, but I promised Bart I'd return before dark. I'm already late."

"Bart is behind this?"

"We both come up with the idea of getting you out of Wild Horse Pass." He shook his head. "You've stirred up a lot of trouble for a little bit of woman. Why, if I hadn't seen you shoot, I'd think you better suited for parlors or the bedroom." He laughed, startling roosting birds from the trees.

Oh, if only Willie had her gun. She was tempted to whip Stormy's head in the direction they'd come and gallop toward home, but the threat of a bullet in her back kept her docile. Her death would result in nothing but heartache for her family and Tom, the man she fully intended to marry someday. She scowled in Parson's direction. How dare he break up her wedding?

"Don't look at me like that." Parson rested his

gun hand on the pommel of his saddle. "You aren't as pretty."

"Oh, is an ornery look all it takes for you to lose interest?" She shook her head and moved as far from him as the road would allow. The man really wasn't the sharpest nail in the box. Staying on the road would make it easier for the others to follow. Oh, where was Tom?

What if he were injured more severely than she'd thought? The bullet had appeared to have gone through his shoulder, which was bad enough, but what if Mama hadn't been able to stop the bleeding? Willie's hands trembled on the reins. Maybe Tom was unconscious or dying. She needed to get free and get to him.

She jerked the reins. If he couldn't come for her, he'd never find Bonnie. She whipped the horse around and, disregarding the chance of a bullet in the back, galloped down the road.

Parson fired a shot over her head, then another, obviously in no hurry to kill her. "Yah!" She spurred Stormy faster. The horse yanked her head. Willie bent over the saddle. The horse's mane mingled with her own hair as they raced away.

Her pursuer caught up to her and ripped the reins from her hand. Stormy was a good horse, but no match for one used to crowding close and herding cattle. Willie slipped her hand into her pocket as Parson brought her to a halt.

He backhanded her, splitting her lip. "Fool! I should just kill you here."

"Then do it." She swiped her hand across her mouth. "Come closer. Show me what you're capable of. Or are you afraid of a mere woman?"

He grabbed the neckline of her dress, yanking her close. She slashed out with the knife, catching the side of his face. He howled, ripping her gown to the waist as he fell.

Willie pulled free and raced away, leaving Parson bleeding beside the road. He yelled and fired another shot. "I will burn that town to the ground and everyone you love with it!" Fire burned along Willie's ribcage.

*

Tom opened his eyes and shot to a sitting position. "Willie!"

"Shhh." Winnie patted his shoulder. "Lay back down. You're in no shape to go after her."

"Who went? Tell me someone went to help her."

"No one." Uncle Theo appeared in the door. "A few of us attempted to go, but Parson and Willie were gone so fast, and the others turned back once it got dark. I came back to check on you."

"How long have I laid here?" Tom searched their faces.

"You've been out all night." Winnie pressed her lips together and picked up the porcelain bowl beside the bed.

He fell back against the pillow. Willie had been gone all night. He laid his good arm across his eyes. There was no telling the horrors her and the child were going through. He took a deep breath and slid his legs over the side of the bed. "Let's go." He peered up at Theo. "We can't leave her alone."

"You have a fever, Tom." Winnie paused in the

doorway. "You're no good to Willie in your condition. If God brings her home, and you've died, she'll never forgive me."

Tom would never forgive himself if something happened to Willie. Just sitting upright made his head spin and his stomach churn. He'd been shot before. The pain was nothing new. The new was the agony ripping through his heart. "Uncle Theo, gather up some men while I get dressed. If no one will come, then we'll go ourselves."

"I can't let you go." Uncle Theo clapped his hat on his head. "I'll see what I can do to find your woman, but you have to stay here." He turned, cupped Winnie's cheek, then marched away.

"Well." Winnie squared her shoulders. "It looks as if we're both going to be waiting for those we love to return. I might as well bring you some soup." She left, leaving Tom with his thoughts.

He tried to remember exactly what had transpired the day before. He'd stood facing Willie, about to say his vows, when Parson rode up causing a commotion. He'd ordered Willie and Bonnie to leave with him, shooting Tom in order to get Willie to obey. Not only Tom, but he'd threatened the entire town, knowing exactly how Willie would respond to that type of threat.

It was no secret how Parson lusted after Willie and how the man wanted revenge for the death of his brother. Still, Tom didn't think he worked alone. The only logical people were the Larson men and Bart Johnson. All of whom had a grudge against Willie. Dread coursed through him. If they had all teamed up against her …"

"Winnie!"

"I'm here." She set a bowl of soup on a small table next to the bed.

"Where are the Hickman sisters?"

"Still in jail as far as I know. I reckon they might be hungry. I feel bad that we've forgotten about them."

"Gertie fed them yesterday. I need you to take the keys out of my pocket and bring those two women here. I want to talk to them. Then, you can feed them."

"Junior, come feed Mr. Miller." Winnie nodded as if all their problems were solved. Within seconds Junior had taken her place in the room.

"I can feed myself," Tom said. "It's my left shoulder that hurts, but you're welcome to keep me company."

Junior nodded and perched on the edge of the bed against the opposite wall. "Do you think my mama's still alive?" He stared at the floor, his young face creased with worry.

"Well." Tom tried moving to a more comfortable position. "I reckon if anyone knows your ma, they also know how thick headed and opinionated she is. My guess is, she'll boss her abductors enough that they'll set her free."

Junior lifted his head and smiled crookedly. "You're probably right. If not, I guess she'll end up in heaven with my pa."

"Yeah." Tom reached for the bowl of soup. The movement tugged his wound and he flopped back empty-handed. "I reckon your pa is waiting for her."

"You were almost my pa."

"I would have liked that." What were they doing? They were talking as if Willie were dead. Until someone brought him her body, he'd never believe it. He would know in his heart if she no longer walked the earth, wouldn't he?

The Hickman sisters, hands tied in front of them, entered the room in front of a rifle-toting Winnie. "They wouldn't come nice," she said. "All these two do is complain."

"I reckon you'd whine a bit if you ain't had your coffee of a morning."

"I wouldn't be in jail in the first place." Winnie stood guard in the doorway.

"Ladies." Tom hated holding council from a bed. Yet, the longer the day went, the worse his head pounded. Maybe he wouldn't have made it far after all. "Let's make this fast. You two have worked with Bart for quite a while. Where would he have taken the sheriff?"

"I ain't got no idea," Verna said. "You, Vera?"

"All we ever done was come to the saloon." She snapped her fingers. "No, I once heard him say something about a family farm over by Billings."

"No, it was Livingston," Verna corrected. "Maybe. Anyways, he has a farm somewhere. Iffen you let us go, we could help you look for the sheriff."

"Not going to happen, you old biddies." Winnie pointed the rifle toward them. "You two already shot at her once. You can't be trusted."

"That was a warning," Verna said. "Time to let that go."

This was a waste of time. Tom shook his head. "Mrs. Baxter will fix you something to eat, then it's back to jail until we can get someone here to escort you and her to the county courthouse. If you think of something that might help us find Mrs. Jackson, please give a yell." He believed that they hadn't meant to actually shoot Willie. They were two cantankerous old women out to make some easy money.

Once Winnie had them out of the room, Tom asked Junior to hand him the soup bowl. He tilted it to his mouth, drank a few gulps of the broth, then handed the bowl back and closed his eyes. He hadn't felt this weak in a long time. "Thank you, Son. I need to rest now. You let me know the minute your ma shows up, okay?"

Junior nodded and stood by the window.

*

"Where is she?!" Bart paced the room. "It should have been a simple thing. Get the kid, get the mother."

"She cut me," Parson whined, holding a rag to his face. "I want her as much as you do."

Bart doubted it. She'd ruined him, running him out of town. Until he could gain access to the money hidden under the floorboards behind the bar, he was as destitute as the folks who lived up the mountain. It was all that woman's fault, too. Now, Parson had messed up what should have been a foolproof plan. That's what Bart got for sending a fool.

"Where are the Larsons?"

Parson shrugged. "I didn't see them when I

rode in. I think I shot the sheriff, though."

"Why didn't you say so?" Bart rubbed his hands together. "Our problems could be over, and here I am wearing a hole in the floor."

"What are we going to do?"

"We hit the town in three days and show them all who the new bosses are."

"How do you propose to that?" Parson dropped the bloody rag on the crooked table and grabbed a cleaner one. "I think I need stitches."

"I'm no doctor. Just pinch it closed until it scabs over." Bart poured a cup of thick coffee from a dented pitcher and glanced out the slit of a window. "Yep, in three days, we ride into town and take care of anyone who opposes us there. I reckon with you, me, and the Larsons, we ought to be able to get the job done. We'll have us a good old fashioned gunfight." Anticipation flooded through him like the finest whiskey.

Something else that darn sheriff took away from him. At least he had a couple of cigars left in his pocket. No matter how much Parson begged, he wouldn't get another one unless he wanted to sneak into the saloon and get the box.

"Yes, sir, I reckon we're going to have one heck of a good time come Saturday." Bart withdrew one of his cigars and ran it under his nose breathing in the scent of tobacco. He'd make sure he had one cigar left for his victory smoke.

The folks in Wild Horse Pass wouldn't know what hit them when him and his gang rode down the middle of Main Street, guns blazing and called out Tom Miller and Mark Netzer. Pastor or no, the man was handy with a gun. If the sheriff had somehow made it back, she could join the fun.

23

Willie found Bonnie shuffling down the road, her chubby fist clutching Bear's hair. While the agony spread across her midsection, Willie reached down, swung her daughter into her lap, and then continued toward town. Since she'd seen no signs of Jim Parson, she'd slowed Stormy to a slower speed.

"Mama hurt." Bonnie wrinkled her brow.

"I'm fine." Willie forced a smile. "Lay your head back and sleep." Thank you, God, that Bonnie had listened to Willie's instructions. If she had ridden much farther without sign of her child, Willie wouldn't have known what to do. She would have been forced to search the surrounding forest. Without knowing the damage Parson's bullet had done, she could have died, thus leaving her baby to suffer the same fate.

She glanced to where Bear loped alongside them. The best gift Sam had given her, outside of the children, was that massive dog. He deserved a giant steak when they arrived home.

Why couldn't Wild Horse Pass have been

similar to their home back in Kansas, at least as far as danger went? Sam rarely left town for any reason, spending most of his time bored in the sheriff's office. Willie had seen nothing but danger since arriving in Montana. Tom hadn't been kidding when he'd said the smiling faces hid something more sinister.

Since he had yet to come for her, he must be gravely injured. She forced despair away. With pain and loss of blood making her dizzy, she had no time to dwell on things that might be wrong. She needed to concentrate on staying in the saddle. She gripped the reins tighter. If she fell, she'd take Bonnie with her.

A cool rain began to fall, helping to keep her awake. She shivered in her torn dress, and slumped over Bonnie to help keep her dry.

"Sheriff?"

Willie opened her eyes to discover the horse had stopped on the side of the road. Theo peered into her face.

"Let me take the little one and get y'all home." Theo cradled Bonnie against his shoulder and took the reins from Willie. "All you got to do is hold onto the saddle. I'll go nice and slow."

Willie nodded. "How far are we?"

"Only a couple of miles." Rain fell from the brim of his hat. He clicked his tongue, signaling the horse to move.

"Tom?"

"Alive, but injured, same as you, I reckon."

Tears coursed down her face, mixing with the rain. She'd feared the worst, and now, knowing

Tom lived, the fear bubbled up and released in the form of tears.

She dozed again, rousing as they entered the yard to her house. Mama and Junior came running. Theo handed Bonnie to Mama, then helped Willie from her horse.

"Land sakes, child." Mama put a hand over her mouth. "This job as sheriff is going to kill you."

"I ain't dead yet." Her knees buckled.

Theo swept her into his arms, and with Junior's worried gaze on Willie, carried her into the house and into the same room as Tom. He placed her on the single bed across from him. "Might as well make it easy on your Mama and let her nurse both of y'all in here, seeing as how there are two beds."

"Mama?"

Willie held her arms out for Junior and grabbed him close. "I'll be fine, son. I promise."

"Did you kill the bad man?" Tears shimmered in his eyes.

"No, but I cut him pretty good." She smoothed the hair away from his face. "Why don't you fetch me a cup of Grandmama's fine coffee?"

He nodded and rushed away. Theo nodded, his face grave, and backed from the room as Mama entered. "Don't leave yet. I need you to string me up a curtain to separate this room so I can get Willie into dry clothes. What if Tom wakes up?"

Willie clutched her hand. "Why hasn't he woken?"

"He's got a frightful fever from his wound, honey. I'm doing my best." She perched on the edge of the bed. "One day, he sat up, drank some broth, questioned the Hickman sisters as to where Bart might be, then went to sleep and hasn't woken up more than a few minutes at a time, and in most of those minutes, he don't know where he is." She glanced toward Tom's bed. "Junior has been a big help, keeping him company and talking to him about the livery. Theo's been taking care of that and his own farm."

"How could all of this have gone on in one day?" Tom could still die. She forced her tears back. Mama needed to dress her wound so she could care for him. There would be no lying in bed for Willie. She would do everything in her power to make sure he kept breathing.

"It's been two days." Mama patted her shoulder as Junior handed her a mug of coffee. "Drink this while Theo strings a curtain, and I take a look at what you've done to yourself this time."

Willie propped herself against the wall and sipped at her drink while Mama fussed over her. She watched Tom sleep across the room, his handsome features relaxed. Except for being pale, he could be taking a nap.

"It's just a graze." Mama straightened. "Won't need stitches." She grabbed clean bandages and wrapped them several times around Willie's midsection.

Once Theo hung a quilt from hooks he'd installed in the ceiling, Mama helped Willie undress. "I'll get your nightgown."

"No. Fetch a day dress. I'll be nursing Tom."

"You've had quite an ordeal, Willie. You need to rest, at least for today."

"I can't, Mama. Please." Willie gripped her arm. "I love him."

Mama nodded. "I suppose I know that. I've suspected for a while now, even before y'all attempted to get hitched. I'll fetch your yellow calico."

Dressed and bandaged, Willie stepped to Tom's side of the room and pulled a chair closer to his bedside. She planted a tender kiss on his lips, then sat and laid her head on her folded arms. Within seconds, her eyelids drifted closed.

"Willie." Tom's husky voice woke her.

"You're awake." She raised her head, grabbing his hand.

"You're here." The corner of his mouth quirked. "I'm sorry I wasn't there to help you. What happened?"

She sighed. "Parson intended on taking me to Bart, but I cut his face with the knife you slipped me and came home. Your uncle found me and Bonnie on the side of the road."

"Are you hurt?"

"No, just—"

"Let me check your bandages, Willie." Mama bustled into the room. "Welcome back, Tom."

He narrowed his eyes. "Bandages?"

"Just a graze," Mama said as Willie rolled her eyes. "Seems as if my daughter attracts them lately."

"I'll be right back." Willie slipped her hand from his and moved to her side of the room.

"I can't believe you were going to lie to me," Tom said from his side of the curtain.

"You're ill. I didn't want to worry you." She held up her arms for Mama to unwind her.

He groaned. "Most stubborn woman—"

"You've ever met. I know." She grinned at Mama. "But, I've gotten under your skin and you can't let me go."

"That's the truth." His bed springs creaked.

When Mama had Willie back to rights, she left to fetch her patients something to eat and Willie took her seat back at the side of Tom's bed. He had scooted to a sitting position, using the wall to support his back.

Parson had no reason to shoot Tom. He'd done it out of maliciousness. Since the man still lived, Willie feared he'd be back with intent to create bigger trouble. "What are we going to do about the threat to this town?" She asked.

"I was thinking on that, until I fell asleep. Maybe we could get Theo to organize the men of this town to set up a road block. Make it more difficult for someone to ride in with guns blazing."

She agreed. "We can't finish our wedding until we know the danger is past." She entwined her fingers with his. "As much as I want to be your wife, certain things take precedence right now."

*

Tom rested his head against the wall. At the rate things seemed to be going, the wedding would never take place. When he got Parson in the sight of his gun … "I agree, but I'm not happy about it."

Willie laughed. "Neither am I." She rested her cheek against the back of his hand. "You still feel warm."

"That's because you're holding my hand." He smiled, knowing the fever had yet to leave his body fully. He needed to heal. It wasn't a matter of *if* Parson and Bart would return, but when. He needed to be on his feet by then.

Winnie carried in a tray with two bowls of soup and thick slices of bread. "You two eat up, then Willie needs to get in her own bed. The town is in good hands tonight. The women are on lookout with orders to shoot Parson on sight."

"Mama." Willie shook her head. "He's proven he isn't against shooting women."

"No, he's proven he isn't against shooting the sheriff." Winnie grinned and set the tray on the bedside table. "We figure he'll try to talk sense into a group of mere women."

Tom laughed, the action shooting nails through his shoulder. "While you might be right, I agree with your daughter. It's too dangerous. Get the men to stand watch."

"Oh, they're out there, too. I just have more faith in the women." She felt Tom's head, fluffed his pillow, closed the curtains against the night, then left the room with orders to eat and she would return in fifteen minutes.

"She loves this, you know." Willie handed Tom a bowl. "Having someone to take care of."

"I think she'll have Uncle Theo soon. Have you seen the way they look at each other?" Much the same way Tom gazed upon Willie, with stars in his eyes and his heart on his sleeve.

"He showed up the day Mama prayed for a husband." Willie dunked her bread into her soup.

"Within a matter of minutes, actually. We were arguing about me turning you down. She said I should marry you for the sake of the children and since I wouldn't, it would be up to her. I'm glad to see she's found love again."

He wanted to ask if Willie had found love, too, but wasn't sure he wanted to know the answer. If she was only marrying him for convenience, it would be enough. Whatever her reason, he would be happy to have her by his side.

He studied her while she ate, noting the exhaustion lining her face and in the slump of her shoulders. Weary or not, Willie wouldn't rest until the work was done. She'd work herself into the grave if she kept going without sleep. He tucked an errant strand of hair behind her ear. "Go to bed, Willie. I'll be fine, the town will be fine, the children are fine. We won't be though, if you collapse."

"I am tired." She heaved a sigh. "A few hours of sleep won't make the sun fail to come up." She finished her soup soaked bread, gave him a quick kiss, then smiled and went to her side of the room.

Tom finished his soup and turned down the lantern, leaving just enough of the wick burning for Winnie to find her way when she returned. He scooted to a lying position and stared at the ceiling until gentle snores came from the other side of the hanging quilt. If the wedding had gone as planned, he and Willie would be recuperating in the same bed, not separated by several feet and a blanket.

He grimaced, thinking of how their wedding night would have gone, or not. With him shot and her kidnapped, they'd be much the same as they were now. Hopefully, Willie wouldn't change her mind about getting hitched by the time everything was said and done.

"Go to sleep," Winnie whispered as she collected the tray. "There's nothing to worry about tonight. The children are in bed, Bonnie none the worse for her ordeal, Willie is home, and the town is quiet. Leave things in God's hands for tonight." She patted his shoulder and left him to his thoughts.

"You asleep?" Mark peeked through the door.

"No. I slept for a full day. Now my mind won't stop turning. Willie's sleeping on the other side of the blanket though."

Mark sat in the chair Willie had vacated. "I'll be quiet. I'm sorry how things turned out."

"Thank you, but I don't think that's why you're here."

"No, it's not." He hung his head. "I'm afraid the Larson boys might be behind all this, too. Oscar's wife came into town this afternoon, saying the men haven't been home in days. She's staying at my place for now. Either Oscar and Henry are dead, or they've hooked up with Bart."

"Alice is better off without that no good scoundrel."

"True, but my point is, we're looking at at least four men, counting Bart. They could cause a heap of trouble for this town, especially with you and the sheriff out of sorts."

Theo leaned in the doorway. "I'm in charge for now."

If anyone could run the place, Theo could. Uh-oh. Willie's snores had stopped. "Men, help me out of this bed and let's take this conversation elsewhere." He held out his hand.

"You three stay right where you are." Willie peeked around the quilt, holding it in front of her for proprieties sake. "No one put anyone in charge, except for me. Now, Theo, Pastor, iffen you want to be deputized for the time being, I'm willing to do that, but I'm still the sheriff for another week."

"Yes, ma'am," Mark said. "We're only trying to help."

"If you really want to, I suggest you gather up a posse. We'll leave first thing in the morning." She dropped the curtain into place, leaving the men to stare at each other.

Tom shrugged, wincing against the pain. "Guess you heard her. I'm thinking she aims to go after Bart before he can come to us."

"You guessed right! Now, y'all leave so I can get some more sleep." Willie called out. "We won't be doing anything tonight."

"Well, that leaves prayer and asking men to ride along." Mark rubbed his hands together. "I'll get right on it."

"And don't let any of the women know what you're doing," Willie yelled. "That's the last thing we need."

Tom laughed until tears streamed from his eyes, whether from humor at Willie or pain, he didn't know. Add in the astonished looks on Mark's and Theo's faces that Willie was giving orders from her bed, and he feared he'd rip out his stitches. Oh, but life with her would be anything but boring. He prayed he'd get the opportunity to find out how much.

*

Bart sat and stared into the fire, counting down the hours until he deemed it safe enough for them to sneak into town, get his money and cigars, then torch the place. The men were getting bored and on each others nerves, complaining about every little thing until Bart wanted to shoot them all.

Oscar Larson barged through the door of the shack and tossed a couple of rabbits on the table. "We killed 'em, you skin 'em," Oscar said.

Parson scowled, the cut on his face an angry scarlet. "Have Henry do it. He's the youngest." He drained a bottle of moonshine.

"Was that the last of it?" Oscar scowled.

"I need it for my pain. My face is killing me."

"It looks infected."

"No!" Parson put a hand to his face. "Don't say that. It's healing."

"Looks bad to me." Oscar shrugged.

"Gentlemen." Bart planted his hands on his thighs and pushed to his feet. "Remember who we're mad at. Save your anger for the sheriff and the town. Parson, you need to scrub that wound and pour whiskey in it."

"It'll burn."

"Then die," Bart said. "Makes no difference to me." He paced the room, aching to smoke something other than the cheap homemade cigarettes Oscar made. How dare the sheriff take away all of his luxuries because of a silly law? What about the old biddies who sold him the stuff?

He hoped she had caught them and they rotted in her jail. Stupid women!

He kicked the leg of the stool, knocking it out from under Parson, who hit the floor with a thud. "I said to go take care of your face!"

"Sure, boss." Parson scrambled to his feet and dashed outside, grabbing a fresh jug of moonshine on his way. He passed young Henry who came through the door, burdened with a pail of water. The boy tossed Bart a questioning look before dropping the bucket on the table.

"Oscar, Henry, go help him." Bart motioned his head toward the door. "He'll be no good to us if he's feverish."

Oscar nodded and he and his brother followed Parson outside. Minutes later, Parson's screams rang through the window. Bart grinned. That's the sound he wanted to hear from the dear, beautiful sheriff. All he needed to do was be patient. His day would come.

24

With her side bound tighter than dried leather, Willie poured a cup of coffee and slid it across the table to Tom before pouring one for herself. Neither one of them wanted to abide another day in bed, not when the town was in possible danger. While Willie was fine unless she sneezed, she feared Tom fared worse and wished he'd stay in bed.

"Your thoughts are spread across your face," he said, accepting the cup. "I'm going with you this morning, and no arguments."

"But you've just woken from a high fever." She pulled out a chair across from him. "I can fill you in on what we decide."

"What if Bart comes today and I'm lounging in bed like a man of leisure?"

"Then we'll handle it."

"With me." The hard glint in his eyes as he peered at her over the rim of his mug said he would take no more against him going.

Willie sighed. Since coming to Wild Horse Pass, she'd been shot at twice and almost burned alive. While those types of dangers were to be expected, to an extent, for someone acting as sheriff, the thought of someone she loved being in the same danger churned her stomach. If she'd been more vigilant that last day with Sam, he might still be alive. She couldn't let the same happen to Tom. He'd already almost died because of someone's grudge against her. If he did die, the town would have to bury her alongside him, she'd never be able to go on without him.

"Stop thinking that way," he said. "I can see the wheels turning in your head. God is with us, Willie. Everything will be fine. Trust Him."

"I do trust God." It was the other guy she didn't trust. "At least this upheaval has taken the town's attention away from your forward actions with the young single ladies," she said, attempting to lift their mood.

Instead, a shadow passed over his eyes. "You were spared from having to follow through on your offer of marriage to save my reputation."

"That isn't why—"

"Folks are gathered at the church," Theo said, making a beeline for the coffee pot. "Standing room only. Everyone's concerned with how the sheriff is going to handle this."

Willie shook her head. Less than a week until they voted on whether to keep her and Bart had presented the biggest challenge to ever face her or the town. What if she wasn't up to bringing Bart and his gang to justice? She pushed aside her insecurities and drained her cup. Setting it on the table with a thump, she pushed to her feet. "Let's go."

She tried not to dwell on how painfully Tom got to his feet or how Theo held out a helping hand. If she dwelled on their injuries, she couldn't keep her focus where it mattered … keeping them all safe. Taking a deep breath, which pulled against her side, she led the way out the door and down the street.

The early morning sun glinted off shop windows. Birds twittered from the trees. A dog barked. A sleepy, picturesque town on the edge of Armageddon. She hefted her gun belt more securely on her hip, made sure her whip was within easy reach, and shoved open the swinging doors to the newly cleaned and prayed over church.

All conversation ceased and heads turned as she stepped inside, flanked by Tom and Theo. Applause greeted her. Tears filled her eyes. Whatever might come in the next few days, she had arrived home.

"Let's hear it for Mrs. Sheriff!" Mayor Bloomfield lifted a bottle of sarsaparilla. "The strongest, bravest woman in Montana Territory."

"Hear! Hear!" The room resounded with cheers.

She was peppered with questions on her way to the podium. Taking her place behind it, she raised her hands and motioned for everyone to quiet. She sniffed and wiped her eyes on the collar of her blouse. "You warm my heart with your greetings. I am truly blessed."

The Simpson family curled their lips but remained, Sally's eyes feasting on Tom who stood next to Willie. Closing her eyes, Willie prayed for wisdom.

"As you know," she said. "Bart Johnson and Jim Parson have a grudge against me. I'm terribly sorry that this has affected all of you. I have deputized Tom Miller and Theodore Grimes until the threat to our fine town has been ended.

"When Parson abducted me, he headed out of town on the road heading east. I'd like to get together a posse and go after them before they come here." She shook her head when Gertie Bloomfield stepped forth. "None of the women's vigilante group will be allowed to come along."

"Why not?" She planted fists on her hips.

Willie smiled. "If you were to go, who would watch out for those left behind?"

"I say we stay and face that gang as a united front," Leroy Brown said, stepping forward. "I'm betting Bart ran out of here with nary a cent to his name. He'll be back for his loot, guarantee it."

"What do you know, Mr. Brown? What if Bart decides not to come for his revenge? Then, we're sitting here waiting for who knows how long."

"Well, see, that's where you might be wrong, Mrs. Sheriff." Leroy stuck his finger in his ear as if digging for gold. "I helped build this saloon and Bart had me put in a hidden vault under the floorboards behind the bar. I figure his money is still there."

Willie motioned for Theo to check out the man's claims. If Leroy was right, they could lure Bart to a safe place rather than go searching blindly through the mountains.

"Leroy's right," Bob Mellon said. "I caught him stuffing a bag of coins in it once. It's hidden good, but you can see the outline iffen you look close enough."

Theo disappeared behind the bar, straightening a few minutes later with a roll of paper money in his hand. "There's a fortune hidden in here, and some of the world's finest cigars, if my guess is right."

Oh, yes, Bart would definitely be coming back. "Take all that to the bank and lock it in the safe. We'll set ourselves a little trap. The rest of you stay here. I've got some rules to lay down when I return." And Tom could get another day or two of rest without riding out of town on horseback. Say what he would, but Willie could see the strain on his face.

She slipped her hand in his and led him to a chair vacated by Mellon. "Please sit before you fall over. I will need you later." She cupped his cheek. "Do this for me."

He nodded, which alone told her he felt a lot worse than he would let on. Willie located Mama standing in a corner with Junior and Bonnie. "Would you fetch Tom a glass of water? I'm worried about him."

"I told him he should stay in bed." Mama marched away.

Willie tucked Bonnie's hand in Junior's. "Don't let go of each other. You two stay right here until everyone has left the building. You hear me?"

"Yes, ma'am." Junior nodded. "I'm a good big brother."

She tousled his hair. "The best." Stepping

outside, she made her way to the bank and supervised the transfer of Bart's money. Frank Simpson glared when she stepped through the door, but wisely held his tongue.

Willie stepped into the safe and breathed deep of polished wood and money. With the rich oaks of the lobby and the bricks that made up the walls of the bank and the safe, the small building looked too grand for a small town such as Wild Horse Pass, but Willie had learned in her three months there that the town had high expectations.

The walls of the safe looked strong enough to prevent outside entrance. If Bart wanted his money, he would have to come through the front door where Willie would be waiting for him. "I'll send Theo over in a few minutes to stand guard while I get my children safely to home. I advise you do the same with your daughters, Mr. Simpson. Tell them to stay there. I'm headed back to the church."

Ignoring the ache in her side, she resumed her position behind the podium and stared over the crowd. Some of her rules would not set well and she wanted the town residents to know she meant business. Tom made a move to join her at the podium, and she shook her head.

"Now that the motive is locked up, there are some things I am requesting that the townfolks do until this situation has come to an end. No one under the age of eighteen is allowed outside of their home under any circumstances."

Groans filled the air.

"We know that Bart is not opposed to taking even children as hostage. For those of you over eighteen, you are not allowed to go anywhere alone. If you own a gun, please leave it at home. We don't want any itchy trigger fingers injuring, or killing, innocent bystanders."

"If we leave our guns at home, how are we supposed to defend ourselves?" Leroy asked.

"By following these rules." Willie narrowed her eyes. "No one, other than myself and my deputies, are allowed on the town street past dark. We will ring the church bell," she said, grateful it hadn't burned in the fire, "if help is required in any shape or form. If the situation is dire enough to require us to ring the bell, then we will need every armed person. Understood?"

Heads nodded solemnly. Mothers gathered their children close.

"I realize I may be predicting doomsday here, folks, but my primary concern is the town's safety until Bart is locked away." She took a deep breath. "I will also be sending a telegram to the Marshall's office requesting further help. The rules are in effect immediately." She marched to where Tom sat, a muscle twitching in his jaw, and offered him her hand. "Time to go home," she said as people filed out of the building.

She led Tom to the telegraph office where she had him wait until she sent her message, then she walked him home, her arm linked firmly through his uninjured one. He remained silent the entire way, his face looking as if he were cast in granite.

*

The fact Tom had to be led home like a child rankled like nothing else. Just standing beside

Willie for a few short minutes had left him exhausted. Still, he refused to be sent to bed and chose a rocking chair on the porch instead.

Willie fetched them both coffee and sat in the chair beside him, propping her feet on the railing. "The meeting went well, don't you think? We don't need a posse now that we are going to lure Bart here. All we have to do is wait. That gives you some time to heal."

"I'm not the only one who was shot, Willie." He tightened his grip on his mug.

"No, but you're the only one who caught fever. Stop being so stubborn and let me take care of you."

"I'm supposed to take care of you!" He threw his tin mug against the wall with a clank, spilling coffee down the side of the house.

"I thought you were past those silly lines about what is expected of men and women." She glared at him. "It must be the fever talking because you're being ridiculous."

"God clearly states in His Word that the man is head of the household. That means—"

"So, if we had gotten married, you would expect me to follow your orders without expressing my opinion?" Her mouth fell open. "Maybe Bart did us a favor." She paled. "I didn't mean that. Forgive me."

"You're right. Maybe Bart kept us from making a grave mistake." He turned away as she gasped and dashed into the house. He could probably explain his churlish behavior on his pounding head, but he'd be lying to himself. The longer Willie remained as sheriff, the greater the danger. Why couldn't she see that?

Could Tom sit back and allow his wife to stay in such a position? He'd thought so until today. Now, he wasn't sure. Having the wedding interrupted would allow both he and Willie to search their hearts and find out what they really wanted in a spouse.

"I'm sorry." Willie stood in the doorway. "I wish our relationship didn't always come down to this. Us not clear in the roles expected of the other."

He motioned her forward. She knelt beside his chair and laid her cheek against his arm. "I'm sorry, too, Willie. I'm headstrong and opinionated, but God is working on me. Let's focus on the problem at hand and pick up the subject of our relationship when we're feeling better and can concentrate on our feelings."

"Agreed." She stiffened. "Oh, no. I am not prepared to deal with this right now."

Tom glanced toward the lawn where the women's vigilante group, or auxiliary group, as they've decided to be called, marched to the porch. He squeezed Willie's hand before letting her stand.

"Sheriff." Gertie tilted her chin. "I am well aware that you thought you could appease me by saying you would leave the town in our hands when you formed your posse, but since that isn't going to happen, we've decided to take shifts in monitoring Main Street."

"I have men selected to do that. Please stay home where it is safe." Willie moved to the top step.

"Will you be doing the same?"

"Excuse me?" Willie glanced at Tom.

He shrugged. There was no telling what the group was up to.

"Well, this stems from us being women, correct? And, since you're a woman, we figured the same rule should apply to you."

"I'm the sheriff."

Tom bit his lip to keep from grinning. While he partially agreed with Willie about the women staying home where it was safe, he could still see their point. He couldn't wait to see how this argument played out.

"And a woman." Gloria stepped forward. "Sheriff, we are behind you with everything we have, but even if you were a man, you couldn't handle Bart and his gang alone."

"Especially if my worthless husband and no-good brother in law is involved." Alice Larson piped up. "They don't have the sense God gave a goose and might just as well shoot first if Bart says so, then worry about the consequences later. I say the entire town, men *and* women, should fight alongside each other."

Well said. Tom set his rocker into motion, keeping his gaze on Willie. From the set of her shoulders he could tell she was mulling things over. How she carried it all on her slim shoulders was beyond him. The duties of sheriff, the responsibilities of motherhood, and being the sole provider for her family had to be a heavy burden, yet Willie carried it as strong as any man. Tom was a fool for expecting her to be anything but what God had created her to be. She was the sheriff of

Wild Horse Pass and deserved to be so until she, not any husband, chose to step down from the role.

He struggled to his feet and took his place beside her. He put his good arm around her waist and pulled her close. "I'll support your decision," he whispered.

She tossed him a grateful smile before turning back to the group. "I will be honored to accept your help."

"Hallelujuah!" The women pulled pistols from pockets and set off down the road.

"Heavens, what have I done?" Willie shook her head.

"You've let them feel important and needed." Times were changing. It was time for Tom to change with them. He looked forward to learning about the future at Willie's side. When the trouble with Bart was over, he planned on proposing again and wouldn't take no for an answer.

*

Bart's need for one of his fine cigars was like a tick bite that wouldn't heal. He barked and directed orders until the others had started spending most of their time away from the cabin. He kicked at a log that had fallen from a stack near the fireplace. They'd leave first thing in the morning for Wild Horse Pass. He wanted his money and his cigars and to see that woman sheriff lying in the street.

"Oscar!" He yanked open the door.

"Yes, boss?" The man snapped his suspenders over his shoulders, clearly having awakened from a nap.

Bart shook his head. "Where's that idiot,

Parson?"

"I think he's down at the crick taking care of his face. It ain't healing right, boss."

As if Bart cared. As long as the man could stand on two feet and shoot when they arrived in town tomorrow, he will have served his purpose. "Tell him to stop goofing off and get the beans on the fire. It's his turn to cook." He slammed the door, shaking the flimsy cabin on its foundation.

His having fallen to such lows could only be blamed on Willie Jack. If the woman had kept her nose out of his business like the sheriffs in the past, he'd still be living in as fine of luxury as Wild Horse Pass could offer. If nothing else, he'd have his money and be able to pack up and move to where a fine gentlemen's establishment such as his had been would be appreciated.

He grabbed another homemade cigarette and puffed as if each puff was his last. With each exhale of smoke, he pictured Willie Jack falling from his bullet. If anyone stepped in to help her, he'd shoot them too. The whole town, if need be. Yep, Bart didn't like to fail, and he didn't aim to this time, either. Soon, he'd be the king of Wild Horse Pass and toss all their silly laws in a shallow grave with the sheriff.

25

Willie shoved aside her plate and studied the stoic face of Tom. He'd said little since returning to the house last night, his face still in hard lines when they'd gone to bed. She wanted to explain away his moodiness on his not feeling well, but wasn't exactly sure that was the reason.

When he'd said he would support her, she had thought their times of miscommunication at an end. Instead, they had gone to sleep without a word, leaving Willie lying awake most of the time, listening to Tom breathe from his side of the hanging quilt. Not only had she thought of his angry mood, but of how all it would take was a few steps on her part and they would cross a moral line drawn only for married folks.

It was time for one of them to start sleeping in the parlor. Since Willie was the least injured, she'd lay blankets on the sofa come evening. She should have done that the first night. How could any red-blooded woman sleep with a handsome man mere feet from her, especially one she had feelings for?

"Do I have something on my face?" Tom

wiped a napkin across his cheek. "You've been staring intently at me for several minutes." He grinned as if he could read her mind. "I feel a lot like a side of beef at the auction and you haven't eaten in a week."

Her face heated. "Finish your breakfast. You're obviously feeling better."

"If I don't move too suddenly. You seemed to have trouble sleeping last night." He winked. "I heard a lot of tossing and turning, a few groans."

"Don't be crude." It was definitely time to sleep somewhere else. She grabbed her coffee. Wait. This was her house. He could sleep on the sofa, or better yet, move back to his room above the livery. Heavens. What would people say if they could read her mind? She'd be tarred and feathered and run out of town.

God said to dwell on things that were pure, true, and lovely. Willie knew He meant himself, but mercy, Tom was all those things and more. She wanted to shoot Parson for disrupting their wedding ceremony. Enough was enough. She slammed her mug back to the table. "It's time to head to the bank. I have first watch this morning."

"Don't you mean we both have first watch?" He adjusted the sling on his arm and grabbed his hat from the back of the chair next to him.

Side-by-side, as Willie hoped they would always be, they made their way first to the jail, where Mama was tending the Hickman sisters, and then to the bank, relieving a red-eyed Frank Simpson. She was more than ready for a Marshall to arrive in town and take control of the two women.

Moonshiners or not, Willie didn't like keeping women of their advanced age behind bars.

"Those meddling women have been checking up on me all night." Frank shook his head. "What were you thinking, setting them free? I'm glad my woman knows her place."

"You are a fortunate man, indeed," Willie kept her face expressionless. "You should hurry home and comfort that obedient woman."

Tom ducked his head to hide a grin, but not before Willie saw. She turned her back on Frank and pretended to fiddle with her whip. Why was the man still standing there?

"Do you want the combination to the safe?" He asked.

"No." Willie faced him, her humor fading. "If something should happen to me, I don't want Bart to have easy access." There were too many people that Willie cared for that the man could use as leverage against her in order to force her to open the safe.

Frank headed home. Willie and Tom set chairs on each side of the wide front window, giving them a clear view of the entire street. With no back entrance to the bank, it would be nigh on impossible for Bart to sneak up on them.

"Have you ever wondered what God thinks of all this?" Tom removed his hat, glancing her way.

"What do mean?"

"This is all going to come down to more violence." He shook his head. "Blood will be shed before this over. You and I, not to mention the town's people, are prepared to defend what is ours with gunfire. I'm wondering whether there is another way."

"I wish there were." Willie stared at the sunbaked street. A sheet of paper danced on the breeze. "I won't shoot first, Tom. I'll try to reason with them. The Bible states in **Psalm 82:4** that we are to *rescue the weak and needy; Deliver them out of the hand of the wicked*. That is what those enforcing the law are doing. God's Word is full of death and violence, a lot of it at God's leading.

"Sam once explained it to me like this after he was forced to kill a man. Using the example of David who wanted to build a house for the Lord, the Lord said he wasn't qualified because of causing the death of Uriah, Bethsheba's husband. Yet, God called David a man after His heart. God won't shun me if I'm forced to kill someone, but maybe I won't be qualified to serve him in certain ways." She drew in a sharp breath. "Sam said it was a good thing he never wanted to go into preaching."

Tom chuckled. "Your Sam had a way with words. He would have made a fine preacher."

"Killing didn't come easy to him, even as sheriff. I don't aim to take it lightly either, but I will defend this town and my family." She prayed he understood; that God understood. Her heart told her she was in the right place, doing the right thing, in accordance with God's plan. She might not be one of those people who walked around quoting scripture, but it didn't mean she didn't meditate God's Word in her heart. On days like today, when she waited for evil to stroll into town, she kept His words close and dwelled on His promises.

Mama and Theo headed for the bank, Theo's head bent over Mama's, the look on his face so tender it brought tears to Willie's eyes. Mama gazed up at him in rapture. It was good that Mama had found love again after so many years. They pushed open the bank doors and stepped inside.

Willie met Tom's smiling gaze. Not only was it good for Mama, it was good for Willie. Now to convince Tom that the two of them would make a good law-enforcing duo. While she was at a point where she would lay down her badge if Tom insisted once they wed, she hoped he'd choose to join her as a full time deputy instead.

Oh, where was Bart? She wanted this over and done with so her wedding could pick up where it had left off.

"Why aren't there any lamps burning?" Mama asked.

"We don't want to alert Bart that anyone is inside. It's Saturday. The bank would be closed." Willie glanced out the window. "Where are my children?"

"Whichever woman is off duty is watching them at the parsonage." She smiled up at Theo. "It's our turn to walk the streets." She turned back to Willie. "Seems a mite lonely out there, though. That fact alone will tip Bart off."

"I know, but I can't risk having folks meandering up and down the sidewalks. I wish you weren't out there."

"We're keeping to the shadows the best we can. Having someone outside will act as an early warning system. Speaking of which, Bear is keeping guard right outside the door. Raised such a ruckus when I went to fix the lunch basket, I didn't have the heart to leave him behind." She slid a basket off her arm. "Here is a canteen of water and another one with coffee. Also, I put in some sandwiches for lunch. We'll be back around supper time to give you a break. Tom, let me take a look at your bandages before I head home. Willie, turn around."

Willie grinned. If Mama only knew how much of Tom she'd already seen she'd want to pack up and move.

*

Tom kept his eyes trained on the street as Winnie applied fresh bandages to his gunshot. Bob Mellon and Leroy Brown lounged outside the saloon/church looking as if they did nothing more than soak up the sun. Tom knew those two wily men knew everything happening around them, despite their drowsy demeanor.

"Healing up nicely," Winnie said, handing him his shirt. "No more fever."

"You're a good nurse." Theo gathered her supplies together. "If not for you, my nephew might have died. We owe you a lot." He grinned. "I aim to collect on that debt shortly."

Winnie giggled. "Oh, you." She slipped her arm in his and allowed him to escort her from the building.

"Your uncle makes my Mama look like a young woman again." Willie turned around. "It's us who owe him."

"Then I'll collect on the debt."

Her cheeks darkened. "Stop. We have more important things to worry about right now than stealing kisses."

"I'm thinking more than just a kiss." He winked and transferred his attention back outside. Flirtation was nice and passed the time, but the morning was passing. If Bart didn't show up soon, Tom feared they'd be fighting the man during the night. All kinds of things could be hidden in the dark.

He pulled his pistol from his belt, thankful again that it wasn't his shooting arm that was injured. After checking to make sure it was loaded, again, he slid it back in its holster.

"I'm nervous, too," Willie said. "Times drags slowly when you're waiting for evil to approach."

Tom didn't know why he hadn't seen it before, the evil in Bart Johnson. It could be the fact he never frequented the saloon, but he'd passed the man on the streets more than once. It had taken a beautiful woman standing up to the man for his true nature to show. It had taken that same woman to show Tom what he really wanted from life.

Not a successful blacksmith shop or livery, not to spend the rest of his days alone, and somehow the idea of his own ranch didn't hold the same appeal with the thought of Willie at his side. This lovely woman had removed a lifetime of bitterness and prejudice, making him a better man, all in the span of three months. Did the people of this town know how lucky they were to have a sheriff such as Willie Jack?

He reached over and took her hand. "There is

no one I'd rather sit here and wait with than you." His gaze locked with hers. "Whether we live or die, Wilhemina Jackson, I am a blessed man to have known you."

"Me, too, Tom." She squeezed his hand. "But, we'll be fine. I feel it here." She placed his hand over her heart. "God has promised. What is wrong? You are usually the one with the strong faith? I've heard of the times you've headed to the pastor's house for guidance."

"That's because I didn't have the answers."

"All you had to do was ask the one with all the answers."

How right she was. He returned her hand squeeze and straightened. Sitting for hours tended to make a body lock up on a guy. He twisted from side to side, taking care not to jostle his shoulder. Fifteen long paces took him from the front door to the safe. Ten paces took him from one side to the other.

"You're making me antsy," Willie stated. "Can't you sit down?"

"Rigor mortis was setting in."

"Not a good phrase to use right now." She rolled her head on her shoulders. "My time here is almost up. The parson is taking the next watch, which I don't like. I'm the sheriff. I should stay here as long as it takes."

"You won't be any good to anyone if you keel over from exhaustion. Since you're the best shot in town, we need you at your best." He dug in the basket and pulled out a sandwich. "Eat this and have a cup of coffee." He knew her well enough to know that when Mark showed up, she'd send him home until dark, if then. Tom intended to stay with her as long as it took.

"I understand your frustration. It's quite possible Bart will cut his losses and keep running."

"But you doubt it."

She nodded. "We took a lot of money out from under those floorboards. I can't imagine him not returning."

"Maybe he's waiting for us to let down our guard."

"Maybe."

Tom grabbed his own cheese sandwich and resumed his seat in his chair. He would have liked something with a little more substance than cheese, but Winnie was as busy as the rest of them. It wouldn't have hurt Gertie to bring over a meal or two from the restaurant, though. He swallowed the dry sandwich, washed it down with coffee and resumed staring out the window.

The summer heat shimmered over the dirt of the street. The wind picked up, rattling dry leaves down the sidewalk and buffeting the skirts of two of the Simpson girls. "What in tarnation are they doing out there?"

Willie leaped to her feet and rushed outside. "Sally Simpson, are you plumb loco?"

"Pa said me and my sister have to do our share of patrolling the town."

"Get back home right now. Sheriff's orders." She pointed and waited until they lifted their skirts to their knees and dashed away.

Tom laughed. "I've never seen either of them girls run like that."

"Fear is a great motivator, even for the lazy." Willie expelled air sharply from her nose. "It's a wonder anyone is left living in this town. I've never met people who make such bad choices in my life."

"They aren't that bad. They're used to doing for themselves, since they run off every sheriff that hangs up their hat here." Except Willie. She'd dug in her heels and hung on for the long haul. God hadn't made many women like her that was for sure. He lifted his coffee for a drink.

"What's going on in that head of yours?" She asked. "You've got a silly grin on your face. A lot like Bear when he wants a steak." She reached down and scratched her dog's head.

Tom choked on his coffee. "I was just thinking of what an extraordinary woman you are. Nothing inappropriate, I promise." Although, he was a lot like the dog with Willie being a juicy steak. Not that he would ever mention that to her, of course.

"You've really turned around in your way of thinking." Willie set her mug back in the basket. "That is very, very promising, Mr. Miller." She straightened and gave him a smile that rivaled the sun.

*

"Get on your horse." Bart kicked Parson, who rolled out of his blanket like an unwrapped Mexican burrito. "I wanted to be gone a long time ago. There's a town to conquer and money to get."

"I think I'm dying, Bart." Parson sat up, the side of his face puffy. Red streaks ran from the wound in every direction. "I'm hot and freezing at the same time."

"It's that sheriff's fault you're infected. She's the one who cut you. Get up and seek revenge." Bart handed him the last of the whiskey. "Drink this. You'll feel better. Once we get to town, there will be a lot more of that."

He headed back to the cabin where Henry Larson dished up yet another meal of beans. Not much longer and he'd force the snooty mayor's wife to cook a meal fit for the king of the town, just as soon as he could get his minions moving.

"Hurry up, you no-good scoundrels. I want to be there by noon." He'd always fancied himself a gunfighter, having a showdown at high noon. They'd have to hurry to make it.

"I'll need to do up these dishes," Henry said.

"Just leave 'em. We ain't coming back here. Whoever owns this cabin can take care of things when they return." Unless they were dead up the mountain somewhere. If so, then they were God's problem, not Bart's.

He wolfed down the undercooked beans, then strapped on his gun holster, tying it low on his thigh for easy reach. He wiggled his fingers, then grabbed the butt, whipping it and aiming at Henry. Yep, he was still fast enough.

"Hey!" Henry glowered. "Careful with that thing."

"It ain't you I'm aiming to shoot." Not in a hundred years would Bart have ever thought his enemy would be a woman whose beauty rivaled the brightest spring flower or one that could out shoot most men. Well, Bart hadn't shown his true colors. He'd be mighty hard to beat in a draw.

He did a few more practice runs, then went in search of his "gang". The four of them, even with Parson barely alive, ought to accomplish taking over a town full of spineless men and bossy women. The worst ones he'd have to deal with were the sheriff, the blacksmith, and the parson. His shooting on the Fourth of July had astonished Bart. Who thought a man of the cloth could handle a gun?

Still, Bart had full confidence in his ability. He swung onto the back of his horse. "Let's go men. Riches and revenge await!"

26

The sun hung high overhead. The dirt street shimmered with haze. Even the women's auxiliary group had given up their patrol. Willie tucked her hair under her hat, trying to catch a breeze in the dark bank building. The day stretched long in front of her. She suspected Tom napped under the pulled down brim of his hat. Good. He was still recuperating and needed his rest for when Bart showed up, if he showed.

She squirmed on her stool, the bandages cutting into her ribcage. What would Sam say if he saw her with a fresh scar on her temple and one across her midsection? Would he still think her beautiful? Tom did, if his heated glances were any indication. She scoffed. Silly woman, worrying about her looks at such a time, but Willie never had done well with inactivity. Her mind tended to head off on strange tangents that would otherwise have no bearing on her thoughts.

Tom sat with his back against the wall, hat pulled low, mouth slightly open, and looking as loveable and endearing as she had ever seen him.

321

She wanted to plant a kiss on his parted lips, but feared waking him. She smiled. Talk about tangents. The last thing the two of them needed to be doing at such a critical time was kiss. She shook her head and stared back out the window, her fingers running through Bear's thick coat. A leaf skittered down the sidewalk.

Mayor Bloomfield peered over the doors of the saloon, then withdrew back inside. No one seemed overly eager to spend time in the hot summer afternoon, but it relieved Willie's burden to know others were at least checking occasionally for signs of Bart. An early warning would be their best chance of coming out ahead of any skirmish.

Sighing, she pushed to her feet and onto the sidewalk, Bear on her heels. Staying in the shadows, she made her way from one end of the street to the other, peering between the buildings for signs of foul play.

Bear growled deep in his throat and stared down the street, the hair on his neck almost standing on end. Willie followed his gaze. Four men on horses rode past her house, headed for Main Street. Willie whirled and dashed back to the bank. She slammed through the door, grabbed her rifle, and headed back outside as Tom bolted to his feet.

Rifle gripped in both hands, she stepped in the middle of the street and aimed her gun at Bart Johnson's heart, or where his heart would be if the scoundrel had one. "Gentlemen."

"Sheriff." Bart leered. "You're looking well."

"Can't say the same for you or your men. Parson looks downright ill."

Parson called her a few unsavory names before upending a whiskey bottle into his mouth.

"Tsk tsk, Mr Parson, such language." Willie kept her finger on the trigger as Tom stood beside her. "I'll have to ask you gentlemen to leave."

"I'm afraid we can't do that." Bart leaned forward, resting his forearms on the pommel of his saddle. "See, you have some things that belong to me. I can't make a fresh start without them."

"I reckon you could hang around for a while and see whether the Marshall of Montana Territory will grant you your belongings," Willie said. "Even you are permitted a fair trial."

He shook his head. "No, that's not going to happen. This is the way I see it. You being such a good shot and all, I figure you and me can have an old fashioned gunfight. Winner takes all."

Willie's heart stuttered. She might be a good shot with a rifle and more than passable with a handgun, but being a quick draw was one skill she hadn't spent a lot of time improving.

"We'll make it even." Bart grinned. "I got four men, you find a total of four and we'll see who comes out the victor."

"You're crazier than a rabid coon." Tom put his hand on the butt of his pistol. "All that's going to accomplish is the death of four people, and I wager those deaths will be on your side."

"Enough talking." Bart slid from his horse and motioned the other three to do the same. They slapped the horses' rumps and sent them racing down the street. "We're doing this now. Either you fetch two more folks or we'll do it this way. I got a beef to settle with you, sheriff, and I aim to take care of it today."

Willie glanced at Tom. The worry in his eyes was almost her undoing, then as if he'd unlocked a secret compartment, a steely resolve took over the worry and he nodded. "Aim for Bart and I'll take Parson. The Larson boys most likely won't draw," he told her in a low voice.

"What if they do?"

"That's a chance we have to take. Whatever happens, God is in control." He ran his thumb down her cheek. "We'll be fine. We have some unsettled business of our own."

She leaned into his hand for a second before straightening and tugging her hat more firmly on her head. "All right, Bart. It would be much easier if you'd just go to jail like a good boy. So, what? We face off at ten paces?" The whole scenario was ridiculous and would most likely leave her babies orphans. Still, this was the wilds of Montana, where anything could happen, especially with God and his angels flanking her.

"Oscar Larson!" Alice stepped from the saloon and marched to Willie's side. "You and your no-good brother head home right this instant. What in heaven's name do y'all think you're doing?"

"You shouldn't be here, Alice." Oscar scowled. "Where's the young'uns?"

"As if you care. You've been gone nearly a week." She planted her fists on her hips. "Give me a gun, sheriff. I reckon I'll stand up with you."

"I can't shoot my woman, Bart." Oscar shook his head. "It ain't right."

One by one, the women of the auxiliary club, armed with rifles or pistols, took up spots on either side of Willie and Tom. Soon, the menfolk joined them, the line stretching from one side of the road to the other, and several folks standing behind. Tears stung Willie's eyes at their support.

She'd managed to thrust aside her fear of succumbing to Sam's fate and faced her greatest foe yet, only to realize she was never meant to face any of it alone. She had friends and family. She truly had come home when she'd stepped foot in Wild Horse Pass.

"Sorry I'm late," Mama said, racing up, skirts hiked to her knees, one hand clutching a pistol. Theo jogged alongside her. "We had to get the little ones settled in at the parsonage."

Mayor Bloomfield bustled forth. "Bart, you've been a member of this community for years. I hate to see it all end this way. You men are outnumbered and outgunned. Mrs. Sheriff has full reign to handle this situation as she sees fit. I suggest you hand over your weapons."

Heads nodded from Willie's supporters.

"It doesn't have to result in bloodshed," Willie said.

"Sorry." Mark stepped on the other side of Tom. "Had some trouble getting the Simpson girls to stay with the children."

"Well, Bart." Willie rested her rifle on her shoulder. "You've got three shooters facing you, any of which could most likely out shoot you on any given day. My arm is getting tired, my finger is twitching, and I'm thinking it's time to put a stop to this whole ridiculous thing." She was almost tempted to shoot him just to shut him up. A bullet to the leg or the arm might disable him long enough for her to cart him to jail to wait on the Marshall.

"The only bloodshed I want is yours," Bart reached for his gun at the same time as Parson fumbled for his.

Willie pulled the trigger, her shot taking Bart in the shoulder. Tom's shot knocked Parson to the ground. Other shots rang out until Willie's ears rang. "Enough!" She held up her hand. What a load of trigger happy people.

She handed her rifle to Mark, then pistol in hand, went to stand over Bart. "He's still breathing."

"Can't say the same for Parson," Tom said, bending over the other man. "My shot took him in the side, but he hit his head on the sidewalk. From the looks of that cut on his face, he was soon to be a goner anyway."

Willie stared down at Bart, thankful he still breathed, and she hadn't had to kill him. "Bart, my Mama is going to take care of that bullet wound, and you're going to jail. I don't know what the Marshall will do with your money, but I reckon you won't need it where you're going."

He coughed. "Just a bit faster and you'd be the one lying here."

"Too bad that didn't happen." She kicked his gun toward Mama. "You might have gotten me, but you couldn't have taken on the whole town."

"All I wanted was you out of my way." He closed his eyes and turned his face away from her.

Willie nodded for Theo and Mark to cart him to the jail. The man was too dangerous for Mama to doctor at the house. She could work on him while he lay on a cot just as easy as the kitchen table. She moved to Parson's body. What a tragedy. She prayed the man didn't have family waiting for him.

The Larson brothers sidled toward the sidewalk.

"You two stay right where you are." Willie speared them with a glance. "I reckon Mrs. Larson might have a few choice words to say to the two of you while I figure out whether to arrest you or not. Tom, would you accompany Mama into the jail?"

He nodded and left her to face the crowd. Willie bit the inside of her cheek and studied the apprehensive faces of the women's auxiliary group and their husbands. What they'd done couldn't be put into words. Most likely, they'd saved her life, and probably Tom's, too.

Swallowing back the sobs of gratitude that tried bursting free, she holstered her gun and faced her supporters. "I can't thank you enough. Not only did one of you step forward," she smiled at Alice Larson, who headed toward her husband, "but you were all willing to risk life and limb. This has to be the best little town in Montana."

Mayor Bloomfield stepped forward, thumbs hooked in his suspenders. "Mrs. Sheriff, do you realize that your trial period was actually over yesterday? I propose you stay on indefinitely as our sheriff. All agreed, say Aye!"

The street resounded with cheers and thrown hats. The women fired their guns into the air, whooping and hollering like a band of Indians. Willie let the tears flow. She no longer cared if anyone saw them as a feminine weakness. She was a woman who had proven herself up to the task of sheriff to a western town.

"Rider!" Gloria Netzer pointed down the street.

Willie turned, wiping her face on her sleeve. The sun glinted off a metal star. The Marshall had arrived. She grinned and stepped forward to greet him.

"I'm Marshall Forrester," he said. "I'm here to see the sheriff, Willie Jack." He eyed Parson's body.

"I'm Willie Jack. We have an injured gunfighter being doctored in the jail. I reckon he'll be able to ride by morning."

His eyes widened. "You're the sheriff we've heard so much about?"

"Yep," Mayor Bloomfield said. "And she's the best in the territory. Was prepared to face four gunmen all alone, until the rest of us stepped in. She can outshoot anyone here and half the time, she's doing her duties with a child on her hip. Yes sir! Our Willie Jack is the stuff legends are made of."

The heck with worrying about the Marshall thinking her foolish. Willie let her tears flow.

*

Tom watched through the window as Willie conversed with the Marshall. He'd thought his heart would stop when he'd spotted her facing Bart and his gang alone. While more frightened than he'd been in a long time, he couldn't help but feel pride at her courage. He looked forward to protecting the town by her side. He shook his head. Three months ago the thought of a woman defending the town, carrying a gun, hunting down bad guys … it all sent a river of fear through his heart. He might still have moments of uncertainty regarding Willie's title of sheriff, but instead of getting in her way, he'd support her. God had brought him a long way from where he'd been.

Alice Larson approached the Marshall, said a few things, then shooed her husband and brother-in-law, at gunpoint down the road to where she'd parked her wagon. Those two wouldn't be causing trouble any time soon.

Willie and the Marshall entered the jail, the Marshall heading to the back where Winnie patched up Bart. Willie sidled up to Tom and slid her arms around his neck. "I heard Mama and Theo are getting hitched."

"You don't say." Tom pulled her closer with his good arm.

She nodded. "Yep." Her husky voice sent shivers up his spine. "And since we have unfinished business of our own—"

The Marshall cleared his throat. "Sheriff?"

"Yes, sir." Willie sighed and stepped back.

"Is there a place I can hang my hat for the night?"

"The saloon, which is now our church, has rooms on the second and third floor. You're welcome to whichever one suits your needs." She faced him. "Bloomfield's Best Vittles is the best, and only, restaurant in town. Your meal is on us."

He glanced from her to Tom, his eyes

twinkling. "You're a lucky man, deputy." His gaze landed on the badge pinned to Tom's shirt. "A lucky man indeed."

"Yep."

"If I didn't have to haul that sorry carcass back to Billings, I'd like to stick around for a while and see what this town has to offer. I haven't met many folks like the ones here."

Tom offered his hand for the man to shake. "You come back and I'll show you the best fishing hole in the territory."

The Marshall pumped his hand. "That's an offer I can't refuse." He tugged his hat brim and headed across the street.

"Now, where were we—" Tom reached for Willie.

"Mama!" Junior ran as fast as his sister's legs would allow him as he pulled her along behind him. "I heard you shot a man."

"Yes, son, and it was very unpleasant." Willie gave Tom an apologetic look.

Junior frowned. "I had to miss the whole thing and stay with the other babies."

Tom ruffled his hair. "They needed a man to look after them. I knew you were the man for the job."

"Really?" Junior's face lit up. "I reckon I did good."

"The best." Willie planted a kiss on his cheek. "Go to the restaurant and ask Mrs. Bloomfield for a slice of pie. You've deserved it. Take Bonnie with you."

"Yes, ma'am!" He dragged Bonnie with him.

Tom snaked his arm around Willie's waist and pulled her close. "Now, where were we?"

"Willie?" Winnie poked her head out of the cell. "I'm finished with this scoundrel, and he's asleep."

"Lock him in, Mama. I'm busy." Her amazing eyes stayed locked on Tom's. "Can you handle all these interruptions? Life with me isn't calm and quiet."

"Calm and quiet is boring." He lowered his head, bringing his lips inches from hers.

"It is?"

"Yep. So, Wilhemina Jackson?"

"Yes?" Her breath wafted across his face.

"Will you marry me?" Tom held his breath, waiting for her to make him the most blessed man anyone would ever meet. "I promise to be your deputy for as long as you want me, I vow to be a daddy to two of the best young'uns this side of the Mississippi, and I promise to love you til my last breath. I look forward to our next adventure as husband and wife."

"Oh, Tom." She laid her cheek against his chest. "Do you know what you're asking? I'm a widow with two children. I'm part Indian, I'm willful, headstrong, and—"

"I'm asking to be the happiest man on earth." With his forefinger, he tilted her face toward his. "Say yes, and kiss me."

Footsteps approached behind them, and Theo cleared his throat. "Those Hickman sisters are harassing the patient about their money, and –"

"Iffen it ain't a matter of life or death, Uncle, I

suggest you keep your words to yourself for a few more minutes." Tom lowered his head again.

"I also thought you might want to know you have an audience."

Tom glanced toward the window where just about everyone in town stood grinning like fools. "Let's give them a show, Willie Jack. Say yes. I love you with everything in me."

"Yes, I love you. You're my heart, my breath …."

He claimed her lips to hoots and hollers from outside.

27

Tom helped the Marshall escort Bart and the Hickman sisters to Billings with a signed statement by Willie, thus prolonging their wedding date by a week. In that time, Willie had signed a permanent contract to much fanfare to be the sheriff of Wild Horse Pass. Alice Larson had 'convinced' her husband and brother-in-law to attend church and stand before the congregation with an apology for their unlawful behavior, and Mama had sewed Willie a new dress that set off her eyes to perfection and shined off her freshly washed hair with hints of blue.

Finally, today, Willie would wed Tom and Mama, dressed in a gown of goldenrod, would marry Theo, moving out to his farm and leaving the sheriff's house to Willie and her family. Willie smiled at her reflection in the speckled mirror hanging on the wall beside her bed.

No longer did two single beds occupy the room. Instead, Theo had built a handsome bed frame of pine to grace the room with measurements large enough to accommodate Tom. Willie's face heated while her heart raced as to what would happen later that evening in that very room.

Would Tom find her as attractive on their wedding night as he did in the light of day? After all, Willie had birthed two children. While remaining slender, motherhood had left scars on a no longer youthful body.

"You're beautiful, Wilhemina," Mama said, tucking a wildflower behind Willie's ear.

"A feather would suit me better." She met her mother's gaze in the mirror.

"I brought one of those, too." Mama handed her an eagle feather. "It doesn't go with your dress, but I thought we could tie it to a strand of hair and let the feather frame your face. Remind the people around here exactly who they hired as their sheriff."

Tears stung Willie's eyes as she spotted a much smaller hawk feather tucked into Mama's updo. She'd decided to embrace her heritage. Willie couldn't be prouder. She turned and took Mama's hands in hers. "We've both been blessed with a second chance at love. Are you happy?"

"Have you met the man I'm marrying?" Mama grinned. "I loved your papa, but Theo makes my heart sing."

Willie could say the same about Sam and Tom. Sam had been as comfortable as a well-worn pair of moccasins, but Tom … he had her cycling through emotions she'd thought long dead. The big blacksmith had truly stolen her heart despite their rough beginning. "I understand completely."

Willie linked her arm with her mother's, motioned for Bear to follow and took Bonnie's hand in hers as she led them to where her wedding should have taken place over a week ago. They slipped into the saloon to avoid being seen by their grooms.

The women's auxiliary group had outdone themselves with swags of wildflowers and a bar burdened with covered dishes of food. Junior, in new pants and starched shirt dashed among them all running errands of one kind or another and swiping a cookie as he went. Willie smiled. He would sport dirt on his shirt before the ceremony took place or she'd eat her feather.

"You look beautiful, Mrs. Sheriff." The women complimented her as they bustled around setting more dishes on the polished surface of the bar. The place still looked nothing like a church, but God met his people where they gathered.

"We've come a long way, daughter." Mama hugged her arm. "We've met the loves of our lives, made lifelong friends, and found a home, not to mention the accolades the Marshall gave you in regards to your abilities as sheriff. God is good."

"Yes, He is." The Marshall's words of approval for Willie's skill in enforcing the law in the town still seemed like a dream. For so long she'd battled insecurities as to how she could care for her family. Now, that had all been taken out of her hands. She had a profession she loved and could share the burden with a man willing to allow her to pursue her duties with him by her side. She wasn't ignorant enough to believe Tom wouldn't still have his occasional qualms about her duties, but their occasional disagreements would keep their marriage hopping.

"Mrs Sheriff, I mean, Willie," Mark said, peering over the top of the swinging doors. "We're ready when you are. Bob, pound away on that ancient piano."

Willie's heart leaped into her throat. Nothing could stop the wedding this time. She wouldn't let it. If someone rode up with ill intent, she'd shoot them. Junior dashed past to take his spot at Tom's side. Bonnie walked slowly in front of Willie and Mama, her small dark head concentrating on the basket of flowers in her hand.

"Don't forget to toss them once we go outside," Mama reminded her.

Bonnie did just that. The doors opened and she tossed the flowers, basket and all, into the watching crowd. Good-natured laughter rang out as Willie and Mama stepped into the late afternoon sunshine.

Willie tried to focus through tear-filled eyes on Tom's face. He looked resplendent in a new suit. When had he had time to purchase one?

"Dearly beloved," Mark began.

Willie let the tears flow.

*

Tom smiled at the sight of the feather in Willie's hair. She'd left her hair hanging free down her back, as he preferred. He couldn't wait to run his hands unrestrained through the silky tresses. It took all of his willpower to focus on Mark's words. It was finally happening. The confirmed bachelor of Wild Horse Pass had met his match and was marrying the woman he thought he'd never find.

"With this ring …" He slipped his mother's gold band on Willie's finger. His heart hitched. His mother would have loved Willie, and sided with her during every argument on what was proper women's behavior. He smiled, eliciting one from Willie in return. He barely heard Mark give the same vows to Uncle Theo and Winnie, so engrossed was he on his bride's face.

"You may kiss your brides."

To hoots and hollers, Tom bent Willie over his arm and kissed her with all the love he felt. He raised her, breathless, high spots of color on her cheeks, to her feet. He put his lips near her ear. "I can't wait to do that again."

"Neither can I." They turned to lead the way into the saloon.

With his hand on the small of Willie's back, Tom steered her toward a table set up for their family. The women of the town insisted on serving the wedding couples and soon handed them plates filled with fried chicken, corn bread, and an assortment of vegetables. While his stomach rumbled since he'd skipped breakfast, and lunch, due to nerves, eating was the last thing on Tom's mind.

Obviously last on Willie's, too, as she pushed the food around her plate. Winnie and Theo giggled like a couple of young'uns as Theo nuzzled her neck. Tom dragged his gaze away.

Mark and Gloria had offered to keep the children for the night, giving Tom and Willie the privacy they needed on their wedding night, and he found he could focus on little else. What if he disappointed her? He was unskilled where women were concerned. He studied his new wife's face.

She raised her amazing eyes to his, melting his insecurities. How could he go wrong with the other half of his heart?

He held out his hand. "Let's walk."

"Thank you." She exhaled heavily. "I feel like a bug in a jar with all these folks staring at us."

They walked until they came to the creek where they had discussed the things of their past that had held them back from fully loving each other. Now, his arms around her waist, they watched the sun set over the trees, kissing the water with coral and lavender. What better place to begin their married life than in the spot where Tom had decided to give up his prejudices and open his heart?

He turned Willie to face him and lowered his head to kiss her as birds flew overhead and settled in the trees, serenading them with song.

The End

ABOUT THE AUTHOR

www.cynthiahickey.com

Cynthia Hickey is a multi-published and best-selling author of cozy mysteries and romantic suspense. She has taught writing at many conferences and small writing retreats. She and her husband run the publishing press, Winged Publications. They live in Arizona and Arkansas, becoming snowbirds with three dogs. They have ten grandchildren who keep them busy and tell everyone they know that "Nana is a writer."